Emma Neale is the author of four previous novels and three collections of poetry. In 2000 she received the Todd/Creative New Zealand Bursary for New Writers, and in 2008 she was the inaugural recipient of the NZSA/Janet Frame Memorial Award for Literature. She works as an editor and creative writing tutor in Dunedin, where she lives with her husband and their two sons.

Fosterling
Emma Neale

VINTAGE

 The assistance of Creative New Zealand is gratefully acknowledged by the author

A RANDOM HOUSE BOOK published by Random House New Zealand
18 Poland Road, Glenfield, Auckland, New Zealand

For more information about our titles go to www.randomhouse.co.nz

A catalogue record for this book is available from the National Library
of New Zealand

Random House New Zealand is part of the Random House Group
New York London Sydney Auckland Delhi Johannesburg

First published 2011
© 2011 Emma Neale

The moral rights of the author have been asserted

ISBN 978 1 86979 485 9

This book is copyright. Except for the purposes of fair reviewing no part of this publication may be reproduced or transmitted in any form or by any means, electronic or mechanical, including photocopying, recording or any information storage and retrieval system, without permission in writing from the publisher.

Design: Megan van Staden
Cover design: Saskia Nicol
Cover image: © Yolande de Kort / trevillion images
Printed and bound in Australia by Griffin Press

For my sons

Contents

Prologue 9

PART ONE
Seek 13

PART TWO
Hide 145

PART THREE
Seek 177

PART FOUR
Hide 205

Epilogue 295

Prologue

Bu

Bu had been walking for more than an hour. He wasn't used to such heat. The sun seemed to find him even through the trees, as if it knew how he had fled his home the night before, and sought to punish him. When he came across a tiny creek with an overhang of rock nearby, he flung his pack into the shade. Soon he was crouched, gulping, gulping, so lost in the water's icy sweetness that he failed to hear the approach of a heavy tread.

A hunter, bowed down by a red deer carcass slung over his shoulders, pushed through waist-high ferns. He froze when he saw Bu. Then, cursing, he dumped the deer and tried to ready his rifle with fumbling hands. Bu reared up, staggering sideways and yelling in fright, but the hunter's ugly words and scrambling steps soon showed his gun was empty. Bu lifted an arm to say, 'Don't be afraid', but the man had already turned and started to run. He crashed through undergrowth, snapping twigs, wrenching at clumps of leaves, skidding down an unstable bank of ferns. Long after the man was out of sight, and he was alone again, Bu's heart still raced.

He hadn't thought he would see people this soon. Perhaps he was confused, had walked farther than he'd realised. The wringing in his gut told him that he had certainly never expected guns, nor to feel a stranger's fear and anger fly at him as clear as blows.

He breathed in deeply and looked down at his wet, shaking hands. Perhaps he needed more time to recover from last night's horror of smoke and burning. He lumbered over to his pack and began another long slog into the maze of the bush, the pads of his feet raw inside his boots and seeping through bandages he'd bound around the blisters.

Even with stinging soles, the rhythm of walking seemed to ease his fright. His thinking sprang back again, like grass from under a lifted stone. He decided to head towards an old, disused surveyor's hut that his father-man had shown him on maps. He would sleep there till nightfall, then make the rest of his way under moonlight, starlight. It would be slow, but night trekking would be cooler. The hut would likely be mouse-riddled and possum-run, but good enough for a day's rest. Yes, in a small hideaway of hours, he could draw around himself the plants, birds, and colours of the wilds one last time, and loosen the tight ache of guilt and sorrow in his belly.

Bu checked his compass and began to shamble east. He took off his boots and walked barefoot for a while, to ease his blisters, but the skin under the bandages broke and bled all the more. Soon a hot thread of pain wound up from the cut pad of one foot and into his leg. Infection and the early onset of fever twisted together. His head swirled. He tried to read the light and shadow around him, but flames and glowing wood appeared where he meant to put his feet.

Perhaps he had gone too far; already wandered closer to the people's bush tracks. Maybe he'd misunderstood his maps. It was taking so long to reach shelter.

Poor goat, *he berated himself.* Stupid mule.

And now a tree root leaps up, stark and gnarled. His leg swings to clear it, but kicks it all the same, and his maimed foot is hooked. Helpless as a pebble, he hurtles down a bank of baby saplings, rocks, ponga, yet nothing is big enough to catch him, massive as he is. Just before he blacks out, he feels a strange, floating thankfulness. That's it, *he thinks.* No more Bu.

PART ONE
Seek

Jane and Greg

AFTER MORE THAN AN hour's walk up a deceptively gradual incline, they agreed to stop for a short rest. Jane was fed up with Greg pushing her. This trip to New Zealand was supposed to be time together, but the pace he walked at, the way he charged on at things without asking her, seemed only another version of all the petty differences that had ground them down at home. Exhausted, her mind locked on little hectoring phrases. You *always*, you *never*, you *promised* . . .

Her throat was papery with thirst. Almost the moment she drank — and ate a handful of nuts and raisins — she felt ashamed at her snappishness. Glad she hadn't said anything aloud, she rested her hand briefly on Greg's upper thigh. He grinned, as if he reckoned the touch promised more, soon. Little jewels of sweat had appeared on his forehead from exertion, but the dark hollows under his eyes had lightened.

Jane looked up the bank beside her, which towered above with beech trees. The lower ferns looked like giant, green shuttlecocks and the air in their shade had a dirt-sweetness she could catch on the back of her tongue, an ancient coolness that slipped over the skin of her hands like water.

Scanning through a stand of lichen-covered silver beech, her eye was snagged by something: the gleam of eggs still improbably cupped in a fallen nest. She swigged some water, then partly to show Greg how much energy she had now, what a great idea this break was, she scrambled up the slope to take a closer look.

High above her was the other-worldly hum of a distant plane. Gradually its thrum drew away, and silence poured back along the funnels of sunshine that came intermittently through gathering rain clouds, and showed here and there between the tree trunks. She had just bent over the nest, when the pale flittering of a fantail's wings made her glance up, over and across.

'Oh my God.'

She stared, then turned and ran, skating and sliding back down the bank.

'Greg!'

At the cry, her husband dropped the plastic bag he'd just fished out of his pack.

'In the trees. Someone's taken a fall.'

'What?'

'Up there.' They began the clamber towards the shape.

She had only seen him side on, from behind — noticed the figure's heavy backpack, his dark clothing, wondered if she'd imagined the rise and fall of his shoulders. She started to take off her jacket, her fleece, in case she needed to cushion the man's head. Greg, who was behind her, called up, 'Keep yourself warm, Jane. We'll use the other gear in our packs if we need to.'

As they drew closer, the colossal size of the sprawled figure stopped them both in their tracks. '*Jesus.*'

They exchanged a glance, then edged near, and knelt —

Greg at the man's head, Jane behind his large pack, ready to help remove the bag, but also frightened, holding off just a fraction longer, not wanting to see whether the face or skull were damaged, too scared to know, straight away, whether he was dead or alive.

Even Greg hesitated. 'Holy shit,' he whispered. The delay seemed wrong. He looked over at Jane, and she felt how the three of them were held there in the leaf light, as if this were the last fragile moment before the onset of wider harm.

Gently, his face intent, Greg reached out for a pulse at the neck. 'Weak,' he said. 'But he's breathing.' His lips moved strangely before he spoke again. 'Janey,' he said, 'come here.'

She stood up and stepped over next to him, moving carefully, as if she already knew.

The face was peaceful, somehow, and youthful — even underneath the covering of silky fur, even given the pronounced eyebrow ridge, the lips and the jaw that immediately gave her the word muzzle. Greg gestured and she saw hair on the throat, visible under the neck of a torn, cotton kurta, on the backs of his mitts, even in the gap at his waist where the shirt fell away from his trousers. Like the shirt, the trousers seemed foolishly thin for the current temperature, which had dropped dramatically an hour or so earlier. But his whole body must be thickly coated in the same rich, glossy, dark-blond pelt that covered his forehead, nose, cheeks, chin, ears.

Jane looked back at her husband in confusion and concern. 'What is it?'

Greg's hand hovered briefly over a patch of hair sticky with blood on the scalp. 'Concussion, most likely. A —'

'No, I mean —' She felt a sudden chill. 'Is it . . . a man?'

'Of course.' Greg frowned. 'What else?'

She stared at the face, though afraid the eyes would open and gaze back. 'I don't know.'

Dismissing this with a gentle, almost amused shake of his head, Greg shifted his balance where he crouched. 'We've got to get him comfortable. Then one of us has to go for help. He's too heavy for us to move on our own.'

Jane stood, running her hands down her fleece trackpants. 'I'll go. You'll know what to do if he wakes.' Greg nodded, but something in his look sent her a stab of anxiety. 'Or maybe we should go together. Just mark the track — tie the survival bag to a tree.' The bag was unmissable: it was the lurid, unnatural orange worn by road workers, air traffic staff.

Greg chewed at his lip. He drew himself up, scanning the collapsed giant. 'Let's see what we can do for him first.'

The man had fallen roughly in the recovery position. Despite his prodigious height, there was an impression of adolescent gangliness. Greg told her to push free the straps of the pack so the chest and shoulders weren't constricted. At the pragmatism in his voice, a quick current of admiration ran through her. Their weeks of pecking at each other now seemed like her own selfish overreaction. She wanted to tell Greg she'd been spoilt, naïve, unmindful of the pressures on him. He held her gaze for a second, as if he sensed something of her thoughts, then gave her shoulder a hard squeeze. Jane slid down off the bank to retrieve Greg's gear. His pack held a sleeping bag, extra clothing, some of their food, his water bottle and a small first aid pouch. They tended efficiently to the young man's wound, then covered him with a sleeping bag, lifting his great, leonine head and pillowing it on a fleece sweater. He was limp, unresisting, silent throughout.

Greg was uneasy. 'I think one of us does need to stay with him. You go. Ditch anything you can from your pack. Make sure you've got food and water, and a sleeping bag though, just in case. Move fast, but be careful. You don't want to twist a knee —'

Jane was zipping her jacket. 'Or fall. I'll try the mobile from the car. If there's no reception —'

'Drive towards Haast. Keep trying it en route.'

'Greg, if he wakes . . .'

He understood her tone. 'It'll be okay, Janey. One ankle's wrecked. Look at it. He won't be up to much.'

She realised she had been pulling her mind away from it, the foot oddly cocked, turned the wrong way, like a flipper.

'Poor creature,' she said. She caught Greg's expression at her choice of words, felt her voice hitch even as she said it. Greg hugged her hard, then she was off, retrieving her pack, leaving a pile of gear in the survival bag, which she tied by its drawstring to the base of a sapling, to mark the site where help would need to turn off the track and head up the bank.

Whenever her legs ached for rest as she pounded along the trail, she thought of Greg left alone with the broken were-man, and tenderness for her husband surged up, galvanised her, kept her moving.

Bu

COLOURED LIGHTS FLICKERED THROUGH his eyelids. He must be moving through trees, the sun hiding and finding, hiding and finding. But there was no scent or rustle of leaves. Why was he gliding, gliding and lying at the same time, and so beautifully blind, seeing only purple, scarlet, green, spill and splash?

Voices echoed, jangled and jarred as if they were being shaken in a metal box. There was no birdsong, no sound of water. No cool air on his lips.

His thoughts made a shape: it meant *leave me*. Bu wanted to let the colours keep flowing, and to sink into their soft silence. Yet a sound kept jabbing at him . . .

❋ ❋ ❋

HE OPENED HIS EYES. He was in a strange room. There was a smell like acrid soap. Blurry lights and noises jumbled together, as the face of a man not much older than Bu looked down at him.

Quickly someone brought a metal dish as Bu retched. The young man held him, a woman offered him a sip of water. Carefully they laid him back down. Now everything turned: the scene came clear of its muddled, swimming lights; sounds found their proper forms.

'Can you understand me?' The young man shone a thin beam into each of Bu's eyes. 'How are you feeling?' Someone wheeled up a metal table full of bright clattering claws and scoops.

'Mmmmph.' Bu's throat throbbed, raw. It felt as if some hard object had been forced the length of his gullet, although there was nothing there now. He wanted to ask about his parent-folk, but an ache at the root of his heart told him the answer. His arm was cuffed with a band of material that tightened. Something held near his ear made a brief chirping sound.

He looked around him, eyes gummy, head stinging. This wasn't what he had been walking out of the bush to find. The terror became quiet and cold, slid solidly inside him.

'You're in hospital, sir. In Dunedin. A long way from home?'

Bu shifted his head a little.

'We had to bring you here — Greymouth Hospital's on an emergency shutdown with norovirus,' said the hovering man, whose cheekbones looked naked as eggshell. 'Queenstown's too, as it happens. It's a nasty bug. The north's bracing for it. And radiography staff are on a rolling strike: Southland's turn this week. Lucky for us. This is a teaching hospital, and . . .' The man, who had been searching Bu's face as if for some recognition, stopped himself and wrote something down on paper clipped to a wooden board. 'You rest for a while more,' he said. 'We'll bring you a meal in an hour or so. See if you can manage to eat something then.'

Day and night merged. Bu's wounds were cleaned and checked regularly, and his fever dropped. Still, he had strange, alarming dreams. In one he was put into a dark metal hood that sent loud, alien noises into his skull, then he was pulled out again, and left in a room with white walls that bulged and shrank. When he woke, he swallowed a small amount of food past the rod of terror that had lodged in his body. At some stage — perhaps when he had first been brought here — his ankle had been covered in a long, stiff wrapping, like a pale branch. Another doctor came with a group of people and talked about what they had done to prepare the leg.

She asked Bu if he had any pain. Everyone in the room waited. The man-nurse. The junior doctors. Another older man-doctor.

Bu swallowed again. Thinking of what had passed before he came here — sick, sore, bereft — he felt every last word trickle away: seed from a slit cloth bag.

He turned his head slightly, watched the doctor's green glass earring quiver as she spoke, and the way it shed another droplet of green on her neck, where the light passed through the dangling berry shape.

The woman touched her neck self-consciously. It changed her, that gesture. Made her softer.

There was coughing, shuffling. The people withdrew. Bu heard them, though. From across the room, from behind the screens with their patterned brown and cream curtains.

'He hasn't talked at all yet, so, given the blow to his head, we did an MRI, to see if there was any brain damage. Everything looks normal, so I think the next step is probably a psych assessment. We'll also need to get a social worker in.'

'You're sure he can hear?'

'Yes.'

'And understand?'

'I'm convinced he does, yes. Although I'm not sure how much.'

'Have you checked the vocal chords are intact?'

'Yes. Perfectly healthy, as are the larynx and pharynx.'

'Right. But clearly there's some sort of genetic abnormality. The gigantism, the hirsutism, the skull structure. Maybe even the aphasia . . .'

'Hmm. We should contact a geneticist and get them to run some more sophisticated bloods. But I'll also put a call through to dermatology. I'm pretty sure the skin condition is some sort of severe hypertrichosis. I treated a patient in Malaysia once who had something similar. Very rare, but fascinating. I'll speak to John Stape.'

A third voice came in. 'Do we know anything at all about his background?'

The pause that followed was like the not-quite-silence of something moving through the bush: a presence, nearing, watching.

'Only what the police have gleaned from looking through his bag. It was a well-prepared hiker's pack. He had food, clothing, sleeping bag, first aid kit, pocket knife, alarm clock, maps. There was even a locket, a photo and a book. Nothing that gives a name, though.'

Someone mumbled, then Bu heard them say, 'The missing link.'

There was a groan, then a leaf fall of laughter.

The woman doctor's voice came in, sharp and disapproving. 'Let's focus, please. If he's able to talk, but unwilling to do so, it's likely he's extremely fearful after whatever he's been through. I'd strongly recommend that we proceed with even more compassion and sensitivity than usual, especially given his . . .'

'Outlandishness,' someone else broke in, and although it wasn't said unkindly, there was more nervous laughter.

'Right, Wayne. You'll be presenting the next case for us on the round.'

Most of the voices moved away, but Bu still heard, 'Told you she was a ball-breaker.'

'No shit.'

He tried to swim back into sleep, the safe den of nothing.

> Police are seeking information that could help to identify an injured hiker found in the South Westland region on Tuesday. The man (estimated age 18–21) who appears to be a selective mute, has several distinguishing physical characteristics. He is seven feet tall (2.13 m), is of darkish-blond colouring, has a pronounced brow, and a noticeably thick covering of facial and body hair. Anyone who has any information regarding the individual's identity or next of kin should notify the police. All contact will be treated in the strictest of confidence.

Corky

TWENTY-FOUR HOURS PASSED. One person came forward: a hunter who said he had seen the strange man in the bush. Gareth Anderson, known as Corky, told police in Haast the man had given him a right scare. Roared at him.

'That's no real mute,' Corky insisted. 'He's not . . .'

'No,' said the duty officer, and slowly, as to someone hard of hearing, 'that's what selective means.' The officer waited for him to offer any other information, but Corky stood looking at his feet, turning his black woollen beanie round and round in his hands. Someone asked the policeman to come away for a moment, so he showed Corky the new water and coffee dispensers, said he was welcome to wait. When he came back, Corky held the beanie twisted like a rope, but had nothing else to add. The officer thanked him and sent him on his way.

Corky felt a sad sort of aimlessness as he reached the pavement outside the police station.

It was like when he was a kid, and he'd been expecting a letter or a parcel in the post, because his grandfather had said he would send him something. But Granddad had got crook, real crook. He had never seen him again.

Corky let his boots scatter some gravel into a flock of seagulls that milled and complained in his path.

But I wanted the cops to tell me what it was out there. What did I really see?

Bu

BU DIDN'T LIKE THE person they called *social worker*. On each of the man's two or three visits so far he smelt of ash and something else — plants rotting. His teeth, Bu realised. They were brown as old fruit you'd leave for the ants. He wouldn't talk to this man. No. He might have talked to Dr Jackson, but she was always rushing. No time for talking to Bu. She was just like the small torch beams that trembled over her skin. Dart and dash.

The social worker had sprung him with the magazine, too. Bu's fear skated close to fury then. He'd been hiding down inside himself so well, silent as a stoat. Now Browntooth thought he knew something more about him.

'Ahh,' said the man, arms crossed over his clipboard as he leaned against the doorway, which he'd approached without Bu hearing. 'We're not quite the real wildman then, are we?' He nodded at the *National Geographic* photo essay Bu had been lost in.

Bu stared at the social worker's name tag: *Brian Jobbes*. Then he tipped his head slightly forward, and looked up from the shading ridge of his eyebrows. He knew it scared the man. It made him fumble in his pockets, searching for something he never found.

'You really can read.'

Bu traced the outline of a picture with an unsteady finger.

'Still not talking, eh?'

Bu tensed into a hunch. Jobbes pressed his purplish lips firmly together. 'I'm sure you have good reasons.'

Bu stared at the floor.

'But we need to help you. The doctors say you'll be well enough, physically, for them to discharge you in a few days, as long as you have help at home with mobility and access and so on. But they've decided to wait, until they're sure that you're robust enough — whole enough — in yourself.'

The *whole self*. Bu's mind saw a white grain, split. A tongue of green rose from it.

'You're very lucky, you know. Normally this place doesn't have the beds for anyone who doesn't tick the right boxes.'

Bu glanced around the cupboard-sized room. He'd already been told how lucky he was to have his own space. It was more like a cage, with its bars on the windows, and its single peeking slit in the heavy door.

'Doctors Jackson and Ali have really pushed the boat out for you.'

Boxes and boats.

'They want to be sure that you've got somewhere to go.' Jobbes sat down at last, on a seat near Bu's wheelchair, which was crammed in next to the bed. 'The results from your MRI scan were fine, apparently — the doctors will go over those with you. But given your reluctance to talk with us, we all think it would be a good idea if you saw one of our psych people. That's our next priority. If you're okay with this, we'll get you an appointment, then go from there.'

Bu stared through the barred window, at the city. He was a little braver about looking out the window when another person was in the room. It somehow held him back from the dizziness that plunged through him because of the height. He had seen such towering buildings in movies, of course, and had read about them, but had never been inside one so high. They were up several floors and could see out over some of what a nurse had told him was the *student quarter*. So many buildings that Bu felt in even more danger of falling, from confusion. She had pointed to the outside tangle and said there were some coffee bars and, over there, pizza places, a taxi stand, a car park. She said that people lived in an old stone building over the road.

He had to remind himself that the window wasn't just a big TV screen, and that if he could bring himself to lean out, real city air would press against his mouth, and he would smell the wet footpaths, the blood tang of metal, the sick swoon of car fumes. If he reached out a hand, into the sky, he wouldn't just touch more glass and feel the prickle of static electricity leap up from its hard curving bubble. *Real,* he said to himself inside his head. *Really, truly real.*

While he was gazing out, someone across the street opened a sash window and placed a pot plant on the broad window ledge. Then they put out a black cat. The cat made no effort to jump. It sat there, basking. Taking the air. The sight made Bu widen his eyes at what a lion the cat must be. He would not want to put himself out on the very edge of the air like that, not without branches or some other hand-holds to guide him down.

Brian Jobbes made notes in a little book he carried, his eyebrows lifting. 'Good. No objections to that.' He pushed himself up, stood there for a moment. 'I've just come over from psych services now, and to be honest I doubt there'll be a consultant free for a while. What I'll do is book you in for an appointment first thing tomorrow morning. I'll take you over there myself.' His mouth puckered a bit. 'Y'know, those *National Geographic*s are ancient.'

The pile had been brought in to Bu by a nurse aide, a thin young girl with hair the colour of silky toetoe heads. She backed out of the room, misjudged the space and bumped the doorframe with her elbow. She gripped her hurt arm, the fear in her eyes hardening in a way that made Bu feel accused of some nasty, secret trick.

'There's a patient library in the day lounge. Bit shabby, but you might want to take a look.' Jobbes crumpled something that crackled in his pocket, his frown saying he was about to test something out. Bu, perhaps.

'Or, actually — if you want, you could borrow something from the public library.' Bu saw how his stare made Jobbes hunt for an explanation. 'That means — to have books for a while. To read them, then take them back. The book bus is here today. It's a new scheme, parking it by the hospital. They have a disability access ramp. If you were comfortable about going out for a few minutes — under supervision, of course, and you'll need help — I'll let you use my card.' He fussed with the crackling stuff again, worry lines on his face.

Bu straightened, like a plant turned to the light. He nodded.

Jobbes left, and Bu watched the small piece of sky allowed to him in this room. He listened again to the way the city made a constant, deep-throated growl, something like the rush of wind or water. Two nights in a row he had jerked awake thinking some live thing was out there enraged or hurt. When his heart slowed from its panicked sprint, he worked out that the sound was horns, sirens, the shriek of tyres.

Raw-nerved, he couldn't trust his ears at first when he discovered that even here, where he could see no trees or shrubs, he now and then heard birdsong. It soothed him, like his mother-woman stroking his head. It was a thread of truth or memory still wound around his wrist, tying him safely to some spool of the past.

He cupped a hand to his chest, as if cradling a tiny, hatchling-sized mother-woman and father-man deep in his heart. *I'm so sorry*, his fingers said. *So sorry*. Then he reached for the backpack stowed in the corner, ran his fingers inside an inner pocket and felt the shapes of the things he had brought from home, their small, solid weights. Their coolness calmed him more. He felt able to wait here a little longer.

❃ ❃ ❃

THE ORDERLY WHO CAME to take Bu down to the hospital's main entrance was a tall, burly man the colour of dark, polished wood. He had a smooth, sloping walk. His name badge said Latu: the second name obscured by a sticker that said *I gave to Cancer Kids*. When he saw Bu he didn't even flinch. Bu felt the tightness in his muscles loosen another stitch.

'Hello.' Latu helped Bu into the wheelchair. 'Jobbes tells me you're off to the book bus.'

Bu stirred.

'Sweet,' Latu said. 'Cruise, or top gear?' He switched from a slow gait to a fast glide to demonstrate, as they went past another couple of men in clothes like his, who were leaning over wheeled shelves piled with sheets.

More and more people.

Involuntarily, Bu lifted an index finger, as if to reach through the space between him and the men, and test the texture of them, the thickness.

One drew himself up to his full height. The glint of pleasure in his face made Bu think of a ferret with a chick in its mouth. Bu dropped his hand.

'Latu, my Tongan brother! What's up with the Wookie?'

Latu whistled back, low and provoking. It wasn't like anything Bu had heard before.

There was another comment from the skinny man, which Bu couldn't understand, but his companion shook his head. 'Leave it, you don't wanna take it outside.'

Latu slowly wheeled Bu past, but gave the low, musical taunt again.

His whistle changed as they passed two women, both in blue smocks, one with the pinky-white skin of sun-tinged cloud, her eyes blue; the other brown-skinned, her dark hair pinned back with a large fabric flower. Bu worked to untangle a tightly wound skein of scents. Apple, vanilla, cinnamon, soap; coconut and warm scalp; the strange, wet, peppery smell of sweat tucked away in the skin's folds. He sniffed, mouth open a little, and the women spoke to Latu, but stared at Bu.

'*Malo e lelei. Fefe hake*?'

'*Sai pe.*' The one with the flower tipped her head back, cheeks reddening, and both women laughed, as if at some joke that Bu was no part of. He felt hot, uncomfortable, yet couldn't help staring at them.

The women were left behind, but Latu still sang to himself. Then, as they pulled up at some metal doors, Bu thought Latu was asking him, 'You like to do the buttons, man?' until he saw the small boy clutching his father's hand, the pair's mouths open, eyes bulging round as mushroom tops.

'If you don't answer me, I'm gonna beat you to it,' Latu said. The boy shot out a hand, smacked the buttons on the wall, but then refused to get in when the doors opened to show a lift. The child pulled back and down on his father's hand, all in silence, until he sat on the corridor floor. His father was arrested there too, staring as the lift doors closed on Bu and Latu.

'Rude,' Latu said, once they were alone. Bu looked down at his lap. *Hide. For his own sake.*

For your sake, thought Bu. *Forsake.*

The lights blipped through the numbers and the lift came to a sliding halt. He felt a strange, delayed bobbing sensation. Latu broke the silence. 'You just tell me if you don't want to carry on. I can take you back to the ward any time.' The doors opened onto a large reception area. Latu wheeled Bu out, then stood in front of him. 'I'm serious. You want to call it quits, just do this.' He touched Bu's arm, then jabbed up at the ceiling with his thumb. 'That'll be the *let's get out of here* signal.'

Bu let his lips curl. Just a little.

Outside, on the street, Bu hardly knew where to look. Buildings shouldered out the sky. People dashed to and fro. He whipped his head about, but the passers-by talked, laughed or clung hip to hip, neither hiding nor slinging frightened looks behind them. Soon Bu saw that their hurry didn't mean he should expect buildings to fall, or some savage form to burst out from an alleyway, teeth blazing.

Mad as starved sandflies, cars, trucks, buses and motorbikes zigzagged from all directions. Every second some strange new marvel swam past him with the easy nonsense of dream: a car with a large, fuchsia-coloured toy duck grinning from the dashboard; a man walking past wearing wings made of crinkled paper in rainbow colours and a toy bear strapped to his stomach; another man biting a fat cigar as he cycled by on the footpath, bags of vegetables swinging from his handlebars; a gaggle of beautiful girls all wearing matching skirts and blazers, their hair mostly shining and long, but two who had just pink and purple tufts, like flowers from his mother-woman's garden. The air tasted cool; his palms felt the spit of a few raindrops as Latu hustled him along the street. His body ached and for a moment he closed his eyes, hardly knowing whether he tasted excitement or fear at the back of his throat.

When they reached the book bus, Latu pushed him up the ramp, asking him what he'd had for breakfast. 'You're giving me a workout,' he said heavily, but managed to move the chair past where a woman stood at a counter. Latu wheeled Bu right along the centre of the vehicle, the walls of which were lined with books.

Latu stood with his hands in his pockets. 'I'd like to borrow something for my friend here today.' To Bu he said, 'You just choose what you like.'

The woman was solid, dressed in loose purple pants and an earthy woollen jersey with pieces of sea-shell and driftwood woven through it. Her mouth hung open. Latu pushed the chair towards a sign that read *adult nonfiction*. He leaned down to whisper, 'Bus must've took a roll on the beach on the way over.'

Bu might have let all his caution crumble — he had a memory of the ticklish unravelling of laughter — but three other customers were entering the bus and Latu was already backing away to make room for them as he said, 'Take your time, browse away.'

A brief yet rich sense of comfort returned as he looked at the books displayed along the walls. He reached out and ran his fingers over the spines, not really reading the titles at first, just feeling the relief of familiarity: *I know what these are.* He realised his body had been in a tense vigil ever since he had woken in this strange place.

He let the mood settle, let the books lull him. Then he saw the simple title *Wood Carving for Beginners*. The letters on the cover began to dance, dissolve. Bu couldn't breathe out. He felt a strange popping sensation in his eyelids. His lips and fingers began to tingle, then the digits cramped and bent up as he watched. He began to lose them. His mouth, his hands: they were gone. Each shock was like another cold wave that made him gasp, until it seemed the air itself was stuffing his lungs, choking him. Yet with sharp clarity he saw and heard the other people who had entered the bus. The extra air turned up the world's colour and volume so that it seemed he had not only left his body, but had copied himself. The selves travelled off: one of him was stationed near the librarian, one was by the newcomers, one was by the shelf where his poor body shook.

'Wow,' said one of the arrivals, an older woman wearing a shirt and top made of shiny, crumpled stuff, her hair a tidy white cap of cream. 'It's not, like, Halloween here, is it? We just got off a cruise ship down at the port. The *Pacific Empress*. I wanted to ask which way back to the Octagon.'

The librarian raised her voice to speak to Latu, who was hidden from Bu's sight by the other visitors. 'No, this has to be a student stunt. There's a graduation parade later this morning. I had to divert the bus away from the main drag down George Street — there's a roadblock. Is this a dare?'

'Hang on,' said a young man who was holding hands with a young woman. 'Is he okay?'

'His *leg* is broken,' piped the tourist, edging closer to Bu.

The librarian called to Latu, her voice shrill with urgency. 'Excuse me, your friend — he seems to be having *trouble*?'

The young man went to step back out of the bus, maybe to make more room so that Latu could manoeuvre Bu's wheelchair down the ramp. Bu saw the man was already clicking at a lighter, a cigarette clenched between his lips. His girlfriend was backing out too. Bu saw a breeze lift her long coppery hair and trail it quickly near the small, sturdy flame.

As Bu's lungs clenched on another breath, the lighter flame snatched successfully at a lock of the girlfriend's hair, travelling it as quickly as it would a strand of dry grass. The man said, 'Shit, sorry, Carrie, watch out!' He began smacking at the flame with a hand covered in the cuff of his jacket. The tourist didn't seem to notice the small crisis. Instead, she reached Bu's side, touched his shoulder, then tugged at a fistful of the long fur on his scalp.

Bu heard the realisation hit her. 'Oh . . .'

Too late. The book; the sting of Bu's injured scalp; the ragged flash of fire; the pungent, burning hair; the small genie of smoke: Bu howled, the sound startling even to him, his head jerking back so that the tourist stumbled and cracked her shin against the wheelchair. Bu's hands cramped up more and more until they made talons. He couldn't move, and the others scattered. Screaming, with a hand to her bruised leg, the tourist tripped out onto the pavement.

Latu lunged along the bus aisle, sent papers and pens on the checkout desk flying as he seized a large manila envelope. He emptied it out, then scrunched it up to make a hole at the centre of a paper ruff. He held one hand to the back of Bu's massive neck and cupped the envelope over his lips and nose.

'Breathe. Slowly. Breathe out. *Out*. That's it. Easy does it.' He kept a grip on Bu's shoulder as his great frame shook. 'You're all right,' Latu said. 'You're all right. It's a panic attack. That's all it is. I see it a lot, man, in my job.' He watched Bu carefully. 'You pick up what to do after seeing it a few times, hey.'

Time passed — minutes, an hour? — and at last Bu felt himself shudder back into the present. He raised both hands to his face.

'There's no shame in this, bro. I've seen it happen to all kinds of people.' Latu kicked off the footbrake on the wheelchair, and started to push Bu back down the ramp. 'Let's get out of here.'

As they descended to the footpath, they saw that a police patrol car had been flagged down. Two officers, a man and a woman, got out. The tourist walked along beside them, breathless, hobbling. 'There he is!' she managed. 'That's the one.' Her hand was on the woman police officer's elbow as she began to explain. 'I was petrified. I thought he was going to turn *violent*, he looked completely *insane*, like he was going to *assault* me.'

'The individual in the wheelchair, ma'am? The one

who can't walk?' The officer's hand dropped from the belt where her radio and incident notebook were clipped.

The policeman asked Latu for his version.

'The patient was in my charge for an outing. That lady grabbed hold of his hair and pulled. He just lurched out of the way. She's lucky he's playing dumb. I'd say *he'd* be the one who should be crying assault. He's the guy they brought in from the bush. It was in the papers.'

The police conferred. 'Mystery hiker,' the man said, and looked at Bu sideways as if, Bu thought, he didn't want to have to solve this sort of mystery at all.

'You've sustained no injuries, ma'am? There's no actual assault to report? You have transport to wherever you're going now?' The woman police officer felt for her belt again, eyes searching over the tourist's head and off into the city, away from Bu, in a way that seemed kindly. 'So everything's actually all right here.'

The tourist gave a small mew of protest, which the policewoman deftly misinterpreted. 'Don't apologise. We're glad it was nothing serious.' She swung back to the patrol car, thumbing at her tiny phone as she went.

Bu felt a pulse of relief as he heard the police slam their car doors. Then at the sight of a man and woman in hospital uniform hurrying over, as people called, 'Over here, over here!', sparks of panic began to swarm under his skin again. *Breathe out*, he reminded himself. *Out, out*: as if he could snuff his dread as easily as he would a match.

'A&E,' the man said. He asked Latu inaudible questions, his back turned on the gaggle of onlookers who had been slowly filling up the pavement.

'He's been in orthopaedics,' said Latu. 'I think he's had

a panic attack. Brian Jobbes is his social worker. He's the one who suggested we visit the book bus.'

'Great, thanks.' He knelt down close to Bu. 'My name's Grant Holloway. I'm a doctor.' He looked at Bu like a child who had turned the page to find an unexpected picture in a favourite, absorbing story. He seemed to be waiting for him to speak. The doctor glanced at Latu. 'Jobbes thought he'd cope with being sent out here?'

Latu shrugged in apologetic agreement.

Searching Bu's face, Holloway asked him a quick series of questions about chest pain, headaches, recurrent blackouts, any other unusual sensations. Bu gave a minimal head-shake to each.

'Okay, sir. Sounds to me as if Latu here is right. You've heard of hyperventilation — over-breathing?'

Bu folded his hands together. Unfolded. Folded.

Holloway's mouth quirked up at one corner. 'You know, I don't deal with the hard stuff. I just stitch people up, slap bandages on them. I think we should get you over to emergency psych for an assessment.' He nodded at the woman who'd arrived with him, saying she could head back to A&E. 'I'll go with these guys, and put a call through to his ward.'

With Holloway leading, Latu wheeled Bu along the road to another hospital entrance. Once they were inside, Holloway carefully tried a joke about Bu making himself comfortable, nodding at the wheelchair. It was like he was touching a sore part with a fingertip, not sure if it would cause a yelp or a snarl. Holloway pointed to a table laden with magazines, and tried to switch on a wall lamp so that Bu could read while he waited. The light trembled and stuttered. The doctor switched it off again, mumbling, 'Always does this. S'posed to have been fixed. Never mind.'

Bu slowly inclined his head, then, hand unsteady still, reached over and unscrewed the bulb and the fitting itself.

'Careful!' warned Holloway, hand out to push Bu's fingers away before they went to the wires, but Bu was already replacing the fitting, then the bulb. He tried the switch. The lamp sent out a steady stream of light.

'Oh, great. Thanks!' Holloway was puzzled. 'You're an electrician?' Bu signalled no, and slumped back into himself.

Bu felt Holloway draw away. When the doctor came back, he said everything was set up for seeing a registrar.

Something in the silence that followed made Bu look up. He felt the man's eyes trying to hold his own. He was reminded of the expression he had seen as a small boy, on his father-man's face, when they had watched the stars together on a warm, clear night — and Bu had wanted to hold tightly to his hand in case they were both swept away by the fever brought on by endless space. *Wonder*. Bu switched his stare to the floor, hearing the whisper of *sorry, so sorry* again in his head, like wind in the trees.

Holloway held out a hand. 'I'd better be getting back. Though I'd . . .' His words fell short. 'Good luck,' he said. An unfamiliar impulse told Bu not to touch him: that the man wanted too much from the handshake. Instead, he waited to hear the sound of the doctor leaving before he looked around again.

A movement in a corner caught Bu's eye. On the other side of the foyer, a woman lay on a bench, clutching a bundle of blue blanket to her chest. She rocked and shivered. The bundle had a face, Bu saw: the woman was cradling her baby. It had moon-smooth skin, but looked soft and warm as owl feathers.

They all waited together for an aching yawn of time.

Eventually a woman came to speak to the mother. She crouched down next to the bench. Bu strained to catch what she said.

'Your husband doesn't have to know. We can visit you when he's at work, use an unmarked car . . .'

Then a man was beside Bu, staring. A spell seemed to hang over him, loosened only when Bu slipped another glance at the woman on the bench. He snapped to, then greeted Latu and said to Bu, 'My name's Andrew Swade. I'm one of the psych registrars on today. Sorry you've had such a long wait. Let's take you through to an interview room.'

Bu's mouth felt parched. The sides of his lips stung a little as he licked them. As he was wheeled past a trolley stacked with hospital linen, he reached out, gripped one of its handles and stopped the chair's momentum.

'What is it, bro?' asked Latu.

From one of the trolley's neat piles, Bu lifted a folded blanket that matched the one around his knees. He twisted himself in the chair, tipping forward at the waist, like a rider urging his horse in a different direction. Latu understood the sound that came from his throat. He took Bu over to the woman shivering on the bench. Bu signalled, *closer*. The care worker's monologue stopped midstream. Bu leaned across, and arranged the blanket as best he could over the mother's stretched out form.

At first, trapped in the rhythm of shuddering and rocking, she barely registered Bu, but soon her eyes locked on him. A hand stole out to draw the blanket around her shoulders. Then, as if the warmth helped to pull her body out of the sheath of fear, she drew herself up, sitting with the child cradled in her lap. Bu caught the sound of her voice as he was wheeled through another set of swing doors.

Dr Swade led them into a bruised-looking, green-walled room with drooping brown curtains. Bu smelt the sharp tang of someone else's fear still lingering, and something else — pockets of air that made him think of dust, ice, shadow, the odour of loneliness. He wanted to pace back and forth between these traces and find another name for them. He must be wrong. In a city so tight-full of people, why was the smell of isolation so strong?

When Latu reached the doorway, Swade said, 'We'll be fine from here.'

Latu frowned at Bu. 'You okay on your own?'

Bu's eyes darted from Latu to Dr Swade, then back again. He could feel anxiety pull at the muscles in his brow.

'I'll find some trolleys to push around.' Latu waved at the corridor and grinned. 'I'll take you back to the ward when you're done here.'

Dr Swade settled in a seat opposite Bu and busied himself with the clipboard papers. He was a big man, with dark hair, large glasses, the buttons of his shirt gaping slightly at his waistband, showing a soft white roll of skin. His face was bland, as if the roundness pressed out any expressive lines. 'I've spoken to your social worker and Dr Jackson. They've filled me in a bit on your situation, and I've got your ward records here. You would have been in some pain after a suspected fall like this. How do you feel now?' The doctor waited. 'Do you remember much about the accident itself? What caused it?'

The tree root, the hunter, the trek.

No. The trek, the hunter, the tree root. Running, the fire. No. First the fire. Bu saw and smelt smoke: dense, rancid, unforgiving. His fault. His heart contracted like paper blackening on hot metal.

Swade heaved his weight to the other side of his chair. It startled Bu and he dug his nails deep into his palms to pin himself still.

'I can see you're feeling very anxious,' said the doctor. 'I just want to say, that's highly understandable.'

Bu watched him.

'Did something specific happen to frighten you out there today?'

Bu licked his lips, bowed his head, shivered. He must be cold: perhaps he'd caught the idea from the woman on the bench.

He looked at the window, the way it was positioned close to the ceiling. There was only a small opening at the very top, and the pane was lined with a net of wires, like a fence preserved in glass. Bu looked at the walls, too, at the black scuff marks in strange places: far too high. The tarry stains made him uneasy. He felt them in his side vision, as if they were somehow touching him, sticky hands pulling at the pelt on his neck.

Swade spoke again. 'You don't have to tell us anything you don't want to. We're not here to pry into your affairs. We just want to know that you're healthy enough *inside yourself* for you to manage those affairs competently and safely.'

The man had too many words. He didn't leave any room for Bu. And when he said *inside yourself* he leaned forward a little, to show that he meant it kindly, but it was clear he was nervous: that he had never come across someone like Bu before.

Bu could have felt sorry for him but the man peered as if he couldn't really see Bu; as if he thought Bu's very face were a disguise, or even as if the Bu inside wasn't truly there at all.

Yes. As if Bu wasn't there. So he closed his eyes, and waited, stubborn as a possum, for Dr Swade not to be there either.

❄ ❄ ❄

BACK AT THE WARD, Latu scanned the brief report Swade had added to the file he was to take back to Jobbes and Drs Jackson and Ali. 'This paperwork he gave me, it says, *Unnamed young male subject presented immediately after suspected panic attack: still very apprehensive, shaking and fearful. Ward records note recent history of injury, poor appetite, disrupted sleep patterns, depressed mood, reluctance to engage socially, and visible weight loss in past several days since admittance. Presented with clear symptoms of anxiety and depression, yet given the subject is still reluctant to talk, and resultant lack of direct personal information, inadvisable to administer medication until after further interview in forty-eight hours.* Whoops. Confidential, my mistake.' Latu winked and folded the paperwork back into its envelope. 'Never mind. I won't tell if you won't.' He came over, squatted down on his haunches. 'It's all right, bro. You just need to rest. When you're rested up, I reckon you'll talk in your own time.' He paused. 'You can understand us, hey? You can talk?'

Bu felt the last six hours clench behind his eyes in a headache. He rubbed at his temples with both hands.

'Yep. You've had it. You rest.' Latu's shoes squeaked on the linoleum floor. 'I'll come and check in with you if I can, before I go off my shift.'

Bu heard him open the door, then greet someone passing by.

'Hey.'

'Hey, Latu. How're y'doing?'

'Good, man, good.'

Bu opened his eyes, saw Latu out in the corridor with a small, slight man in a blue hospital uniform. They shook hands, pleased with each other.

'You working with the mystery guy in there, hey? Any word on him yet?'

'Not so far. No name, no connections, far as I know.'

'What do you think? You believe what people are saying? That he might be some kind of, you know, link?'

'What? Shit, man. He's just a frightened kid.'

The other man rolled his shoulders uncomfortably. 'Yeah?'

'I wish his family would show. Boy needs looking after.'

Bu was glad when they finally remembered to close the door, and the voices receded. Again he tried to pull the silence down around him like warm, dark camouflage.

❈ ❈ ❈

HE WAS WOKEN BY a sudden blast of voices, the pounding of feet and the rattle of wheels. He lunged upright just in time to see an old man's face squinting through the window slit high in his door, the white burn of a camera flash through the glass. Then the door was shoved open, a chair was sent skidding into the room, and the elderly man fell after it, spread-eagled, his camera still held aloft.

Bu's heart slewed in his chest. Medical staff stood over the man on the floor, Latu among them, the sight of his familiar, burly form — and of Dr Jackson — only just holding Bu back from bellowing with fright.

Brian Jobbes was there too, and a female nurse Bu didn't recognise. Dr Jackson had red blots high on her cheekbones. Hands on her waist, she was all angles. Anger spat from her. 'Who are you? What do you think you're doing?'

The gaunt, rangy old man, thin hair plastered close to his scalp even after the scuffle, looked furious.

'The public has a right to know!' he said. 'Medical misadventure? Or state secret? Do you know,' — his eyes fixed on Dr Jackson — 'how much radiation our national hospitals use?'

Dr Jackson's arms dropped to her sides. 'Sir, I will ask you only once. Please leave immediately, or we'll call security and the police.'

Latu went over and hauled the old man up by an armpit. Bu saw the orderly's jaw flex as he bit down hard on his anger.

'I have a right to be here! I know this *one*!'

'What?' The medical staff exchanged glances.

'I know him!' The old man searched in his trouser pockets and brought out a business card. He handed it over to Dr Jackson. 'My name is Victor Forsyth. And I know this — being! He has been sent to us all as a portent. The public has a right to know him too. I am on assignment!'

Irritated, Linda Jackson flipped the business card over to Brian Jobbes. 'These aren't even your details, sir. The card belongs to some woman — Four Corners Real Estate. It's advertising guff. Christ, Latu, can you get him out of here, please? But don't let him leave the ward — I'm calling the police. We'll be with you in a minute.'

Though the old man struggled and protested, Latu removed him easily. 'Crackpot,' Dr Jackson muttered, once he was gone.

She held out a hand to Jobbes, who returned the card. Frowning at her, he said, 'I'll help.' He left the room quickly, hurrying to catch Latu.

Dr Jackson approached the bed. 'It's all right now.' She watched Bu for a while. 'But I suppose your story must be getting around.'

Bu knew he mustn't take his eyes off her. It was like balancing on a high, narrow beam, nothing but sky above and below. If he looked away, the blue nothingness would come rushing at him. Her earrings today were clear glass, but close up, he could see they held a cluster of pollen-coloured flecks. Like gold dust in a river pool. He fixed on them.

'The nurse will get you something to drink. Is there anything else you need?'

Bu lifted his stare from her earring to her eyes, then quickly lowered his gaze. He began to feel nausea again and gripped hard onto the sides of the bed.

'Just — breathe out. It's all right. Breathe out slowly. That's it. Good. Are you okay?' Linda Jackson sat with him for a while, taking his pulse. She seemed reassured, and said, 'There'll be an afternoon tea trolley round soon. And I'll get someone to pop in on you every half-hour or so, just to make sure everything's still all right.'

She watched him, her mouth softening. 'You know, we're here to take care of you. But perhaps we haven't done such a good job so far. Perhaps there's somewhere else for you to go, somewhere you'd like us to help you get to?'

Bu turned away. Too tired for this.

The nurse came in with a plastic water jug and a clean cup. 'Thanks, Anna,' said the doctor, and both women moved away to the door. 'Can you wait with him for a while?'

'Sure.'

Then, just audibly, Dr Jackson added, 'I don't think we can legitimately keep him here in an open ward much longer. We might have to look at moving him over to psych properly. Easier to protect him there.'

The Crowd

HOURS BEFORE, THE TALK had begun about Bu. Spectators began their telegraph as soon as he was wheeled away from the book bus.

'Did you see that guy?' said someone in academic robes, as his parents tried to hustle him off to the start of the capping procession.

'No, not really, Cohen. Come on, you don't want to be late.'

The young man shook his head in disbelief. 'Wish I'd taken a picture. I could've sold it to the papers. It's like, Nicole Kidman's boyfriend. You know, from that flop movie, *Fur*. Some carnival guy maybe.'

The cream-haired tourist turned to the small, balding man who stood next to her. 'I saw him. I *touched* him. I thought it was a prank, see, but he just went completely *insane...*'

And so it grew, from a cluster of sources on the spot, to hotel receptionists, academics, taxi drivers, petrol-pump hands, shop assistants; in conversations at pubs, to family and friends; via emails, phone calls, texts.

The rumours began to mutate.

There was a strange, unidentified man at the public hospital. He'd been glimpsed between wards. A mute, a recluse.

'Didn't you read about some guy like that in the paper the other day?'

'Same one, maybe. I heard he looked really unusual.'

'Poor guy.'

'He did. They said he looked like — well — an animal,

really. Covered in hair thick as fur apparently. Massive. Walks upright. Some sort of wild man from the bush.'

'Works for Search and Rescue, does he? Like that TV ad. *Dave, there's no such thing as yetis.*'

'No, you lot, this guy's for real.'

'Freaky. Some kind of throwback.'

'Or alien.'

'Sounds like the maero.'

'Maero?'

'My koro told me these stories. The maero had crazy tangled hair, and long, long nails. Used them to kill their prey . . .'

'A bit like Big Foot.'

'Get real. He's probably just some random bloke with an outsized beard. And they've never proven any of those things, have they? Disproven, more like. Y'know, scientists have run tests on supposed yeti fur samples, and worked out they're just from antelope or bear or something.'

'So what, you're the yeti professor now, are you? I saw on Discovery Channel just the other day, people reckon in like some of the really remote regions of the world there could still be undiscovered species, and like, if they can find whole new monkeys that they never even knew existed, why can't they find a yeti?'

'What, in New Zealand? We've never had prehistoric people here. The first humans came on boats.'

'What's to stop a yeti making a boat too?'

'You're having a laugh. Just buy us another beer, y' daft arse.'

Sandrine

SANDRINE MOREAU PULLED HER socks back on behind the hospital room's changing screen, then roughly shoved on her slightly mismatched shoes, feeling herself veer between anger, awkwardness and a sense of how absurd her own mood swings were.

'There's really nothing more to be done,' the young clinician had said to her, before pointing her to the chair behind the modesty screen, as if even he found the exposure of her foot an embarrassment.

She wished she could ask to see her old consultant, Professor Hendrickson, of the soft voice and comforting, badger-like stripe of grey in his beard and hair. But apparently he was overseas on sabbatical, and this brusque, athletic man (enviably good bones — how unfairly fitting for orthopaedics) had been assigned to take her last post-surgical appointment. Dr Lloyd completely lacked Professor Hendrickson's gentle, jokey ways: he hadn't smiled once, hadn't even used her name. After all these years of investigations and failed operations, Sandrine felt like nothing more than an annoyance: the one-too-many on Dr Lloyd's Tuesday schedule. He didn't look up from his computer screen when she gave her automatic thanks and goodbye — not even when she repeated them with a catty-sour twist in her voice.

Nothing more to be done. She guessed she'd half known — okay, three-quarters known — that the doctors would say as much. Yet leaving the consultation she still felt the welling of disappointment. A giant moth lightly made of tears tried to batter its way along her arms, into her chest, up behind her mouth. She pinched the skin on one forearm, hissing at herself under her breath, '*Stop* it.'

As she rounded a corner, she almost bowled over a very thin, young Indian man roaming the corridor, selling flowers from a bucket. Flustered, she bought a bouquet in apology, also thinking it might calm her down. It didn't. She found herself back at the wrong end of the ward, so had to double back past reception again. As she went by, her glance flashed over to a white board listing room numbers and patients' names. One entry with a 'Mr' and then a long, thickly drawn dash made her hesitate. Something started to tease at her memory.

That morning, the community newspaper where she worked had been asked to run a further missing persons notice about the injured tramper from South Westland, but nobody could provide a mugshot. Mark, her boss, argued that with a description like that, there would hardly be cases of mistaken identity, but Sandrine had countered that more readers would notice a picture than a tiny sidebar at the edge of a page. As if snooping around would somehow exact a small fillip of revenge against the medics who couldn't mend her hobbled foot and lopsided, rolling walk, Sandrine found herself deliberately stopping at the enquiries desk.

The girl on duty looked so young that Sandrine wondered whether she was someone's daughter on a day off school, left in charge for a moment while her mum or dad nipped out to the loo. The whippet met Sandrine's 'Excuse me?' with a jerk of the head and an attempt to cover up something she'd been reading.

'Yes?' She widened her eyes.

Sandrine's thoughts darted in and out of possible stories. 'Um — I've just — uh — brought in these flowers for one of the patients on the ward.'

'Oh.' The girl stood up, smoothed down her skirt, then shielded her chest self-consciously with one arm. She gazed at the bouquet in confusion. 'I'm just a temp. Should I take them, or —?'

'No, that's okay, I'll take them in myself. I'll leave them in his room if he's sleeping.' Sandrine gave the girl a beaming, comforting smile. 'Thank you.'

The receptionist smiled back tentatively, one hand still gripping the opposite arm, but she didn't sit down. Sandrine walked away quickly, then ducked around a corner. Still feeling a weird buzz of illicit excitement, she began to search for the injured hiker, peering into each room as she passed. A nurse carrying a medicine tray came by but barely tossed Sandrine a glance, her mouth set in a mournful cast.

When Sandrine found the young man, in a tiny room tucked away in a corner, she couldn't quite believe it was that easy. She kept looking over her shoulder, in case someone was about to halt her and pull her away.

He was sitting up in bed, his hands folded over his lap, his gaze turned away to the high window.

Time slowed, and she took the chance to absorb his appearance without him witnessing the way shock spilled through her — or the shame that quickly followed, at the lack of genuine motive or need behind her curiosity. What had she been *thinking*? Was she mad?

Even seated he was strikingly tall and broad-framed, yet with a kind of slenderness in the shoulders and a fine muscularity that suggested his youth, as if he hadn't entirely filled out yet. It was sobering to imagine him even larger, stronger.

His dark-blondish, silken pelt seemed to cover everything except his lips. It grew in whorls over his cheeks and forehead, so that it swept up and over his scalp away from his eyes. Lower, near his jaws, it formed a kind of double cowlick, so that his full mouth was visible. Luxuriant, smooth, glinting, the hair reminded her vaguely of the tail feathers on a golden retriever.

She'd automatically fallen into breathing deeply. *So I must be afraid*. She realised her throat was crowded again with bizarre, held back tears: almost as if the disarray she'd felt after her appointment had been some kind of premonition of this scene, and the erratic emotions had pulled her here, to their real source.

She tried to regain self-control by tracking his gaze. He was watching a wood pigeon, its breast stout as a cream jug, sitting in profile on the outside ledge. It was odd to see one so far from the town belt and where there was no real space between hospital blocks for it to perform its breath-stopping arabesques and sky-dives.

Sandrine squared her shoulders, lifted a hand and, with her heart racketing in her chest, knocked on the already open door.

The stranger flinched, palms quickly splayed flat on the bedcovers, giving the impression that he'd have sprung into a crouch if he weren't hampered by his injured leg. His eyes were huge, dark, hectic with fear.

'I'm sorry. I startled you.'

Silence.

She stayed in the doorway, trying to keep all her actions slow and measured. 'I didn't mean to.'

She waited. She could feel his eyes dart over her, up and down. Then he lowered his head, wary.

'Do you mind if I come in for a moment?'

His gaze scampered to the corridor behind her.

'These are for you,' she said, embarrassed, thinking he would easily guess that she'd made up the offer on the spot.

She entered slowly, arranged the bouquet in a plastic water beaker, then wiped off her hands. When she stood back, she realised he was panting in quick, bewildered breaths. His fear helped her to imitate courage.

'Sorry, I haven't introduced myself. My name's Sandrine Moreau. I — I've read about you, and I was just passing.'

As Sandrine heard footsteps approach, then divert down another corridor, she felt the kind of self-consciousness she might experience if caught talking to a cat. Did he understand?

She plunged on. 'I was thinking, if nobody's come forward to identify you yet, you could do — could do —' Her cheeks felt hot with deception. She should just leave the flowers and go: he'd know she was little better than a gawping tourist.

He met her eyes. His breathing had relaxed. This time the silence seemed so full Sandrine was sure it would have to split, leak some sound, any sound at all — breath, murmurs, fragments of language. She waited. His eyes moved to her clavicle where a pendant nestled, a silver fuchsia, the stamens made as four thin, separate pieces, loose like the clappers of a bell. Her hand went nervously to her neck, and his eyelids flickered before he looked away.

He had seen her fear, yet she knew, as tangibly as if he had spoken, that she shouldn't be afraid. An uncanny contentment filled her, akin to the joy she sometimes used to wake with as a child.

A knot untied beneath her ribs, and she sat down carefully in the chair near his bed.

Watching his prodigious form, she remembered a childhood visit to London. One night she and her parents had taken an evening stroll to Greenwich Park with family friends and settled on the grass while one of the men played his guitar. As the melody lengthened, a fox crept out of the dusk and edged closer, circling them. Because it held her stare for several bars, she was convinced the animal knew she was a child. She somehow knew, too, that it had young of its own nearby, waiting. She never forgot the cautious awe of that moment. The sensation that ran along the blood, from her to the fox and back, had an impossible tenderness.

What brave new world is this? she wanted to say now — Caliban the real marvel. *Where do you come from*? As if he could answer, as if he would understand English . . . Was he even a man?

The paper, her boss Mark . . . to be first in print with an investigation, to get a chance to answer all the questions crushing towards her . . .

She leaned over to see what was on the bedside table pushed up against the opposite wall, already nosing about for clues, for background detail. It took her a moment to accept what she saw. Nail clippers, coloured pens, newspaper, a small pile of books and magazines, even a little transistor radio, with *hospital property* lettered along its side in red Vivid marker. She saw, too, a sizeable backpack shoved into the space beneath the table.

'What are you reading?' she asked, still half expecting

blankness. The belongings might have been left for him by someone else.

Keeping his eye on her, his hands felt for the pile of books, brought it over to his lap and took out a slim volume a couple of titles down. He passed it to her hesitantly.

In her eagerness to accept the gesture, she almost snatched it from him, but then, seeing the sad listlessness of his hands as they drifted back to rest on the remaining books, she felt predatory, crude. She read the title aloud. '*The Hawk in the Rain*. Ted Hughes.' She turned to the back cover. Poetry.

Sandrine stared openly at the otherworldly face she'd assumed was untutored, dumb, and felt another swift flow of shame. She subconsciously tucked her right foot under her chair, adjusting her long skirt so that the hem touched the floor in a concealing tent.

Outside, the wood pigeon stirred, a riffle of white and greenish-grey, with an almost musical thrum audible even through the room's old, rattly windows. It flew off a short distance, then circled in return. The bird regained its balance, shuffled into place again, bobbed its neck.

Sandrine felt the questions jostle, but not how to frame them. *Who are you*? *Where do you come from*? They all seemed too blunt.

The quiet slipped up over her, immobilising, but calming.

Strange. She felt almost sleepy. Could have sat there all afternoon, feeling the stranger's presence like — like what? Like an unexpected package. The thought made her smile, but there it was. Wrapped up in his silence, his secrets were still whole.

The noise of wheels and footsteps from the corridor

broke Sandrine out of her reverie. She didn't want to be asked what she was doing there. Instinct said she should keep to herself the curiosity the young man had piqued. Quietly, she took her leave.

Outside the hospital, on a South Pacific blue day, she felt the kindling of energy and intuition that sometimes came when a feature idea began to take form. She knew she'd find excuses to see the timid giant again.

Bu

HE BEGAN TO THINK of her as the quiet one. She visited again, the very next day, with another gift.

It startled him, the way people could just come and go, like fantails from a clearing or light and dark from the sky, when it had taken him so much planning to leave his own home.

Alert with surprise at her reappearance, Bu noticed something tilting in her gait as she made her way across the tight space of the room. She was like a bird with string or wire wrapped around its ankle. Was she tired, hurt, or sad? He couldn't smell sadness, only something like crushed mint, fresh baked bread, and the she-scent that would have to take her own name.

Sandrine was that name, she reminded him again, as she put a box of chocolates on the bedside table. 'Cliché, sorry. I'm not sure if you can eat these. Would you like them? Is there anything else I can bring you?'

He almost wanted to answer, yet fear and distrust still gagged him. Again and again he heard his parent-folks' words, the ones he'd had to ignore to find the courage to leave. *It would be too dangerous, out on your own. Most people are cruel — crueller than you can imagine.*

The doctors had been in and out of his room all morning with talk of trials and research; pushing at him, looking at him in a way that made him wonder about the difference between questions-questions-questions and being unkind. They asked him to sign consent forms, said they needed his signature before they could run further tests on IQ and genetics, and a nurse asked him if they could take 'just a tiny teaspoon of blood for fuller analysis'. Such a strange way to talk of blood that his thoughts fell into a troubled clutter, in which he imagined the nurse delicately sipping at the measure of his juices, leaving her teeth plum-stained as she told him he tasted of soot and sin. He had growled, giving a wave of his fist that had quickly cleared the room.

Everything they asked made him less and less willing to talk, made his gut ache with need for the man and woman he had been raised by. They had known all along. '*You don't realise how free you are,*' his mother-woman had said. '*With us, you're safe. Here, you can be real. Not just some monster in a mask.*'

He heard her voice; he saw her opening a box of the very same sweets Sandrine had brought him, treating them like treasure. They were a rare, town luxury, bought on one of his father-man's carefully planned expeditions from the bush.

Even though he knew his refusal to talk bothered everyone around him here, the loss of his parent-folk wouldn't fit into words.

When Sandrine visited, it seemed she wanted to match his silence. She sat there, bristling with caged-in energy at first: bees of eagerness humming from her, until, after a while, her eyes stared into a dreamy, hazy nowhere. And as with the first encounter, he felt he had just found enough ease to listen to her properly, when she left the room.

He wished he were brave enough to call her back.

On her third visit, she brought him something else. It was an ice-cream container full of dirt, fern roots, berries and decaying bark that was fat with white huhu grubs.

'Here,' she said. 'One of the nurses told me you're not eating the food they give you. I asked a friend who knows about native, well, birds and plants and things . . .' Her voice was uncertain, but her eyes were lit with anticipation. 'Eat?' she said, and mimed it for him. He blinked at her rapidly. She reached out, carrying one of the grubs too close to his mouth. He turned his head swiftly aside as his stomach heaved.

Her face was woeful. 'Oh. Okay. That's okay.' She sealed up the container again. Her blush stole under his pelt, and warmed his belly. He pressed a hand there.

He had to give her something — some sign that he understood, though grief and the grey weight of guilt still pressed on him. With great mental effort he reached for the drawer in the narrow cupboard at his bedside and brought out the paper and pens someone had left him. Quickly he sketched a picture — he wanted it to be a flower the colour of her blush, but some misjudged lines made him change it into a kind of sprite: a girl-woman with a crown of petals around her head, and at her ankle-stems, leaves that were too long, looked like misshapen wings. A piece of nonsense, a peace offering.

After she took the picture with a small frown, she stared at the page for several moments. The colour in her face drained. She raised her head.

'Who are you?' Earlier she had crossed her legs, one foot propped up so that it almost touched his bed. Now her hand stole protectively to her ankle.

He plucked at the bedclothes. Then he pointed to where her hand was cupped.

Her eyes glittered as slowly she slipped off her shoe, then her sock. She lifted her leg slightly, raising her ankle even closer to his bedside. Her foot was twisted and knobbled like an ancient tree root, and it carried the lines and weals of old scarring. Someone had cut into her, but had failed to mend her.

Briefly, her fingertips rested on the back of his hand, her skin bare and white against his pelt. It was like someone testing for the heat of metal — so different from the way everyone else here had probed him, with their measuring and prodding. He felt his heart thump once, hard and painful. Then unconsciously he reached out to feel the bumps on her foot. Were they as hot as the fiercely red skin said? His fingers glided, trying to smooth away the lumps and contortions. He heard her quick intake of breath, saw what his hands were doing. As if at the release of some hidden lever, he and Sandrine sprang apart.

While she put her sock and shoe back on, bent to her task to try to hide her confusion, he felt he had done something terribly wrong. He sat rigid with embarrassment until he saw her carefully fold the sketch he had made and slip it into her bag. When she managed to look at him again her face had changed: it was accepting, peaceful.

He thought she was about to leave, but instead she asked, 'Tell me, where is your family?'

He lowered his head.

'You do need to talk to someone.'

He looked out the window. He concentrated on the rag of cloud he could see in the sky, waiting for it to change shape, hoping it would show him something else to think about.

'Isn't there anyone who can come and help you?'

The noise that escaped from his mouth was crude, yet she didn't pull away. 'Hey. Hey there,' she said. 'What is it?

Can you tell me?' Then, over his sobs, she asked, 'What's your name, hey? What's your name?'

A nurse swung in with a tray of meds in her hand, drawn by Bu's cry. 'What's going on?' she said. She put down the metal tray with a clatter. 'You're distressing him. What did you want?'

'I — no, nothing. I'm just a — uh — friend.'

'Really? Since when?' The nurse quickly gave Bu some tissues and went to take his wrist. 'What's she done to you?' She stood between him and Sandrine.

He shook his head.

'Like I said, I'm a friend,' said Sandrine, and though he was cuffing at his eyes, he saw her trying to crane around the nurse.

'A friend would know when he'd had enough.' The woman looked at the watch pinned to her uniform as she took Bu's pulse. 'We don't need any looky-loos here, Miss. If you genuinely know this young gentleman, you should be contacting the police.'

Sandrine rose abruptly, 'Right. Well, I have to go, anyway. Get back to the office.'

The nurse refused to acknowledge Sandrine as she left, but her face was kind as she sat next to Bu on the bed and asked the same questions: 'What's the matter? What's upset you? Can you tell me?'

The sensation of Sandrine's touch seemed to stay with him, sending out tendrils and spirals of warmth as he thought of it. He would hold onto his tale until she returned.

Sandrine

OUTSIDE ON THE STREET the hard lines of the buildings and the iron grey light of a sudden sou'westerly change broke her trance. Yet neither the bravery of showing her foot, nor the warm release she'd felt at the young patient's touch, had evaporated. Her step almost felt lighter. He was like some kind of drug. Each time she'd seen him, she'd come away disoriented, heart racing.

She'd quietly been working through how to win his trust. If she could reveal his story, whatever it was, publication could be her ticket into a better job than her role at the community weekly, the *Southern Mercury*. After a tough stint freelancing, she still wasn't saving much, even with steady pay. Yet the dumbstruck man wasn't some marvel, some freak-show exhibit. Acknowledging how she had hoped to use him, she felt the kind of dismay she would if she'd slept with a friend's boyfriend. If you can't even live by your own code of honour . . .

When a woman turned her head as she walked by, Sandrine realised she'd been muttering a string of *shits* under her breath. She swung into one of her favourite bars, found her way to a small table in a corner and, with a notebook and pen beside her, waited for the first sips of chardonnay to float some understanding to the surface of her thoughts.

If she did visit him again, would it be as a friend or really for a scoop? She knew what some of her friends, and her parents would think: if she followed up on him, she'd be taking on yet another hurt stray. There had been 'social crusade' stories for the paper, and her various irregular bouts of volunteer work at a homeless shelter, the Red Cross op shop. Thinking Sandrine was out of earshot, her mother had once said, 'Does she think she's one of them? A lame duck, like them? Because she isn't.' Sandrine had stomped out of her parents' house, her gait as exaggeratedly awkward as she could make it.

She wished Faber were here to talk it over with. Her ex-flatmate, he was her best friend, really, since her main confidante, Deborah, had left town to live with her boyfriend. She missed Faber's level-headedness. But he was on a ten-day holiday to Sydney, pursuing an Australian woman he'd met last winter. He hadn't even texted Sandrine to say how it was going, which probably meant he was too enraptured by what's-her-name to think of his friends back home.

Well, at least Deborah was still in the country, even if she was a three-hour drive away. Sandrine flipped open her mobile to call her, but was put through to voice mail. After another consoling sip of wine, she decided maybe it was just as well. Deb was often refreshingly blunt; but just as often she steamrollered right over important ambiguities. Sandrine let herself slip into a long, introspective lull.

Bu

ON THE DAY SANDRINE brought the grubs, his misery seemed worse after she left, as if her warmth had shown him just how bare and windswept his solitude really was. He was suddenly cold. Although a nurse aide brought him a meal tray, he hunkered down under the covers, wrapping himself away from the light.

The following day slipped by, then the next, and the next. The doctors came and went, asking their questions, trying to press the same consent forms on him, saying *research* and *syndromes* and *long-term prognosis* and *to your advantage*. But he still snarled at the needles, so the staff said, 'In your own time', and kept their distance. In one respite between intrusions, when he had been left alone for so thankfully long that Bu believed they might have forgotten him for an entire afternoon, he fiddled listlessly with the radio someone had brought in, and found a station playing a violin concerto. *Mendelssohn*, the announcer said, and the sweetness of the repeated motifs made Bu feel as if pincers were loosening their grip along the length of his spine. He lay back, closed his eyes, let the patterns of the notes fall easily into his mind. He hummed the refrain quietly to himself, again and again.

'*Listen!*'

'He's vocalising.' A nurse and a doctor stood there. He knew then, in miserable surrender, that he would have to comply a little. He would have to fill out one of their stupid tests. Only one. He still refused to give them any blood, and he wrote unevenly on the bottom of the form he conceded to, '*Now leave me alone.*' There was close-reading and checking of his work, many excited hand-waves and head signals in his room, and then talk in the corridor that he could hear far too well.

'So he's fully literate.'

'Well, we'd already surmised as much. I think the most intriguing result is the intelligence quotient. That's a high score.'

'Yes, the musical ability — and these answers — extraordinary. There's clearly no mental impairment.'

'Exactly. He's poked his nose out of his burrow. We need to tell Keith Peterson from psych, and get him to start some work with him. He might actually make some progress now.'

'Not before time. I've been asking psych to take him almost since he came in — same story as elsewhere, though: no beds.'

'Once Peterson has had a chance to do some head work on him, I'd still like to push for some genetic screening. I'm bloody curious about what's been shuffled around in this guy's chromosomes.'

Bu felt an irrational dread about being moved from one ward to the other, especially when he learned that the new unit had to be reached by mobility van. He found himself wondering if Sandrine would ever visit again. *Foolish cub*, he told himself. *How will she find me, and why would she try?*

Keith Peterson

THE YOUNG WHEELCHAIR-BOUND MAN in the small ante-room was the most disfigured patient Keith Peterson had seen outside medical journals. Words from myth and fable leapt out at him: *troll, griffin, satyr*. He blinked, waiting for their echoes to diminish, as if they might slip off his tongue if he spoke too soon.

Yet it was hardly as if he was inexperienced in such matters. He was used to the flattened, almost leonine facial expression of advanced schizophrenia and the blank mask of some degrees of autism; and of course there was a raft of congenital disorders that caused malformed skulls, markedly abnormal facial features, tortured body shapes. All too often, for the afflicted, the struggle to deal with these also brought compromised mental health. Yet Keith still had to check himself with this young man, actively search for empathy.

Another reason for Keith's uncharacteristic hesitation, he knew, was the visceral pulse of fear he felt. The man loomed from his wheelchair. His form had the shaggy pelt of something ursine; yet the thick, glowering brow, the skull's dimensions and the length of his limbs verged on the simian.

The patient's age was guesswork, although some of his symptoms were typical of younger clientele — the aphasia, for example. But there were other clues. His enormous frame still lacked the thickness you might expect of a much more mature candidate. Despite the size of his skull, it also had an almost — Keith wanted to say delicate — narrowness that seemed youthful. There was even something about the eyes: they were huge, as a child's are in proportion to the size of its head.

Still, Keith was pleased that the psych nurse chosen to escort the patient in was himself something of a mammoth. A former rugby prop, now a bodybuilding fanatic, Tarn was rumoured to eat something like four eggs, eight pieces of toast and two bowls of cereal for breakfast — his first breakfast, before training. He looked as if he could handle just about anyone. This was perhaps another irrational reaction, given the young patient's broken leg, but Keith knew all too well how strong even apparently frail patients could be, when the disturbance of psychosis, or common rage, surged through the mind's wires.

He'd read the patient's slender medical file, but there had been no time to think through possible types of diagnostic and treatment methods. The notes suggested a kind of selective mutism. Two staff had heard the man humming, so they knew he could vocalise, and in a series of relatively complex patterns — he could carry a tune.

Keith had dealt with a couple of cases of selective mutism before, but both instances were in young children. The condition was much rarer in adults. He was already aware that some of the therapies he'd used weren't going to be appropriate here.

It was possible, of course — although unlikely — that the boy-man would talk to Keith, despite the fact that he hadn't spoken to any of the staff over at public. He would need, perhaps, to establish in what contexts speech became crippled for him; work out how to reduce his anxiety, increase his confidence in social situations. But as the reality of the man's physiognomy and physique sank in, Keith knew 'talk therapy' was going to have to come much later in the piece. And another crucial tool would be useless: he wouldn't be able to read the subtleties of facial expression. Keith felt the pressure and responsibility of the man's care tightening around him.

A light yet rapid tic started up in his left eyelid. It was like a memo sent by the body, reminding him of how, with his other two mute patients, he'd learnt to lower his gaze, looking benignly to the left or right — not directly at them. He did so now, but not before he'd taken in several important details. The man set aside a tiny plastic Spiderman motorbike, which he seemed to have been idly fingering. It came from a basket of toys and knick-knacks on a side table that were sometimes used for play therapy or to entertain waiting children. It had been broken by one of the other clients but Keith saw that, just now, the young man had fixed it.

'Good morning,' Keith said. The patient sat tensely in the chair. One thumb rubbed nervously at the base of the other. There was none of the hand-flapping sometimes associated with the speechlessness of autism and, crucially, he had also been able to meet Keith's eyes for a short moment before his gaze drifted away. He thought of a small child watching at a window, waiting for the long rain to end.

Keith kept his voice measured and low as he thanked Tarn, asking him to wait with them, and told them both about the protected blue gums in the hospital grounds.

Keith kept his gaze on his hands as he explained to the man why he had been moved to this clinic. He calmly outlined the concerns for his mental health, his welfare and his ability to care for himself, especially with his broken leg. 'Your doctors from the medical wards and I all agree that you're a valid case for hospital assistance,' he said, 'but you can, of course, discharge yourself at any time.'

When Keith let his glance alight on the young man, who lifted his eyes briefly, he caught what he swore was a spark of irony. Keith stopped mid-flow and found himself raising his eyebrows at Tarn, who looked confused — not sure what was expected of him, like a sixteen-year-old whose name has been called in class when he'd been happily thinking about the pie he'd ordered for lunch. With a small, amused cough, Keith turned to his desk for a leaflet that gave details of the rhythms of the psych centre: meal times, small group activities, possibilities for various types of therapy. 'You can choose, too, which events you take part in. There's no rush. This is for you, if you'd like it.' He pushed the pamphlet across his desk. After several beats, a thickly furred hand stole out and clutched it.

'Hmmm,' Keith said aloud, as if agreeing to something the patient himself had suggested. 'These might interest you, too.' He took some other literature down from the shelf above his desk. 'Not all of it will be relevant, I know, but see if there's something that you think rings a bell.' These were more photocopied sheets about the most common conditions dealt with at the institute. 'Ah, yes, and one nice thing that's happened here recently is that we've installed a small new sound system in the shared day room. And — I came across these at home. I thought they might be something you'd enjoy.'

He pulled out four or five CDs from one of his drawers. Violin concertos: Beethoven, Mendelssohn, Mozart.

Again, he set them on the desk, and waited.

He had the sensation of holding out an enticement to something both as imposing and yet as fragile as a baby giraffe, leaf by careful leaf, through the bars of silence and mystery. The young man tipped his head down again and some of the long, pale strands of hair that grew in whorls away from his face fell forward. It was the way any other boy might try to hide his expression with his fringe, or the visor of a cap.

Keith felt a pang of self-recrimination. He might have overdone it. The humming incident mentioned in his notes was one of the few clues so far to the young man's interior life, but Keith's acknowledgement of it might have made him feel vulnerable, exposed.

He turned to Tarn again. 'Shall we go for a bit of a wander around the buildings and the grounds? It's a quiet time for most of the residents at the moment — many of them will be resting. But it seems a pity to waste that sunshine out there.'

'All-righty,' Tarn said. 'Bit of a breeze, but it'll be nice out round by the rhodos.'

While Keith looked for his keys and picked up his coat, he and Tarn talked about the chief groundsman, who had apparently fallen off a ladder while pruning but was still hobbling around with a sore hip, saying that if he stopped, he'd rust up.

Keith saw that with the focus away from him, the young man's hand slid out to the desk again. His fingers lipped at the CDs, like an elephant's trunk testing their texture, and then he drew them close to his chest. Although he clutched them tightly, and his furry brow was rumpled, his response filled Keith with the quiet glow of a small achievement.

The sun seemed to agree. Light shinned up a lamppost in the grounds, and leapt, dazzling, from the top.

Beneath the quick compassion he now found for the man, there was the thrill of something else — something he tried to censor even from himself. *What I could make of this, once he talks.* There came a quick vision of a conference podium, somewhere in Europe: Keith rising to speak of, say, an extraordinary modern-day Kaspar Hauser, not autistic, but a half-feral savant; colleagues' faces tilted towards him, enraptured by discovery, eager to ask questions, make suggestions. He felt his pulse speed up already with the adrenaline of academic exchange, the advance of scholarship.

'Doc?' said Tarn, behind him. 'It's this way. That way's the staff library.'

Keith managed to laugh at himself. 'Sorry. Distracted.' And he smiled towards the patient. All the same, he heard the words clearly in his head: *Tell me your secrets, and I'll help to make you whole.*

Bu

THE NEW WARD HE'D been moved to across town was in a specialist institute, they told him. There he was given another cubby hole room — awkward for him with a cast and crutches. Over several days he had a number of interviews with someone called Dr Peterson, a lean, tall man — though like all the people he'd seen, not as tall as Bu — with pitted skin that showed through his beard. At the first meeting, he said to Bu that there were concerns for him, but that 'You can, of course, discharge yourself at any time'.

Like a bullet or a bird from my own hands, Bu thought, and he kept to nods, head-shakes, shrugs, still not sure whom he could trust. Increasingly he felt that even if he had wanted to speak, he couldn't. His throat was constricted, like the neck of a balloon pulled into the tightest of knots.

Dr Peterson seemed to sense something of this. At their second or third meeting he suggested that Bu use either finger taps, humming or even popping noises to communicate with him. Bu didn't at first, still too wary, but during their fourth or fifth encounter, Dr Peterson asked about his family and Bu's tears dripped like a leak that couldn't be plugged.

He felt the doctor draw himself back, like a man who had finally seen what he was looking for, and wanted to get full view of it. Peterson passed him some tissues, saying, as if to himself, 'I think sometimes the people we love the most are the hardest to speak of.' He watched

Bu's tears. 'You've had a pretty rough time these past few weeks, hey? Maybe have done for a while.'

He leafed through a folder of papers open on the desk beside him, reading silently. He jotted down a few notes, then looked at Bu over the rims of his glasses.

'I think you've been losing more weight, son. Can you signal to me how you've been sleeping?' He waited. 'No. Okay.'

He put down his pen, and swung around on his swivel chair so that he faced Bu. 'Look. I'm going to be frank. I think it would be a good idea for you to stay with us until you can talk about what's happened to you. How you had your accident.' He paused, and Bu could feel him searching his face, despite the fact that he kept his own head bowed. 'Where you come from.'

With a start he felt Peterson circle his forearm with both hands. 'We need to get you eating. *Mens sana in corpore sano*, hmm?'

When he let go, Bu rubbed at his arm, then cradled it close to his body.

Peterson chewed at the inside of his bottom lip. 'You're telling me you just want to be left in peace.'

Bu gave a small *mmmph* — half sigh, half irritation — and the doctor straightened.

'How about we cut a deal? I'll make sure you're given some real rest for a few days — no consultations, no activities — if you'll just answer a few questions for me. But you must try to understand. We really can't give you what you need unless you start opening up.'

After a deep silence, slowly, Bu raised an index finger and tapped once: the signal for yes.

Peterson seemed to take this in his stride. 'You agree

that you've lost some weight recently?'

Tap.

'Have you been sleeping well?'

Tap, tap.

'Do you have other symptoms?' Dr Peterson clasped a hand to his own chest. 'Racing heart? Dry mouth?'

Bu wondered how the man could possibly know. Did one of his strange electrical instruments read through the walls at night, then through fur, skin and bone, to light up messages on the computer screen here, in his interview room?

Tap.

Peterson's own index finger slowly mirrored the *yes*. The doctor talked to him for a while about words Bu recognised from some of the leaflets he'd been given. Peterson suggested a brand of medicine with a name that sounded like Arrow Packs: he told him it would reduce his worry and panic. Bu imagined it shooting off little weapons to kill his bad dreams, bad thoughts.

'How do you feel about being prescribed something like this?'

Bu dipped his head, *yes*.

The consultant's entire posture changed. 'So we're on the right path, then. That's very, very good.' He made some more notes in Bu's file. 'We can take our time. Perhaps once the medication kicks in, it'll be easier for you to talk. It's hard to think clearly when your mind is clouded by these reactions.'

Yet Bu kept the tablets under his tongue. When he tried to swallow them, he found his throat thought better — he just couldn't. He wasn't sure why he'd nodded to Dr Peterson's suggestion, except that agreeing seemed to be a way to delay the need for other, bigger decisions.

Things he had believed he could work out once he arrived in the city now seemed impossible. He thought himself an idiot, a child. Where to live, how to befriend others, what he might tell them about himself, what they might teach him about his kind: the number of obstacles in the way grew. He would have to allow himself to be looked after for a little longer, until some answers came to him. Surely they would come . . .

After this meeting, when Bu was taken back to his room, he reached into the inner pocket of his backpack to find the comfort of the keepsakes he'd brought from home: the only ones he'd allowed himself. A pocket knife, a small clock, a hand-carved, beautifully polished wooden box, with a locket inside that held a photo. He couldn't open it just now. He knew the image inside it would detach the last, fine fibres of self-control and make them float away on the air, broken spider's silk.

Over the next week, he tried to swim his way up through the deep sea of grief and guilt that washed over him still. If, one morning, he could surface in the first seep of light, he might see clearly enough to know what to do. He might remember what his intentions had been when he first set out from the South Westland cabin, with its odds and ends extensions he and his father-man had built together when Bu was still a boy-cub. He might even find the language to explain himself to the people around him, people who wanted to be kind but were always running; even when they sat down they were running: their eyes racing, their legs and hands fidgeting, their heads bobbing at one another as if to speed the conversation to an end. *Where are they all rushing to? What waits for them at the end of each day when they leave here?*

He was finding it harder and harder to fill the time. He couldn't concentrate to read — sadness pushed at the sentences, then the words, then each separate letter, so newspapers and books became a scattering grey blur. At first he made an effort to move around on the crutches he'd been given, but often he was like many of the other patients on the new ward — sitting motionless in the day lounge, listening to the radio, staring out the window at the cloudscapes, or pointing their faces at the TV.

After a few days, Dr Peterson visited him again. He reminded Bu of a worried heron.

The doctor said it could take up to ten days for the medication to start having a noticeable effect, so it was understandable that there still hadn't been any great improvement in his mood. 'Given that we're diagnosing you in the dark, also — I mean, given you've been unable to give us specific answers about your situation — I've started you on a very low dose. I should reiterate, it's hard for us to know exactly what to prescribe, or how much, if we don't know the full extent of your condition. You will tell me, though, won't you, if you feel the drugs are having any negative effects?'

Bu nodded again, and Dr Peterson sat forward in his chair, hands open. 'I want you to feel that you can contact me, anywhere, any time.' He reached inside his suit jacket and drew out a wallet. He slipped out a small, printed piece of cardboard, circled a line of numbers with pen, and placed the card on Bu's bedside table. 'Please. I don't want you to feel you're alone.'

Bu retrieved the card, held it in both hands, looked at

the words that were like black ants neatly marching in a line. The consultant left with a dignified nod.

As he stared out the window at the patterns of leaves against the sky, Bu thought about the woman's — Sandrine's — visits. He thought about them so hard that they grew unreal, as if he had heard someone say a word aloud over and over until it became broken up into its small puffs and whistles: nonsense.

After nearly three weeks, with his leg gradually strengthening, he saw she was just a stick of hope he'd whittled for himself out of desperation, loneliness, the fear that savaged him sometimes. Dr Peterson said Bu might have a *chemical imbalance* after *recent stress, perhaps?*, or after the blow to his skull, and the *whacking great painkillers they've given you at public* . . .

So when Sandrine walked into the day lounge, bringing her special scent, her expression uncertain, both hands tightly gripping the strap of her satchel, as if it helped to keep her upright — '*Ahh.*' The strangest things could happen in his new world. The city growled like an animal made of metal parts. Buildings cluttered the air. You could like someone, and they would walk in the door as if you had thought them there. '*Ahh.*' Exhaled, like the sound of deep ease, or of something found, something understood. Nearly a word.

He saw her straighten with a small start.

'Hello,' she said.

Bu smiled. Something full and warm rose in his chest.

Sandrine glanced around, checking who else was in the room. The nurse who had escorted her was drawn out into the corridor by a man asking for warmer bedding for his son. In the lounge another man was asleep in front of the TV, and a woman watched the dance show as she slowly sipped tea from a cup. A third man in an old duffel coat stared out the window; he seemed waxen, unblinking, unaware. Sandrine gestured at Bu's crutches. 'Can you go very far with those?'

He shook his head.

She turned on the spot. 'I'll see if I can find a wheelchair and arrange to take you for a walk in the grounds. Is that all right?'

She was back soon with a chair. 'I struck gold,' she said, though she looked a little flushed, as if it had been a fight. 'Let's go.'

She took him by the elbow, and with a rattle of the crutches, a lurch and a squeak of wheels on the shiny floor, they managed to transfer him to the wheelchair.

Along a corridor, down a lift and past reception, they found their way outside. They stopped at a quiet bench under a birch tree that filtered the fierce southern sunlight through a web of shadows. They sat together, looking over at the institute buildings, out towards the road, down at the grass, watching this crescent of the world as if they were waiting for something else to appear.

Bu could smell fruit and flowers from Sandrine's skin — a sweetness she used on top of her own scent. She tucked her hair behind her ears. He wondered what it would feel like, wound around his fingers. His hands tingled with wanting to know.

'It wasn't that easy, tracking you down,' she said. 'I loitered around the orthopaedics ward for quite a while, making a nuisance of myself. Eventually, though, I found a lovely guy named Latu, who gave me a few clues about what might have become of you.' She leaned forward on the bench, swung her legs a little. 'I actually wasn't too sure you'd be here.'

He looked at his hands, left cupped in right, one brother protecting another.

Bu felt the silence go hot. He didn't know what to do. If he made no sound she would vanish again — water drunk by the sun's parched tongue. But he had waited so long to speak and now there were too many words to choose from.

She rubbed at her forehead with one hand, speaking so quietly he didn't understand straight away. 'This is crazy, me being here. Talking to myself. When I first saw you before — I thought things must have improved for you. But this isn't helping, I —'

'Pretty. Ache.' His first full words to her. The constriction in his throat fell away, but what came out sounded to him like grunts and growls. He hated himself. He scowled, gripped the arms of his wheelchair, waited for a look of disgust to cross her face. He knew she would leave. But she stayed there and her smile, though bewildered, was a charm. Even his self-revulsion lost a little power before it.

'Sorry?' she said. She hadn't even understood him. He tightened his grip on the padded handles of his chair, tried to focus the swimming sensation in his stomach into courage.

'I d-ho talk,' Bu said.

He tensed at the brief sensation of her hand on his arm, closed his eyes against the dizzying swoop. She took her hand away and Bu opened his eyes again. He wanted to tell her that her voice fitted perfectly with the patches of sunshine, the scrapings of shadow, around them. Sometimes words came out with creaks at the back of her throat: faintly reedy surprises, like the notes in tūī song, or a boy's voice breaking. For some reason he was reminded of the gingery fur his mother-woman's old black cat grew as it aged, and of the crystallised ginger his father-man bought for Christmas: sweet opposites. He wondered if the reediness meant she was older than she looked, her voice gradually drying into something crackling and leafy. Or perhaps it meant that life kept bringing her things she didn't expect.

Sandrine took some time to collect herself. In the quiet, an early cicada started up its busy call.

Memory unpeeled a paper thin layer: he thought of the sizzle of fat in the pan as his mother-woman cooked with the windows thrown open on the summer; the rhythm of his father-man's saw as he worked away at repairs to the cottage. *Burn-ing, burn-ing, burn-ing*, the cicada sang under the sun.

Have you followed me? Bu hunted around for where the cicada might have pinned itself, bright green on a twig or a grass blade. *Did you see what happened because of my mistake?*

Sandrine said something he didn't catch, and then, 'Do you think this is really where you belong? I mean, is this place going to help?'

His tongue felt fat with lack of use. 'There is nowhere else.'

She bent forward, elbows on her knees. 'Where is home?'

'Gone.'

She hesitated. 'Your family?'

It caught in his throat like a sharp, alien bone. 'Killed.'

He could tell how carefully she held herself now. Her hands drew away, closed up like mountain lilies hurt by the cold. She was afraid.

'It was — an accident.'

She was still pale. 'It was very recent?'

'In a fire.'

He watched as her thoughts tried to find firm grip on this.

'A house fire.' He could hear his own voice next to hers: a deep, buzzing growl, a huge dog prowling, warning her off a boundary. He wished he could just show her what had happened, have it roll out on a TV screen, safely tucked into a cube: no smell, no taste, no heat, no touch. He fingered at the healing patch on his scalp.

'I'm so sorry,' said Sandrine. 'This is upsetting you. I meant to come here to help, but —'

He looked down at his knees, the loose drawstring trousers, even their thin cotton uncomfortable in the sun. 'You can help,' he said, heart pounding.

'Yes?'

'Where to go, in this — *country*,' seemed to be the best word for what he meant, although he knew it wasn't correct.

She bit pensively at the inside of her lip. 'You mean, you do want to leave the hospital?'

He nodded and she frowned at the ground. 'Do you have money? Or will you need . . .?'

'I will hab money. Yes. There are papers. My parent-folk, they made eh-sure I would be all right.' He realised he was wringing his hands. 'My parent-folk — they were bery careful. They were always eh-scared it would be hard for me alone.'

She frowned. 'Because —?'

He didn't like the way he troubled her already. It robbed her of some prettiness, made him feel unkind. Disappointment at himself fell into envy. With a sudden, savage stab at how untouched and protected she must be, he sneered, 'D-ho you not eh-*see* me?'

She sat up, reddening, and yet made braver too, it would seem, by this rapid change in him, as if his ill temper had taken away the need for careful politeness.

'Yes.' And she held his stare. He pulled back a little. 'But you're smart, aren't you? You must have some skills. The newspapers said your tramping pack was highly prepared. I've seen what you read. You're hardly an ignoramus.'

He stared at her.

'What's your name, anyway?'

He licked his dry lips. 'Bu,' he said.

'French?' she frowned.

'No, my mother-woman — she chose it.'

'Were your parents, what, Indian? Canadian? *American*-Indian? It's just — your voice — I can't place your accent.'

He watched her, wondered if the black seeds of his own eyes glittered, like hers, with uncertain lights. He took in the blush of her skin, its nap smooth as ngaio petals.

'It is bery hard to ex . . . eh-splain,' he said.

Sandrine nodded, still frowning lightly.

'Perhaps — when I hab a quiet place, away from all that is . . . eh-sad and wrong, here — I will be able to.'

She bit her lip again. There was a long wait. He watched an ant zigzagging on the arm of the bench. Sandrine fiddled with the zip on her boot.

'Your foot?' he asked, to break the silence.

She straightened again quickly, defensive. 'It's nothing.'

'Here,' he answered.

She took a moment to understand, then gave a short, self-conscious laugh. 'Look, I'm not the guy with the broken leg, right?'

'Here,' he said again, hand out.

Warily, she slipped off her boot, and showed him her foot.

He gestured *up*, and after another hesitation, she cantilevered the weight of her leg on the opposite knee, lifting her foot cautiously towards his hand. Remembering the glow that had come into her face last time, the peace that had stolen into the room, he pressed and massaged again at the poor, contorted root of this woman-tree.

He remembered, too, his mother-woman rubbing at the knots in his father-man's shoulders and arm muscles with one of her healing creams, when he had overworked, trying to rush a slew of small orders — a side table, spice racks, mirror frames — for two coastal towns. Soon Bu had travelled too far back into other memories to sustain the rhythmic kneading. He stopped and looked up into Sandrine's face, which trickled with tears.

He felt shock lodge a cold fist in his stomach. 'I'm eh-sorry,' he said. 'I am rough? I —'

'No,' she said. 'Look.'

The surface still appeared to him as if it boiled furiously with scars and strange lumps made of malformed bone and muscle. Yet she dipped and flexed her foot at the ankle, as if testing its freshly oiled joint; the toes, perhaps, were a little less clenched and twisted than before. She gazed down as if the foot might have belonged to someone else.

When her eyes met his, they gleamed. 'Let me help you leave here,' she said.

Sandrine

WHEN SANDRINE AND BU were granted a meeting with Keith Peterson, the psychiatrist ushered them into his office with a neutral expression. That swiftly changed once Sandrine began to speak on Bu's behalf, explaining that he no longer felt the ward was the best place for him, and that he had asked her to help him find somewhere to stay.

'He's told you his name?' Keith interrupted. 'He's speaking?'

Sandrine felt momentarily guilty, as if she'd unwittingly done something to harm Bu. She wished she could say to the doctor in private, *he's hard to understand, sometimes, some words*, as if to lessen her trespass, and offer him consolation for not hearing Bu talk first.

'Just exactly who are you?'

She took her time to answer, watching the man carefully. *How readable we are, we with our naked skin.* She saw how the astonishment on Peterson's face rapidly moved from disbelief to disappointment, irritation and — she felt sure, afterwards — jealousy.

'I'm really just a friend,' she said. 'I've taken an interest in Bu since — well, since I chanced on him, at the public hospital. My name's Sandrine — Sandrine Moreau.'

'How do I know that name?'

'Uh — perhaps from the *Southern Mercury*. I work for the community paper.'

Keith Peterson tossed down a pen he'd been repeatedly clicking. 'A *journalist*. And you expect me to believe that this young man, who's been unwilling to speak to anyone since the start of his ordeal, has suddenly found it in himself to trust you? Look, Miss. *Bu*' — he said the name as if he disbelieved it, as if it were transparently an alias — 'may be vulnerable and naïve, but *I*, I can assure you, am not. Just what exactly do you think you're after?'

Sandrine felt her eyes smart with indignation. A certain breed of people mistrusted all reporters and yet how often had she been told by colleagues from other papers that hers was a kind of social work, not hard journalism? Arguments about the voice of democracy fought with her composure, but she pushed them aside. 'I'm not *after* anything. I just — it's hard to put into words. Bu simply has — I think he's an extraordinary person. I think . . .' she glanced at Bu, then down at her hands. 'I think he has a gift.'

'For?' He had picked up his pen again and she had the feeling he'd like to strike out her answer in red before she'd even said it.

She shrugged, helplessly. 'Perception.'

Peterson stared from one to the other.

'I haven't said this to Bu yet. But he — *affects* people. The way I've felt since I met him, the way I feel when I'm around him, it's just — it's different.'

She saw then how Peterson misunderstood. It wasn't attraction. She'd felt —what? — *lifted*, since she'd met Bu. There was another possibility she was skirting around, wary of its taint of new-age optimism. It was as if some part of her were healed, although that sounded too thorough, too final: too physical. Since he'd noticed her twists and scars, she'd felt not only compelled by him, but as if some restlessness, some inner dissatisfaction, had grown still.

She glanced at Bu and a skein of apprehension

unspooled in her stomach at the sight of his huge, liquid eyes turned on her. Still, she could explain to him later: what she'd meant when talking to Peterson. That it was both correct, and a feint, a way of persuading the doctor that she meant no harm, had Bu's best interests at heart.

She spoke the truth again, but using words: those enticing, yet misleading shape-shifters. 'I've — I've never met anyone else like him.'

Peterson exhaled through half-closed lips, then shook his head gently, adjusting his tie: loosening it, tightening it, loosening it again.

'I think I see,' he said. Did his glance graze over her figure, and down to her foot? In the interests of winning him over, she pretended not to notice.

The doctor rolled his pen between his fingers. 'My main concern,' he said, in his careful, laboured way, 'when you say, Bu, that you want to leave us, is that if you do, you'll be going away without having worked through the trauma that brought you here, and which meant you lost the ability to talk.' He turned to Sandrine. 'It's a condition we call selective mutism,' he said, pronouncing the words with even more deliberation.

'I know all about it,' she lied, terse and defensive.

'I did explain at the start of your visit, Bu, that legally we can't keep you here against your will. But I would highly recommend that you stay. And if you don't —' his reluctance to offer another option was clear. 'Well, if you were to choose the *much less recommended* path, I would still very strongly advise that you continue with regular counselling.' He watched them both, balls of determination pressing at both sides of his jaw as he clenched his teeth. Sandrine saw, then, how much Bu mattered to him, so she let herself relent slightly.

She turned back to Bu. 'That sounds sensible. I'm more than happy to help you, but there are probably things that only someone like Dr Peterson will understand. And I might not be able to do everything on my own, anyway.'

Dr Peterson lowered his eyes, appeased, she thought, but covering it up — at least until a psych nurse came to take Bu to the lunch room, and he called out casually as she reached the door. 'Sandrine, can I just have a quick word?'

'Of course.'

He waited until the nurse had escorted Bu around the corner of the long, cool corridor, then looked at his shoes as he spoke. 'We have various links to social services, of course, who can help patients — clients — with the transition into independent accommodation. I'd be happy to help you get through all that. But I — ah — I'd be very grateful if you could do me a favour in return.'

'Yes?' She half expected him to say, *Just keep well away from him outside these matters* or *This is all off the record, of course — not for your shoddy little rag . . .*

'When you have some spare time over the next week or so, could you book a time to see me?'

'Excuse me?'

'I'd like to get your account of how Bu started to talk.' His chin and neck angled out with the slightest hint of a plea. 'It would help me greatly with some research.'

Relieved that she'd misunderstood him, she quickly agreed.

Smiling broadly now, he held out his hand and they shook. Yet the decisive pressure of his grip, and the small frown that still sat between his eyes, left her with a niggling sense of gravity, a warning that she should tread with care.

Bu

'PAPERWORK...'

'Conference... care-worker, supervision...?'

'...the right channels. Delicate, responsibility...'

'Independent... quantifiable... intelligence, indubitably...'

'Further interviews and eligibility would require...'

'Patient's choice, however. So despite my doubts and his relative inexperience...'

Meetings, meetings, forms and forms. A gale had blown through his life, knocking everything down, and sending him these endless white leaves. He gave the people his father-man's last name: now they knew him as Bu Finlayson. They wrote it down a dozen times.

'Correct procedures... client's interests... health benefits...' How ugly words can be, Bu thought, in the middle of another meeting with the always-worried Dr Keith Peterson, and Bu's own plump, blonde care-worker, Carly.

He listened to their words dart and zip past him, like little swarms of flies. When Bu grew tired, the flies would land and change into something like a thin, knuckle-jointed bramble that grew and grew as the other people in the room continued to move their jaws.

What kept him sitting in his chair? He would have been rocking and moaning under his breath with confusion if it weren't for the gentle ripple of surprise he felt every time he looked over at Sandrine. Whenever the itch and irritation of the words pressed too close, the promise of her was there.

'I just want to help you,' she had said, when he asked, as if it was the simplest thing. 'Like you helped me.' Though he noticed she still walked with a limp, it was leavened, somehow — lightened. And at her matter-of-fact answer, he felt, *I will get there. Steady-go-steady. We will find me a home.*

❊ ❊ ❊

STRANGE AS A DREAM, one day, they did. In a room in a house: a *boarding* house, a *double* room for a *single person*. He swung himself on his crutches to the middle of the room and stood there, blinking. Had he been drugged, or without realising it, asleep?

The last few weeks had been a sluggish drag through something he couldn't see, a thick fog pulling at his waist and legs like water. Still afraid for much of the time, he knew he should move quickly because there was something pursuing him, and Sandrine was there, close enough to touch, but even his hands and arms wouldn't work . . . yet, *hey presto* — there he stood: in a clean, dry room, with a bed, a wardrobe, a desk and chair, and a high, white, plastered ceiling.

Sandrine had driven him there. During their trip he had felt himself gradually surfacing. There had been so much to see — even more of the city she said was small, but which to him seemed a sprawling maze. It was like a film that never ended, yet where scenes and images went by so quickly that they left him with a bittersweet ache. He wanted to know what that needle-topped building was for; what all the people were doing milling around there; why the couples didn't always seem to match up the way he thought they should; why a pair of shoes had been slung over those power-lines; why that man there, dressed like a giant chicken, was trying to give away pieces of paper; and why most people refused to take them. Sandrine seemed unmoved by any of it so he thought, *These things are ordinary? They happen all the time?* Then there had been the traffic jam, all the cacophony of horns and voices, when it was such a simple problem that even Bu could fix it. There had also been all of Sandrine's talk. She had told him that the half-hour trip took them to the outskirts of the city, just touching the rural zone. There was a combined training farm and small factory site nearby, she said, where people with intellectual disabilities were taught job skills. The last stop for the suburb's city buses was outside The Gables, the boarding house that held Bu's room.

Every fact was a wonder he had to line up with what he'd read, or seen on his parent-folks' old TV. He had to test what he saw against the raw shapes and colours of his imagining, the odd way he had grasped some things. It was like when he'd say words he'd found in books, and his mother-woman had to teach him how to pronounce them properly. The city was like a language he'd learnt without hearing it spoken. Its whole cast and lean was bigger, busier, more bewildering, yet it was also brighter, and drew him in more enticingly. He wanted to sniff it all, bite it, lick it. His hands kept lifting involuntarily to play on the air — he still wanted to run his fingers over everything, to test it was real.

'Do you like it?' asked Sandrine, about the room. Her hand cupped his shoulder briefly and he felt as if he had landed back in his body, fully awake. He gave a small *uh*, nearly a breath of laughter.

'Come and look out here.' Sandrine showed him how the long windows were also doors that opened onto a small balcony with room just for two people and a couple of worn wooden chairs. He touched everything, then stepped out beside her.

There was a garden, a fence, then more trees: the green belt, Sandrine called it. 'There's a lovely native bush walk right there.' And far off, there was the city — even the harbour, a blue tongue in the distance. A gentle wind stirred, and Bu peered into it, sniffing at all the secrets it carried. Manuka bringing a strong sway of memory; pines, eucalyptus, cut grass; and, beneath the burn of distant traffic, salty air — even from here.

Sandrine told him again how the boarding house was run. If he needed help, there was a man called Derek. The government was giving Bu money, a *benefit*, until the papers from his parents' lawyers were all sorted. *More papers.* Derek was used to managing people's benefits. Money went to him straight away for Bu's room, and there was some left over for 'personal essentials'. Sandrine and Derek had helped to get him an *account* and *money card*, from the bank he knew his family had belonged to for years: a place his father-man had always talked about with the same frown he used for fevers, garden pests or customers who didn't pay in time.

There was a kitchen; there were communal meals; there was even someone (Maia, Derek's wife) to clean Bu's room if he needed it. He could come and go as he pleased, but there were organised trips to town if people wanted them. 'Supported accommodation', she called it; the five other men here needed help too: men who found things hard on their own, and whose families were lost to them in some way.

There was a shared lounge and Derek and Maia lived on the property, but down the back, in a place they called the lodge.

He had another *counselling appointment scheduled* with Dr Keith Peterson, back at his private clinic. That too was *voluntary*. But if he decided not to go, he should phone Dr Peterson first. 'He's really very concerned for your welfare.'

Welf-fare. It made him think of a miniature beast. A fair, mouse-sized wolf. He pictured Dr Peterson cupping a *welf-fare* in his palm, protecting it. He laughed when the picture in his head changed to a tiny Bu, peering over Dr Peterson's thumb.

Sandrine smiled back at him. He liked the starry crinkles beside her eyes. 'I should get to work. I have a couple of meetings this afternoon. Shall I call you in a few days, to see how you're settling in?'

'How many days?'

'Two or three?'

'Two, yes.' He stepped closer to her, wondering at how, when he did so, she seemed to warm him — not through his pelt to his stomach, as a hearth fire would, but the other way round: from inside to outside.

When Sandrine turned a shoulder to him slightly, digging in her satchel for keys, he had the impression of a bird lifting a wing, cloaking its head, shutting its eyes tight. 'Right. Till then.'

The temperature dropped when she left. Bu listened to the creak of the stairs as she hurried down to her car. He looked at his backpack, stowed in the corner, and sank down onto the brown coverlet on his bed. He thought of going over to unpack the bag, to set out his keepsakes on a shelf as a way of trying to mark this room as his own, but he saw how the air seemed to close back over where Sandrine had stood, as if she had never been there. He waited, ears stretched to catch the last footfall of her shoes on the gravel outside the building, and finally, the click of the gate, the cough of a car engine starting.

Alone in his very own room, in a town full of people, just as he had wanted for so long, Bu crammed his knuckles into his eyes, and shook.

Sandrine

AT FIRST, DRIVING BU to The Gables, Sandrine had felt the kind of jaunty self-importance she associated with childhood, when charged with ferrying messages from teacher to teacher at primary school; or, more recently, when she had been allowed to take her baby niece out on her own and she imagined strangers thinking the child was hers. Being Bu's chaperone gave her the same sensations of significant change and momentous responsibility, yet it also brought a fresh, unexpected sense of innocence.

She glanced at Bu's profile as they pulled out from the institute to a wide, sweeping hill road. Helping Bu did make her feel as if she were making a contribution to some worthy cause, but with him, she felt — chosen. And by someone who surely had every reason to be cautious about, even hostile of, new encounters.

Yet it was only minutes into their drive across town when she began to feel that she had somehow been touched by his lack of worldliness. Perhaps it came from having dealt with him only when he was under the protection of people like Peterson: concerned, intelligent, empathetic professionals aiming for the greater good. For when she braked in a line of cars held up by vandalised traffic signals — wires and one of the coloured lenses dangled from one set of lights — she realised that, even sealed away in the car's metal and glass pod, Bu drew bug-eyed looks from other drivers and pedestrians. She tried to ignore them, but the longer she sat there in the stalled traffic, the more she began to feel their stares.

She glanced apprehensively at Bu. If she had been the object of attention, she would have wanted to slump lower and lower in the car seat; or would have felt the coursing of adrenaline, telling her to run. But at first, his head just turned slowly from side to side, surveying the scene with a kind of pent-up wonderment, his hands out a little, as if bracing himself for a fall — no, as if he were somehow letting the sights trickle over his fingers like warm water. Then, when the sound of horns started up all around them from frustrated drivers, to her disbelief, he opened the car door, manoeuvring his crutches out as props.

'Bu, what are you doing? You can't get out here!'

Peterson's initial warnings came back loud and clear. Bu must have been hit by a kind of claustrophobia: rising panic.

Cars were trying to edge past each other, or doing tight U-turns; tyres squealed and horns blared. Was he trying to get himself killed?

'Bu!' she bellowed through the car's open door. Ignoring her, he looked around like a small boy slightly stunned by his arrival at a fair. Then, with his swinging, loping walk on crutches, he reached the faulty light.

There was nothing for it: she had to leap out after him.

'What are you *doing*, woman?' bawled a shaven-headed tourist from the window of his 'Wicked' hire van, as if the traffic snarl-up had somehow become all her fault.

'None of us are going anywhere. Just get a grip,' she snapped, then hurried after Bu.

Bu managed to reach up to the broken green light, even though he was encumbered by crutches.

'Bu, stop! Those wires will be live. You'll get yourself electrocuted!'

He seemed to probe and twist something, then, with two firm thrusts, he clipped the black cover back into place. He peered at the pole as the light turned green, just catching his balance as one crutch threatened to tip sideways.

Afterwards, several things stayed with her. The first was that the traffic failed to move again for some moments. The second was that all the horns and voices fell quiet. No yelling; no cheering, either. The initial silence meant that when a shout did peal out behind them, it was all the clearer.

'Where'd you get your gorilla, lady? What other tricks has he got?'

Although it sounded empty of real menace — maybe the heckler was genuinely amused — she hustled Bu back into the car as quickly as she could. When they both reached for their seatbelts, she saw his hands were trembling. Perhaps he'd only now realised that he had walked out alone in front of a crowd, in broad daylight. Yet his eyes were bright, like those of someone who'd just finished an exhilarating race. She had to help buckle him in.

As they merged with the traffic, and cars pulled farther apart, she let music from the radio fill their small shared space for a while. Then she swallowed hard. 'Do people often say those things?'

He turned his head and stared out the window for so long that her comment seemed to singe on the air. She whispered *damn* under her breath. Then he answered, 'It's maybe better if they think that way. Better than if they are eh-scared.'

Eh-scared: the short 'e' like the start of 'estuary'. Was his pronunciation a stutter, or an accent? She'd tried, a few times, to correct him, and although he said he could hear the difference between, say, *estuary* and *story*, the short, hiccupping 'e' always turned up before his 's'. Likewise, his 'v's were 'b's; often his 'd's sounded breathier, both more emphatic and somehow more interrupted than they should. Was it connected to his physiology? Or was it something that could be helped by a speech therapist, maybe even related to the selective mutism Keith Peterson had talked about? *Eh-scared*. The mixture of vulnerability in the pronunciation, and the resilience in what Bu had said, made her puzzle over his answer for some time after she had dropped him off at The Gables, and helped him to settle in. That night, her thoughts kept catching on his lack of resentment, and yet the fear signalled by his shivering hands. How can he not be hurt, angry?

Cooking dinner in her flat — glad that her flatmates Chelsea and Eileen were out so she didn't have to engage in small talk — she heard a brief item on a local radio station, reporting that somebody's large pet ape had been spotted in traffic that afternoon. A Ministry of Agriculture and Forestry spokesperson had been contacted about regulations governing exotic pets in New Zealand. Teetering between laughter and discomfort, caught in the bleak absurdity of it all, she thought maybe Bu really didn't see the gorilla comment as heckling. Maybe he was right to take such things literally. They were more easily dismissed as simple misunderstanding then and perhaps that gave him a kind of privacy.

Privacy; concealment. Sometimes she thought of his face as a mask, because it was so hard to read. Yet it wasn't something he 'wore' to keep people out. On the other hand, he spoke so little about himself . . . the more time she spent with him, the less she understood, and the more complex and daunting his situation seemed. She needed to talk to someone about him. She left pots bubbling away on the stove, and sent Faber a text.

When r u back?

Even imagining Faber's reaction to the story gave her a sharp tilt in perspective. A new discomfort, almost a premonition, began to simmer up. She rubbed her eyes and spoke aloud to the empty room. 'What on earth am I doing?'

Don't get involved, that's what Faber would say. *You've got enough on your plate. There are head doctors for people like him. This is probably bigger than you think.*

'Okay,' she said to her silent mobile. 'You're right. Maybe I should pull back before I get in any deeper. Maybe I should.'

But she kept her phone right beside her throughout her meal, hoping the real Faber might call to offer fuller consolation.

Bu

IT SEEMED AS IF many days passed before Sandrine visited again. Each hour surely had hidden panels sewn into it, so that it stretched into something longer than promised. Yet there was plenty for him to do: learning the names and habits of the other boarders; watching them sideways for cues about when to laugh, what to talk about when they were men together; learning the scents they gave off that sometimes contradicted their words. This one seemed rough, loud, confident, but underneath he gave off the tang of fear; this other one, who seemed quiet and calm, underneath was like fire waiting inside a lump of coal.

Bu also needed time to recover from the reactions the men showed on first seeing him. One backed away, talking high and fast, until he saw that Bu meant no harm. One bunched his fists; the one like cold, waiting fire laughed; the others stared, long and hard.

Bu retreated to his den and unpacked his few clothes, along with a couple of other possessions. Not all of them. As if it might expose him too much when Maia came in to clean, he decided not to empty his pack altogether.

He thought about Derek's offer to accompany him down into the town centre, and how he would manage this. Derek was kind: he smelt of the garden, and wool, and his pale, freckled skin was scrunched all over with lines from where his smiles set in deep. Yet Bu wasn't ready to walk around the town in daytime. He spent all available sunlight calling up courage: perched on the edge of his bed, clomping back and forth in his room, sometimes venturing out to the small balcony, but soon retreating again, away from the sensation of being watched when there were people working in the grounds.

One night, as a feeling of greater ease rose with the dark, he decided he might be able to try visiting the town centre when deep winter came. In the cold he would be able to wear full covering, even over his face, without too much discomfort. Perhaps, if he put on the light silk gloves and balaclava he had in his pack, he could even manage the scheduled visit to the hospital in a couple of days, to get the cast off his leg. The idea gave him a surge of energy, and he decided he would tell Sandrine when she came. He hobbled over to the window, and looked out at the blank face of the moon. If she came.

❆ ❆ ❆

SEVERAL DAYS AFTER HE moved in, Sandrine did visit. He noticed the change in her at once. She had pulled back into herself, watched him as if from behind a protective shell. His thoughts ran from side to side, trapped, as he tried desperately to think of what he had said to her last time, what he might have done wrong.

She was reluctant to come into his room yet someone else had visitors in the shared lounge so after a quick glance around, she agreed to accompany him as long as they sat on the balcony. Derek and two of the boarders were working in the garden below: she must have noticed this when she arrived, and decided the option was a good compromise. He didn't mind being out there, so much, with her beside him.

'I won't stay for long,' she said, as she eyed the wooden chair and failed to look at Bu.

'I am happy you came,' he responded sadly.

'Has it been all right here?'

He nodded. 'Yes, all right.'

'Good.' She frowned out at the garden, watching the men rake, bend, gather. She shifted uncomfortably. 'I spoke to Derek when I came up the driveway. He mentioned that you've been very quiet. Keeping to yourself. You haven't tried to go into town yet, or see Dr Peterson again?'

'No.' He wanted to put a hand out and brush off the invisible frost but it would bruise her. Ruin her. 'I will go to the hospital, eh-soon, about my leg. It's nearly time for that.'

They sat there silently and the layer of ice over Sandrine thickened. She shuffled forward in her chair again, as if to lever herself up to say goodbye. Anger billowed under his ribs, surging and driving through all sense of caution. He pushed awkwardly from his chair first, shoved it out of the way and barred her path to the French doors.

'I can't go into town. You watched the people in their cars. I'm not ready to be eh-seen. You *know* that.'

Her look of wariness and fear made him point at her. 'Eh-see yourself. Eh-see *yourself*. You are afraid of me, too. You know my eh-secret, d-hon't you? Here,' he pushed a fist at his chest. 'You know.'

She shook her head, stunned. 'I — I hardly know anything *about* you, Bu. You've told me almost nothing.'

'Then why hab you been eh-so kind?' In one movement — despite his moon boot cast — he was over beside her and had taken up both of her hands. He patted them backwards and forwards between his own, like somebody gently palming clay. 'Not eh-so cold now. Not eh-so cold to me.'

She held his eyes for the briefest moment, but in a way that he thought meant maybe she understood. Still holding one of her hands, he reached out to run the pad of his thumb along her lips. 'You are eh-so beautiful. Eh-so . . .'

Sandrine pulled back into her chair and tried to tug her hand away. 'Bu, that's enough.'

'Tell me the right things. Tell me what I must d-ho, eh-so that nobody is afraid. Tell me what your happiness is, eh-so you will eh-stay. Please. *Please.*'

She did understand now, he could see that. But she didn't want to. She managed to free one hand. 'I don't believe this. I'm not too sure where you got the idea that —'

'I d-hon't know. You teach me. Please.'

The tone of his voice made her drop her head. 'Okay, maybe I do know where you got the idea that — that we might be heading — But this —' she paused. 'This friendship is — I mean, perhaps we've skipped a few crucial steps. Perhaps I should have made it clear that I'm not interested in . . . And that's my fault. I know it is, and I'm sorry if I've hurt you. I really am.' This time, with her free hand, she touched the one that still gripped his. 'I've already said it, Bu. I know nothing about you. I've just been — I warmed to you, I suppose. I've been charmed by you. I wanted to help, like you helped me. You know? Simple kindness. I'm just — I'm glad you're somewhere safe. But that's all, now. I can't — I've been letting things slide at work; I'm very busy . . .'

He was going to lose her. He swallowed down the trembling that had started again; breathed deeply to silence the roar in his ears. Still holding her hand, he closed his eyes.

He would keep her here. He would tell her something that would make sure of it.

Sandrine

SANDRINE WONDERED IF SHE was safe to drive: she was disoriented to the point where she overshot the turn-off to her suburb. Cursing, she did an illegal U-turn and sped back. She was due at a public debate in an hour: would have just enough time to get home, shower and change into the new dress she had bought with the ignoble intention of saying *Tough luck, you had your chance* to the debate's guest compere.

She wasn't sure whether she was more flustered because she was running late; because there was the very real possibility that she would get to speak to her sort-of-ex, Jake Grenfell, afterwards; or because of what Bu had told her.

Yet halfway through drying herself, she sat down with a thump on her bed and whispered, 'Holy shit, what do you *think*?' to herself in the mirror. She stared at her own face framed by the long strands of wet, dark hair, as if the pared back, cleansed self might speak out of the reversed world and clear the mist from her head.

Instead the woman in the mirror seemed to crumple at the sight of her flesh and blood sister on the bed, the blue towel accentuating the vulnerable bones of her shoulders.

'Poor bastard,' both Sandrines said. The woman on the bed cried quickly, sparingly, until the pain from Bu's words somehow dispersed, and with a tremor, she felt herself return to her own skin. She stared at the red weals and knots in her bad foot: flat, resigned. On the drive home, as if on cue, the habitual, deep ache in her muscles and tendons had begun to creep back.

Drying her face, Sandrine recalled how Bu spoke to her in the steady, solid voice of someone who had decided to stop stepping slightly behind the truth and letting people assume they knew the facts. He told her how he really differed from Sandrine and her kind.

'I am no man,' he said. 'I never knew my true mother and father. The ones who raised me, they brought me to your country, and treated me as their own.' Sandrine thought he was speaking of a gap in the self, a lack of knowledge about his true origins. She felt a tightening screw of pity in her stomach, wanting to say to him, 'You're still so young, that's all. The years will tell you who you are . . .' but then he said, 'In my own people's tongue, I am known as *Meh-teh*.' He paused. 'The Nepali eh-sometimes call me *Bonmanche*. Wildman.'

The large black orbs of his eyes held her gaze steadily, waiting for her to understand. Then, as if she were a child who had to be given the answer to a simple mathematical question, 'Yeti,' he said.

Sandrine felt a small twister tighten, then flare in her skull. Thoughts and images were picked up, whirled and scattered. She found herself stammering something about *running late, just remembered, so sorry*, and then, not waiting to see her own disbelief mirrored in his eyes, she turned and left.

Now, with her hair still to dry, she flipped open her appointments diary, and double-checked the start time for that night's debate. Her eye caught on the entry she'd made saying 'drop in on Bu', and with a pang of guilt, she visualised him: prodigiously tall, glossily hirsute, his constant look of troubled broodiness, or if not that . . . what was it? Doubt? Depth? She remembered how he gripped her upper arms, his eyes boring into hers, and how the sense of healing she had felt around this man — so kind despite his own afflictions — seemed to sour, corrupt. *What happened to him, what's wrong with him, who is he, really?*

She hurried through the rest of her preparations, whipped up house keys from her dressing table and walked as quickly as she could down to the street corner to catch a bus. She needed people, babble, lights, wine. She made for the hubbub of the crowd gathering at the university to hear Jake Grenfell introduce a team of scientists and climate change experts.

Jake Grenfell. Of course when she'd received his email at work, she'd wondered how wise it would be to go along to see him. He'd attached an ad for his event, and the message: 'Coming down south this Thursday, chairing climate talkfest. Drop by if you can and let's arrange a drink.'

At first she'd decided not to go — with the inside-out logic that her life would seem more attractively rich and full to him if she didn't show up. Of course she had no idea whether that was how Jake's mind would operate . . . If only Faber were back from his trip already: he knew how the male psyche worked. But in that maddeningly accurate way of his, Faber would probably have more to say about her own psyche: that she was so eager now only because she needed a distraction from Bu, and he'd ask whether she thought Jake was really the best antidote.

You're a bleeding heart, Jake had said, at their journalism school graduation party: the messy after-ceremony drink and dance. Over the years since they first met, his shelves and walls must have started to look like a trophy engraver's display case. Qantas Young Journalist of the Year, Barclays Award for Best Political Journalism in Australasia, Best Current Events TV Presenter . . . He had seemed like such a prize himself, back then, with his quick wit, vast general knowledge, energy for argument with the lecturers. His craggy, 'rocker' features, rugged squint, his four years' seniority on everyone else working towards the diploma: it all seemed to say he had already divined things about the world that the rest of them could barely grasp.

Sandrine and Jake gravitated towards each other only in the last half of the course. The tension between them had tightened until it was a given that they would arrive at the graduation party together. As they stood there, drinking side by side, Jake appraised her with a look that shifted the evening on its rails. Then he said, *I just can't see you still in this game in ten years.* It was like a slap. *Don't take offence, Sandrine. It's a compliment. A lot of guys* like *that softness.* He'd put his hand on her waist.

She was weak. He'd got her home to his place — God knows how she'd walked there, given what she'd had to drink and smoke and how totally she'd lost all sense of time or self-preservation. Then, in a lovely, long, deluded moment, she'd believed that *this*, and *this here*, all *this* meant he could be . . .

Yes, it's okay. Of course it's okay.

Until he saw her foot. Her stump of clay, her cloven hoof. Bathos made flesh: it let people down with such a bump. She'd had treatment, of course — surgery, exercises, braces, orthotics in one slightly widened shoe — but it was still, she knew, a horror.

Jake Grenfell, blazing comet, rough-edged pin-up boy of the Wellington Polytechnic Journalism Diploma and now one of the 'faces of the nation' for his TV work, had been tender and polite, had drawn the sheet up over them both, and lain back beside her. Kind, yes: his arm around her, yes: but just talking now, about jobs he'd applied for; who else in their intake had offers and how actually, he'd accepted one, based up north. He'd be gone in three weeks. She could have cried at the sensation of his skin so near, and so unstarved for her.

Next day, as soon as it was light, she'd slipped out of his bed and left him asleep, with his back turned. She'd gone home to her flat, hating every step, but walking for punishment, hardly believing he hadn't realised how one shoe was built a little more broadly, hadn't noticed the slight rolling motion of her gait. For he can't have noticed, can he? If he had, he wouldn't have been so plainly stumped — *ha* — when her foot came out of her shoe.

The foot once had a fused clod of contorted toes, as though bound since birth. Yet after all the surgery it was just as disturbing, just as misshapen, and when she unintentionally caught glimpses of herself in shop windows, her stride seemed to beg for every insult she'd ever had flung at her: Peg-Leg. Hop-Along. Clod Foot. Quasimodette.

Now, in light of Bu's situation, she felt ashamed for that old self. She had thought herself so burdened, but at least she hadn't been driven to build herself a protective delusion; at least she still interacted normally with other people, with men.

For there had been others since Jake, of course. Users, most of them, even the one married guy whom she'd really fallen for. Yet even amidst all those entanglements, something about her time with Jake still lingered. She stared through the bus window as it pulled up near the university. He was like the tattoo you get when you're drunk or stoned, trying to impress some hard crowd, and then you're stuck with it. Even removal procedures leave their own blemishes.

If first love was hard to forget, it was even more so when his name and face cropped up all the time in her own line of work. Usually when he was winning something. Or, as now, being the draw-card celebrity to broaden the appeal of a public event. And they'd kept in touch, peripherally, turning up on each other's radars every now and then.

Bleeding heart. It had been echoed down the years by others. Her first boss: 'I just don't understand it. You write well at feature length. But your news stories are just — garbled. How can you mangle something this short?' He'd rolled her printout into a baton, whacked her on the head and told her to get the bloody thing into better shape before he set the nicotine-coloured sub-editor onto her. 'Toughen up, girlie. This isn't a job for princesses. He'll have you for dinner, then want dessert.'

Then there were her job applications to the national dailies. All were turned down. She took that to mean she wasn't made of the right stuff; somehow they too knew she wasn't tough enough. At times she felt she'd made a kind of peace with it, but at others she still hankered after the myth of the big break, the lead story that would make everyone notice. She wondered what Jake would think of her still working at the *Southern Mercury* and toyed with the idea of spinning the line that she was on the move, had a job in Melbourne, or was contacting recruitment consultants in London.

A fresh sou'westerly pressing her skirt tightly against

her legs, she trotted behind the last of the crowd streaming into the lecture hall out of the metallic grey dusk. Despite her efforts to direct her thoughts away from Bu to Jake, a sting of conscience made her stall. Holding open the door to the building, she thought, *I shouldn't be here. I should be making a call to Dr Peterson.* The sense of something amiss crept over her skin, as if she were being watched, followed. She dropped back, hesitating, let someone behind her go in first, then through the glass door, she saw Jake himself being ushered across the foyer, with a gaggle of MPs and scientists, the guest speakers. Her heart skated. Deliciously tall and trim still, Jake, in his white shirt, charcoal trousers and jacket with mandarin collar, looked like — he looked like *quality*. He looked *now*. She wasn't even sure if mandarin collars *were* now: Jake just carried that air about him. Her hesitations were forgotten.

She eased into an empty seat and was soon drawn in by Jake's performance. Far from being easy on the participants, he reined them in and interjected, swung back repeatedly to the Minister for the Environment: 'Minister, am I getting a recorded message, here? When does the public get to speak to a *real* member of parliament, instead of this tape you're running?' He hardly referred to his notes throughout the whole hour and cut off self-important contributions from the floor during audience question time, miming the opening of an envelope, Academy Awards style: 'And the question, please!'

Sandrine found herself grinning openly despite herself, even after the forum was over. She slipped out of the hall after the speakers left the platform, trailing behind them as they made their way to the university staff club. One of the women professors held the doors open for her, looking at her in surprise.

'Are you —?'

Jake turned to see what the hold-up was.

'Hello, Jake.'

Without missing a beat, he flung his arms wide, theatrical, borne up by all the praise he'd been hearing from his fellow speakers.

'San-*drriiine*!'

She laughed, embarrassed and pleased; Jake double-, then triple-kissed her: 'Continental, continental, darling.'

'Or televisual, Jake?'

'Oh, the same, the same. International medium. How lovely to see you. I wasn't sure you'd got my message. Are you coming in for a drink?' He accepted another inner door being held open for him, leaned against it to keep the way clear for Sandrine.

She stalled. 'Are you sure?'

'Of course, of course. Come on.' He crooked his index finger and beckoned her closer. She obliged. His voice fell back into its normal tone. 'I could do with a friendly face.' As she passed through the door, he put his hand on her back, tentatively: the pause was curiously seductive. Was there a flash of vulnerability to Jake now, a new uncertainty?

'You're looking stunning, Ms Moreau.' The lift of his chin slightly mocked his own words, and his smile was at once inquisitive and conspiratorial.

'You're not looking too shabby yourself, Mr Grenfell.'

His smile deepened. *Oh how he loves to be loved*, thought Sandrine, warm and cool in turn. *Play him, Sandrine. You can do it.* 'And that went very well, didn't it? The forum.

I thought you made an excellent chair. Not an easy job.'

Laughing, he answered a question about what he would like to drink by turning to Sandrine. 'Champagne, I think, don't you?'

'Absolutely. You should celebrate.'

She watched how well Jake worked the crowd: introducing her to all the academics, polishing up the little he knew of her CV so that she felt, with each introduction, like the tiny ballerina that springs up in a music box: a debutante, mint and shining, every time.

As the evening wore on, and one verbose, monotone lecturer began to dominate a conversation about the difficulties in communicating science to the public, Sandrine's thoughts wandered. As if it had been there all the time, she felt the shadow of her experiences with Bu crowding up behind her: so vividly, in fact, that she found herself, more than once, looking uneasily over her shoulder.

Jake took it to mean she wanted a refill. As he signalled for more champagne, Sandrine forcibly drew her attention back to the circle and chafed away the goosebumps that had peppered her arms. On the spot she invented a pet project she claimed she had wanted to kick-start for ages: a popular science column in the *Southern Mercury* that ranged over the full scientific community from week to week. The lecturers beamed. She took names and contact details, and as if that were the final note to the evening, the group soon began to diminish. A dinner invitation Sandrine overheard at the start now had just four takers. Jake promptly wilted. He apologised to the organiser, gesturing to Sandrine.

'We've double-booked, I'm afraid. Sandrine's reminded me that we've promised to attend the after-party at an old university friend's wedding. I'm sorry, so rude of me . . .'

Sandrine transformed her genuine surprise into a hurried glance at her watch. 'Oh, help, yes, Jake. It started ages ago. We'd better head off.'

Thanks and farewells sent everyone in various directions. Jake's step picked up once they were out of sight and earshot of the others. 'Had enough of all that,' he said. 'Thanks for covering.' He walked with his hands in his pockets, scanning the littered, rundown student and semi-industrial area they walked through. He had an animation and curiosity that seemed to want to penetrate everything he saw. Where most of the city had fallen into the equivalent of background noise for Sandrine, Jake's manner and queries made her look twice at the grotty flats, one with its front windows painted with cartoons — SpongeBob meets Mickey Mouse — the settee placed squarely in the window as if it were an Amsterdam brothel; at the long, dull walls of the chocolate factory — nothing as enticing as Willy Wonka's Oz-like towers; at the stooped, long-bearded, ageing man who always seemed to walk everywhere with hurried intent and always wore shorts, even in the bitter winter snows. She told Jake that she'd often seen him stop along the harbour-front to take photos of seagulls, looking, each time, as if he couldn't believe his luck in having stumbled upon such a wonder as these plain, black-backed birds.

Jake swung around to stare at her for a moment. 'So. Where shall I take you for dinner?'

She tried to conceal that she felt cut off mid-observation. 'The party was a complete fiction?'

'Faction. Who knows what the evening will bring?'

'I guess we should get as far away from the north end as possible.' She thought about where she'd last been to a genuine wedding reception. 'The Crown Roller Mills?'

'How far is it? Walking distance?'

Sandrine's hip and foot might intensify their ache, her step drag noticeably, if they went that far. 'I bussed into town tonight. Hired a designated driver for a dollar or two. Let's catch another.'

'How déclassé, my dear.'

Sandrine stopped. 'Hypocrisy! *What* was the forum you were just chairing?'

Jake sighed. 'Oh yes. Being ethical can seem so — drab.'

'You're a natural hedonist?'

'Unnatural. I blame the alcohol. It's dissolving my principles. Fortunately, I have a good woman to take me in hand.'

Once they were at a stop and an empty bus turned up — the driver giving a double-take and then a stony show, Sandrine thought, of *not* recognising Jake — Jake took her hand and arm to support her up the steps. He said, 'Let me help you,' but she ducked out of his clasp, so that he wouldn't see the stiff lurch as she mounted the stairs.

'Hypocrites first, please.'

He made a prune-mouth at her, but was entertained, impressed even, by the barb.

After they descended at the end of Princes Street, Sandrine glanced at the departing bus over her shoulder. 'Unusual to see one of those that doesn't look like you, at the moment. Your face is everywhere — on billboards, in the papers, even the rear ends of buses.'

Jake rocked on his heels and flung his head back to stare at the sky. 'A face like the back of a bus. Are you flirting with me?'

She sighed. 'It's been so long. I've forgotten how.'

He raised an eyebrow as he opened the door and waved her through. 'I give lessons.'

Their banter dropped away as they were seated. They ordered food and a bottle of wine to follow the post-forum champagne. Until the meal came, Sandrine determined to leave her wine glass full and to sip water. She could feel caution unravelling, hope climbing perilously, and yet the evening also had an insistent sadness, an edge of uncertainty.

She pulled herself back to Jake, as he worked to surround her in a warm glow of interested questions, and personable, open answers to her own. When he told her that he was engaged to a woman who worked in PR in Auckland, and that the engagement had hit the rocks a couple of times, a tiny clapper of warning tried to sound through her enjoyment. She muffled it.

He and his fiancée were officially still together, he said, but there had been a huge row just before he left on this trip: 'I'm floundering, to tell the truth.' Sandrine was surprised by how candid he was — surprised and pleased. She poured him some more wine.

'These bust-ups don't bode well. I think the main reason I'm not ending things once and for all is because I'm a coward.' He fidgeted with his cutlery, swapping the knife and soup spoon as if trying to solve a logic problem. 'But frankly, the reasons for the cowardice are good, solid, human reasons. You know, fear of old age. Fear of loneliness. Having let too many good things get away.' His eyes held hers briefly before he looked down.

'Anyway.' He took a breath. 'Enough. How about you, Sandrine? There must be more to your life than the *Southern Merc*.'

She tensed a little at the way he said the paper's name, all too quickly feeling criticism. Deflecting it, she hoped, she rabbited on at him about her flatmates, her parents, her volunteer work. He was watching her steadily, which made her talk too quickly, too *confessionally*. She felt heat creep up over her collarbone.

When she paused, he pushed his chair back slightly and crossed his legs, kicking one foot lightly. 'No romance?'

She took an incautious slug of wine and tried to delay an answer for as long as was comfortable. 'Not exactly. Not from my perspective, anyway.'

'Ah. Someone else thinks there's romance?'

The tone of intrigue and what seemed like mild affront in his voice made her think that she might have inadvertently laid some sort of bait. In a gabbled rush, she said, 'I mean, I think someone is interested in me. But —' she took a deep breath — 'this someone doesn't think they're a man.'

'It is a bloke, isn't it? You're not — you're not getting it on with a woman?' He paused. 'Lovely if you are, of course. I just thought you were straight.'

She smiled, rolling her eyes. 'I am, Jake.'

'Bloody hell. A transsexual. Or a man who wants to be a lesbian? Well, we've all heard that one before.'

She gave an involuntary laugh, half protest. 'It's not funny, Jake.'

He held up his hands. 'I didn't say it was. All power to the rainbow of humanity. *I* didn't laugh.'

'No. I know. I wasn't laughing either — or not — because it's comic. It's a — what? — a darkly nervous reaction, if you like.' She leaned her elbows on the table. Another step towards the intimacy she wanted: she would tell him, draw him in. She took a deep breath, then pressed a thumb and finger over her eyelids, at the ludicrousness of what she was about to say.

'A man I've met made the weirdest confession to me just today. I've got myself mixed up in a situation that I've no idea how to handle. It's so stupid. And I suppose I'm worried that if I do try to extricate myself, it's going to be even worse for the poor sod.'

'Go on,' Jake said. His face was less guarded than she'd seen it so far tonight. She indulged herself in a long gaze at his intense green eyes, thick black eyelashes, strong features.

'Well. For a kick-off, he's clearly got mental health issues.'

Jake frowned, waited. 'What, depressive? Bipolar?'

'Biped, but not bipolar.' She gave a raw 'ha!' then said, 'Sorry. It's just all so odd.'

He shrugged. 'Laughing in the face of adversity.'

'Mmm.'

'Let's start at the beginning. What's his name, and how did you meet him?'

'He calls himself Bu.'

Jake looked as if he was trying to suck the pip out of something tart. '*Bu.*'

'Yes. And I met him — well, it was sort of random. I just bumped into him, really, at the hospital, after I'd had a check-up there — but he's — you see, Bu's pretty unusual. He's — he's got some kind of genetic condition, I suppose. He *has* been a bit depressed, and he discharged himself from hospital — psych hospital — before doctors could name his syndrome. He's almost seven foot tall, and his skin is completely grown over with hair. It's so thick, it's like a kind of pelt.'

Jake's face went through a number of efforts to conceal his scepticism. He looked at his watch.

'You need to go?' she asked.

'Just double-checking the date. It's not April Fool's.'

'No.' She drew in a breath. 'Bu thinks he's a yeti.'

Jake's eyes lifted from watching his hand fiddle restlessly with his knife. The silence between them filled up with talk from the other tables, the sound of the espresso machine, bottles and glasses at the bar, waiters taking orders.

Growing awkward, Sandrine carried on. 'He seems perfectly sane in every other way — he's harmless — though there are odd little things about him, you know, he's kind of socially awkward, there are speech issues . . .' Jake's face remained expressionless. 'He's at a kind of halfway house for single blokes now. I helped him find it, and I suppose having discovered some kindness in someone has confused him a bit.'

'What do you think?' Jake finally asked.

'Sorry?'

'Do you think he's a yeti?'

Her mouth dropped open slightly. 'Of course not. The yeti's a myth. He's deluded. He's a gentle, *extraordinary* guy. I mean, he has a kind of indescribable, well, *I* find it's almost a magnetism — but he's — he's really ill.'

'Where's your proof?'

She huffed with disbelief. 'This is not the conversation I expected.'

He looked around the room, thinking, then his eyes came back to her. 'Have you talked to experts about it?'

'What, like psychiatrists? His own doctors don't actually know what he believes. He hasn't told them. He's only told me.'

'And what about, say, anthropologists, zoologists? Or even, what would they be — mythologists?'

'Mythographers?' she said wryly, assuming he wouldn't be able to maintain a straight face for much longer.

'Do you have pictures of him?'

Her laughter was less confident now. 'No. Look, I know it's hard to believe, but —'

He tapped his fingers on his placemat. 'That's not what I meant at all. It's just, it sounds both fascinating and well, very worrying, Sandrine.'

She fell quiet for a moment at his concern.

'Where does he come from?'

'He's — you might have read about it. He was found injured in the bush, in South Westland.'

He looked away. 'I've got a vague recollection . . .' He nodded his thanks to the waitress who came to clear away their plates.

When she replayed the night later in her memory, she tried to see Jake's face again at this point, tried to recall if his expression had changed, but she was sure that he was still warm, engaged, even protective. He frowned. 'He's not going to turn into a stalker, is he? You seem to have a lot of sympathy for the guy. But if he's not well — I mean, do you think he's threatening?'

'No, not at all. Honestly, it's nothing like that. He's a complete innocent. I'm more concerned for *his* well-being than mine.'

Jake seemed to be absorbing this. Then his hand reached across the table and he cupped his palm over her knuckles. He said something she couldn't quite hear and she was far too distracted by her cartwheeling nerves to ask him to repeat himself. Even the lure of Bu's story was pushed aside and every last molecule of sensation seemed to surge to the place where Jake touched the soft lobe of her ear, saying that her earring was working itself loose, then running the side of his finger over her cheek. Almost as if Jake had prearranged it, the waiter brought their bill. It was time to move on: to let the evening develop elsewhere.

'I'll cover half of this, Jake, please.'

'No, let me pay. Honestly, I said, "Let me take you to dinner" and that's what I meant.'

He performed for the approaching maître d', swinging Sandrine's bag out of her reach, clutching it under his arm and saying, 'I *insist*. I've enjoyed tonight. It was my pleasure, and I want to pay. Just let me. Maybe you can buy the nightcap.'

Jake ushered her up ahead of him to the counter and reached for his wallet. In a haze of expectation, she forgot to drop behind him to conceal her limp. As she halted, so that he would draw ahead of her, she collided with a waiter trying to slip past with a heavy tray full of used wine glasses. There was noise, confusion and embarrassment and then the redoubled bewilderment of Jake seamlessly calling for two taxis, not one. With the jarring sensation of a stop button being hit in the middle of a song, she felt his cool, platonic farewell kiss on her cheek.

Many hours later, at 3 a.m., there came the small-hours jolt of having drunk too much wine.

She was thoroughly, unforgivingly awake: raking over the evening, then picking over her entire past. She *was* too soft. Too naïve, too trusting. Just look at her. Look at all her failed love affairs. Take John, the married man who swore he loved her, but said he couldn't leave his wife, because she was still his *best friend*, and who said his marriage was devoid of sex but then one day announced that he was going to be the father of twins. Take Brendon, whose biggest ambition was to move up the indoor soccer league at work; or Callum, who wanted to build a scale model of the London railway system. Weekends with both of them had been very dull. She would *not* let herself think about the brief, alarming fling she'd had with the parcel courier who, it transpired, was attracted to her not despite her twisted hoof, but because she was lame. His mermaid, he called her, but it left her feeling shabby, somehow broken.

God. She, who'd been taught to question, to dig, to verify sources, to spot contradictions in a story, discrepancies or flaws in a statement, should know about professional veneer, about the difference between a work persona and the at-home, casual, unguarded self. How many times had she fallen for someone because of the beautiful package they came in, or perhaps even more desperately, just because they were physically attracted to her? She pummelled her pillow, flipped it over, flapped the duvet to cool her skin. She tried to push her mind away from its self-pecking metre, by making herself imagine retelling the whole failed Jake encounter to Faber — turning it into a *Black Books* style comic episode, with herself as a limping, provincial version of desperate, kooky Fran. But no matter how she rewound, exaggerated, embellished, she just couldn't laugh at herself. Instead, a new kind of loneliness leaked into her bones. 'This has got *nothing*,' she hissed at herself, '*nothing* to do with missing Faber.'

She lay still for a moment, listening to the aftershock of her own words. She trusted Faber. She could *read* him.

How valuable that seemed, how safe she felt just thinking about him.

She admired Faber, was deeply, deeply fond of him. But desire? If she let the anarchy of lust arc between them, there was just too much to lose. Admiration, fondness, mutual respect and dependability — in her experience none of these had ever sat for long with desire. Would she ever feel them all at once, for one person?

She fiercely told herself one of the adages she relied on, despite her own family's anxieties and pronouncements. When you're feeling low, go and help someone worse off: you'll soon see what colour your luck runs.

※ ※ ※

AFTER WORK THE NEXT day — her head surprisingly clear, given last night's wine — Sandrine switched on the car radio on the way to The Gables, and caught the tail end of an item they said had just come to hand: something only vaguely coherent about South Westland, missing link. She turned up the volume but the weather came on. Groping to fit together what she'd heard, she felt a sick, dragging sensation in the pit of her stomach.

She told herself it could have been about anything, but the guilt was already gathering. As she walked into the boarding house, with her pulse hammering, she found an eager audience around the widescreen TV in the shared lounge, a disoriented Bu among them.

One of the other residents called out cheerfully to Sandrine, 'Come and see! We think The Gables is going to be on TV. Some of us saw that Grenfell guy and a film crew wandering about today.'

Nausea made her sit down on the battered arm of a couch. 'What?'

Bu gave her his perplexed stare and she had a swift, sharp intimation of the vulnerability within his great bulk. She went over and laid a hand on his wrist. 'Are you all right?'

'Eh-someone, he eh-said, your friend. He came to talk to me.'

The sense of her own misconduct wound tighter. It almost hurt to look at him. 'What did you tell him?'

'I d-hon't know, I —'

'Did he take pictures of you?'

'He came when I turned from the bush, back to the garden. I went to look only, the track eh-seemed too rough.' He lowered his head to look at his leg, which Sandrine belatedly realised was out of its cast. 'Your friend, he had . . .'

'Sshhh! This is it!' a resident said. There was barely time for Sandrine to register pleasure or surprise that Bu must have felt robust enough today to have managed another medical appointment at the hospital, and to walk on his newly released ankle.

Jake Grenfell filled the screen. He was in a clearing in native bush, wearing a heavy green Swanndri, a warm beanie, walking trousers and tramping boots. The focus dashed away from him as if the cameraman had seen movement in the trees, then it staggered back again. Jake's chest was rising and falling, as if after a long hike. The lines on his face were taut with exhaustion, concern, the sobriety of his message. Barely composed, he began his coverage.

'Reports have come in today that claim sightings in some of the densest bush in southern New Zealand of something many say is proof of the genuine existence of a creature until now only known through Māori legend and world myths.' He crouched down, laid his hand next to a broad yet shallow depression in the soil: it was twice the length and breadth of his hand. 'Locals claim this print was left here today by a maero: a creature sometimes known as the mairoero or mohoao.' His perfect pronunciation lent the whole report an air of grave authenticity. 'To Pākehā here and overseas, that term could even be loosely translated as yeti or sasquatch.'

He frowned, glanced into the trees, recalled himself and eyeballed the camera. 'Of course this is the sort of story, which, over the decades, has entertained audiences, and wasted the time of many scientists — and journalists.' A rueful sliver of a smile appeared, one for which he seemed barely to have the energy. He stayed hunkered down in an earthy, woodsman's squat. 'Forty or so years ago, our own Sir Edmund Hillary was even funded by an international corporation to mount an expedition to the Himalayas, to look for evidence of this fabled hairy, upright, primate — the Abominable Snowman. Hillary's expedition, of course, was fruitless.' Jake swallowed; his eyes darted to the side. Again it was as if he wrenched himself back to his task from a nagging unease. He lowered his voice. 'Perhaps he should have looked closer to home.' Sandrine felt a coil of anger in her throat.

The screen changed. *Archival footage*, the running subtitle read, as the viewers saw an aerial view that moved from Fiordland to South Westland. Jake's voice-over continued. 'This is New Zealand's wildest flank, the south-west coast: a designated World Heritage Area. Here you'll find everything from the mighty Milford Sound and

Lake Te Anau to the ancient Fox and Franz Josef glaciers cradled amidst primeval rainforest. The lakes, rivers, bush and beaches of this untamed hinterland are as pure as you will find anywhere. Fiordland and Westland are increasingly popular destinations for tourists and film-makers. Yet what has the ancient forest on this coast been hiding until now, and for how long?'

The image on screen shifted to black and white stills of a Māori family in a mixture of traditional and Victorian dress, standing next to their horses, then to Pākehā men from the same era, at a sawmill: pipes in their mouths, fists on their hips, trousers belted tightly around their narrow, undernourished waists. The stills dissolved to modern film taken from a moving vehicle: wooden houses along a coastal highway, a tumultuous grey and white beach.

Jake's narrative continued. 'The people on this coast are known for their hardy, pioneer spirit and a close-knit sense of community. Initial investigations suggest that many locals have known of the potential existence of the maero for some time' — the screen switched to Jake's pale face again — 'but most refused to be interviewed.'

Jake stood and the camera drew back as he started walking forward. 'Many experts — primatologists, anthropologists, cryptozoologists — agree that most yeti or Big Foot film stock from overseas has been the work of pranksters. And frankly,' he said, 'I would have placed this local rumour in exactly the same camp, if I hadn't been sent out here myself.'

Jake's expression looked hunted. 'Late this afternoon, our team acquired footage of a most extraordinary phenomenon.'

There was Bu on screen. The picture framed him from waist to head, shambling through trees. He was shirtless.

Sandrine's head shot around as she asked, 'Bu, why . . .?', but Derek, leaning in his bulky gumboots against the doorframe, cut her off as the on-screen Bu stopped in a shaft of sunlight, blinking happily into the trees, following something — the flight of a bird, perhaps. It looked as if he were going to find a place to rest, when he obviously heard something, whirled around, caught sight of the camera, startled backwards, baring his teeth, then began to lumber away. The picture snapped back to Jake before the camera could gain any full-length shots of Bu.

Jake stood now, rattling off the end to his piece, nearly losing control of his mike in his haste. 'This sighting raises many questions. What exactly have we caught on film? If this is indeed the maero, what is it? A new type of human? Another species of primate altogether? What has driven it close enough to civilisation to have risked contact with humans? What does this mean for our view of our prehistoric past, geographically, ecologically, culturally?'

The camera gave a close-up of Jake's face. 'This sighting is nothing short of *history-making.*'

The shot changed. Jake's co-presenter swivelled his chair from where he'd been watching Jake's report back at the studio, and looked out at the viewers, his jaw set. 'After the break, in an unscheduled half-hour item, we'll bring you a panel interview about these claims with some of the nation's top scientists.'

Sandrine put her head in her hands, muttering a single, drawn-out *shit* to herself. What had she done? How desperate was she, to have dropped every guard that instinct and training should have given her?

Derek said, to nobody in particular, 'You've got to be joking.'

'Tell 'im 'e's dreaming,' someone else cracked.

'This is awful,' said a thin, grey-faced man who wore a black cloth cap. He tugged at his frayed jersey cuffs, pulling them over his hands, clutching his arms tightly around his stomach.

Somewhere a phone started ringing. 'Don't answer it,' Sandrine said, needlessly. Everyone sat stock still.

'Hab I d-hone — eh-some wrong thing?' Bu asked.

'It's not your fault,' Sandrine said unsteadily.

Derek looked at her. 'Well, what the hell are we going to do now?'

His wife, Maia, glanced around the men. The slim, oblong lenses of her glasses, and her frizzy red-gold hair, seemed to spark with irritation. She gathered up some empty coffee mugs. 'Best we discuss this somewhere else.'

Sandrine was shown out to the hallway with Derek and Bu, Maia saying on the way to the kitchen, 'It's Barry, the man in the cap. He gets very distressed. Better we don't take him through the blow by blow.' Each sentence was punctuated by a series of quick, insistent nods. Sandrine wondered how a tense, strung-out character like Maia could appeal to Derek, with his gentle, worn face and a personality that seemed as accommodating as his loose cable-knit jerseys.

Once they reached the kitchen, Maia crossed her arms and leaned against the sink. 'Right, missy. You're the journalist.' She said it with an edge of hostility and suspicion. '*You* tell us how to handle this.'

Sandrine felt her heart go out of rhythm and into edgy palpitations. 'I know this is largely my fault. I did talk to Jake about you, Bu, I'm sorry. But really I had no idea —' she flinched as she said her next words — 'that he would believe me.' She ran a hand through her fringe. 'I feel like such a born fool. What a *bastard*.'

She had heard once, from one of her first flatmates — a trainee nurse — that it was usually harmful, perilous, to affirm the fantasies of someone in a florid mental state. Yet she was still unsure, and a little frightened, of whether she was about to say the right thing. 'Even though your story isn't true. It's not, is it, Bu?' She wanted release from this situation — wanted to hear that Jake had been sucked in, would have the proverbial all over the fan and his face.

Bu was stroking and stroking at his luxuriant beard, his gaze abstracted but serious.

'Bu, look. You don't want to get caught up in all this. You're barely through the drama of the last few weeks. It'd be foolish — dangerous — for you to speak to anyone else from the media.'

'You're the media, girly.' Maia's glasses glinted coldly as she gave another double-pecking nod. She looked smug as hell.

Sandrine fought the urge to shove her. 'Yes, but I want to fix all this. I want to *help* him.' She turned to Bu. 'I think we should get you away from here, find somewhere for you to stay where Jake and his contacts can't reach you. Keep you away till this whole thing dies down.'

Derek and Maia exchanged a long, silent look. Derek drew his wife aside, towering over her nervously thin form, and they talked in low voices. Sandrine was still aware of the tension between them as she heard her cellphone buzz. She quickly checked who the text was from. *Faber.*

```
Am back in the Land of Dun. U free 2
meet? Tales 2 tell.
```

Sandrine thumbed back as quickly as she could.

> Thank god u r back. Might need yr help. Keep phone on!!!

Maia shook her head, turned her back on Derek, busied herself with wiping the bench. His arm went around her shoulder and Sandrine heard — mild, rumbling, but with an unexpected tone of telling, not asking — 'Please, sweetheart.' Maia's hands stopped working. She stared out the kitchen window. Derek kept his arm around her. They stood there for a while, then Derek raised his head and said, 'We know a place.' Maia dropped her pale, sharp little chin just once, in agreement.

The place was on a large tract of land in the Catlins, which they joint-owned with extended family. There was an old farmhouse there, and a couple of caravans.

'Plenty of space,' said Derek. 'Well hidden from the road, and it's pretty well surrounded by native bush. The nieces and nephews love climbing up the hill to the back of our property, but we never let them go alone. Bush is too dense.'

'Will anyone else be using it?' asked Sandrine.

Maia shook her head. 'The relations we share it with drive down from Christchurch usually, but this year they're saving for a trip to the Gold Coast. We've got it all to ourselves for the next twelve months.' Her mouth set in a crisp, satisfied line, as if she had arranged the property's vacancy for just this sort of emergency.

The three looked at each other, then at Bu, who stood watchful and puzzled in the corner, his great brow wrinkled beneath his fur. The pelt itself, Sandrine thought, somehow shone and bristled with attention, as if his mood could alter its texture and appearance.

Derek leaned against the bench, arms crossed, all grim concentration. 'We'll need to get supplies and so on. We'll get organised in the morning.'

'Who's going to go with him?' Maia seemed unreserved about talking in front of Bu as if he wasn't there. Although she'd been solicitous for the man in the cap, now it was as if they were discussing the fate of an imbecile. 'Girly here can't take him on her own.'

Sandrine bridled at the condescension.

There was a knock at the front door.

Everyone froze.

'Who the blazes?' Derek looked at his watch, then strode heavily through the hostel, the old, sloping wooden floor vibrating as he went. Even from the kitchen the others could hear his tone — stern, brooking no argument. The door banged firmly to and a lock slid home.

He came back, shoulders squared with annoyance. 'No time to get organised for the farmhouse,' he said. 'We'll have to get Bu out the back way right now. Before there are any others.'

'Others?' asked Bu.

'Journos,' said Maia, reading it from Derek's face.

'Where do we take him?' Sandrine said.

'*You* got any ideas, missy?'

Not a one. 'All right. Leave it with me.' *Shit.*

Derek nodded. 'Maia'll distract them at the front of the house. Bu, you go and get your things. Keep away from the balcony. The three of us will get into the car.'

'How do we do that without them seeing?'

'There's an internal entry to the workshop and garage.

Once Bu's in the car, he goes under blankets. Then,' he raised an eyebrow at Sandrine, 'you tell me.'

While Bu went upstairs, Sandrine texted Faber again.

```
Weird emergency Faber plse b @ my place
in 15.

U ok?

Yes & no. Can u make it?

Yep. C u in 15.

Thanx
```

Sandrine, Derek and Bu bundled into the car. Derek and Sandrine had gathered up a pile of rugs that smelled of wool, salt and diesel. They passed them to Bu and told him to lie down on the back seat.

'But why?' Bu asked. Since the news broadcast, he seemed to have been going along with instructions lethargically. At first Sandrine had assumed this was her own bogged-down perception of things but now she realised it was as likely to be Bu's genuine confusion, his inability to judge the situation.

Derek turned around in his seat. 'There are people outside who are after a piece of you,' he said.

Bu's eyes looked huge: even the irises swollen with some shadowy knowledge. Sandrine wondered, with a sudden pulse of the irrational, if he were seeing through the garage walls, tracking the footsteps of the people waiting outside, anticipating their next action.

She began to buckle herself in. 'They'll want pictures of you,' she said. 'More stories. To prove or disprove what Jake Grenfell has said. If it's someone from a rival channel, they'll want to get their own exposé: "Innocent sickness beneficiary exploited in yeti hoax".'

Bu watched and listened in silence, but with a straining concentration that made Sandrine think she must have used phrases, concepts, that were unfamiliar to him.

She twisted round further, leaning harder against her seatbelt. 'They want to know who you are. What you are.'

'Why on TB?'

She and Derek exchanged a look.

'Some people could get a lot of kudos — attention — and money from a story like yours.' She turned back in her seat with an exasperated 'plump'. 'Whatever it is,' she muttered.

Derek eyed Bu in the rear-view mirror. 'Best you lie low for a while, mate. We're just trying to keep you away from the spotlight till you sort yourself out, get yourself into a good head space, eh?'

Sandrine looked over her shoulder again. 'Please, Bu. We're doing it to protect you.'

He refused to meet her gaze for long. His eyes glowered — she felt a twinge of disorientation, and also shame again, that she had brought him to this — but just as she thought they might have a time-wasting fight on their hands, he threw himself down on the back seat and covered himself with rugs.

Without looking at her, Derek said, 'Best we call up Peterson once we've got him somewhere quieter too, eh?' Then he pressed the button on the remote for the garage door, turned the key in the ignition and drove out. Staring straight ahead, he refused to open the driver's window or slow down for the woman who ran over and waved at them to stop. He drove straight past the two TV vans and the crews hovering on the driveway. Just as if he were on a country highway trying to get courteously past a flock of sheep, he nosed the car through the rabble of other people who came at the car with notepads, microphones and cameras.

Sandrine swore, swinging round in her seat to get a better look at one of the women reporters. Someone else came into view. '*Holy* sh—'

'What?' snapped Derek.

'The station logos on some of those mikes. They're not ours.' She sat back in her seat. 'There are overseas stations here. Already. What did they do, teleport?' She peered into the wing mirror. 'I recognise that guy, though. They must be local stringers working for overseas stations.' She looked at Derek. 'This is big.'

He just concentrated on the road.

Sandrine's cellphone buzzed with another text from Faber.

```
Am at yours. Eileen let me in. Where r u?
```

Sandrine clicked her tongue — *damn*. She'd thought her flatmates would be out: this was meant to be netball practice night for one, and late shift for the other. She wished, not for the first time, that she had her own place. She thumbed in a reply.

```
Need privacy. Meet me at yrs instead.
15-20 mins.
```

Faber's reply seemed to take so long that she imagined him getting fed up, flipping his phone shut. Even the super-loyal can be pushed too far, after all. She gripped her phone tightly, biting at her lip.

The mobile vibrated as if in protest.

```
Wldnt put up w this frm any other
chick.
```

She grinned: here was an ember of normality to keep her spirits up.

'You'll need to head for Port Chalmers,' she said to Derek.

They hurtled through a solemn, grey stretch of the city where motel neon seemed the only flash of optimism. They drove in silence, Sandrine's thoughts in a welter. She took a call from Keith Peterson, who'd seen the broadcast; he pushed her to tell him everything she'd gleaned from Bu: a conversation that made her squirm, given Bu was listening, but which she managed to cut short by saying yes, he was with her, and they were heading off to find a safe house. She wanted somewhere comfortable for Bu to wait while they did a food shop for the Catlins, while she made some quick calls and sent a few texts, where she could guarantee mobile contact: Derek had said reception wasn't great out at the farmhouse.

When she hung up she was already thinking over another dilemma. Someone was going to have to divert the media on Bu's behalf. She stared at the passing football fields, cement works, the fertiliser factory, the cold, hollow-looking wooden villas, a takeaway shop, its windows streaming with condensation — as if the view were a screen that would soon light up with an answer.

Who was she kidding? There was no one else. She flipped open her mobile again and started to compose a text message that she could fire off to people who might help to stir up doubt, spread the word, about Jake Grenfell's report.

There was the lovely Alistair on TV3. He'd twig to the potential compassion fallout of this whole shemozzle. There was an old friend working for *Mediawatch*; another at the *Dom Post*; a contact at the *Herald*. Her old university Russian tutor, she had been amazed to discover, now worked at Radio New Zealand National as a producer. There was a former flatmate, Davie Shay, who ran a blog called *Media-tor*, recently named as the current events blog with the most hits.

```
Hi
Re yeti: TV hoax. Subject = ex-psych
patient. Don't get stung. Backlash will
hurt Grenfell.
```

She saved the text as a draft. She'd need to work out exactly who to send it to. Some contacts would react better to a personal call or an email.

As they reached Sawyers Bay, the alcoholic hippy woman Sandrine had often seen hitching around here staggered along the Port Chalmers road in the dusk, can in one hand, white plastic bag heavy in the other. She stepped out into the road, tipping the can up over her mouth to drain the last dregs, red dreadlocks falling back, plastic bag held up and out, trying to flag Derek down.

'Not tonight, sunshine,' he muttered. In the wing mirror, Sandrine saw her fling the empty can after them. She was glad Bu was still hunkered under the blanket, so hadn't seen: she wouldn't know how to explain the woman to him. What exactly was his reading level of the world? Child, adolescent, or damaged man? The woman's anger tripped some switch in her, so that she felt uneasy, diminished.

Bleeding heart, Jake had said.

You bloody wait! Pressing in a few names on her phone, she hit 'send' with a small burn of satisfaction.

When they reached Port Chalmers, the streets were relatively quiet. A few people headed into New World, one couple strolled towards a café; most shops were dark, but the streetlights glowed. Yet its familiar face was altered by Sandrine's tension. Although the working part of the port was floodlit for a ship loading up with logs, she felt a vague sense of threat in the old stone buildings, the church, the museum, and in the pubs' façades, the massive industrial cranes, the sawmill, the mountain of wood chips. She shivered, saying abruptly, 'Turn here.'

When they drew up outside Faber's house — a tiny, beautifully restored early twentieth-century cottage — Faber himself was standing at the front door, key in the lock. He wore a new, black, down jacket, and crammed over his usually neat, cropped head of blond hair, an orange and brown striped beanie. He'd pulled out his winter clothes already, probably adjusting to the south after his jaunt in Melbourne. Usually he took pride in being one of the last people in Dunedin to resort to coats and hats. 'We haven't even seen a frost yet,' he'd say, with a kind of contented stoicism, and an impish anticipation of how everyone would *really* be suffering when black ice formed, frost glittered cruelly as powdered glass, schools opened late because of snow, and rain was welcomed as a sign that things were warming up. In other circumstances, Sandrine would have been delighted to tease him about how quickly he'd weakened in ten days across the Tasman. Today she was just relieved to see him.

When she called out, he turned, with a quick start of pleasure.

She hurried along the narrow concrete path to greet him. They hugged and he said, 'You're okay, then?'

'Yeah, I'm okay. I'm sorry about all this. It's just — we've got a situation here.' She looked back over her shoulder at the car. 'I wanted to hear about your trip, first . . .'

'Later, eh?' He pointed a thumb at his door. 'You going to come in?'

'Yes. I'll just get Bu and Derek.'

He gave her a mischievous grin. 'Bo Derek?'

'You wish. *Bu* and Derek.'

'Who are?'

She rose up on her toes, bobbed there nervously. '*Don't* spin out, please, Faber.'

He held his expression in a careful neutral. 'Your love slaves.'

'No! Derek is married.'

He shrugged and his mouth gave a small, sour quirk. 'As it turns out, so's Alison.'

'Oh, Faber. I'm sorry.' She reached out to touch his shoulder.

He closed his eyes. 'Don't.'

She swallowed a small, bruised *oh*.

He looked at her again. 'What do you need me to do?'

'I'm looking for a place for Bu to stay. He's in trouble.'

'Trouble?'

She fidgeted at having to explain. 'Have you seen any TV tonight?'

'No,' Faber said cautiously.

The pressure under her ribs was annoyingly like a sob. 'Bu was shown on it. Jake Grenfell has done a story about him, saying that he's some kind of . . . mythical freak.'

Faber's expression hovered between suspicion and the expectation of a punch line.

'He's — Bu's extremely disfigured.' She quickly looked at the ground, uncomfortable with her choice of words. 'It's all a horrible kind of prank. But more media have turned up at the boarding house Bu was staying at, so Derek —' she gestured to the car with an elbow '— the caretaker, he thought it best to get him away, find him a place to stay where nobody could track him down. We were going to get him out of town, but we just need a kind of staging post tonight. To think properly and get ourselves sorted.'

She paused at last. Faber was staring at her with bald scepticism. She clutched his arm. 'Please.'

He puffed out his cheeks, shifting his weight on the spot. 'How did you get involved in all this?'

'I heard about — no, I was visiting hospital . . . Look, it's too hard to talk about out here, on the goddamn doorstep, Faber. The poor guy just needs a break. He needs help.'

Faber was looking down at her from the top step. He was much taller than her anyway, and in this position she felt momentarily like a petitioner pleading with a remote, doubtful king.

'Another one of your causes, hey?'

'Oh, never *bloody* mind then.' Awkwardly she spun around.

'Sandrine, hang on. It's okay.' He caught her arm. 'He can come in.' Without releasing her, he said, 'Because I can rely on you. Can't I?'

She squeezed his arm in reply, then hared off down the steps.

'Careful,' Faber said just loud enough for her to hear.

When Derek and Sandrine had helped Bu out of the car, and walked with him up to the front door, Sandrine couldn't look at Faber. She didn't want to see his reaction — the shock, the inevitable delay as his very picture of the world rearranged itself. Faber could take his cues from her and Derek, treating Bu as normally as possible.

'This is Faber, an old friend of mine. Faber, this is Derek — he works at The Gables boarding house. And this is Bu.'

Derek held out a large, freckled hand. 'Gidday.'

'Gidday, Derek.' Faber was swift on the uptake. Unflappable, he held out his hand to Bu as well. 'Gidday,' he said again.

Bu tipped his head to the side and gazed down at Faber's palm as if wanting to see what he held in it.

'Right,' said Faber, slipping his hand back in his pocket. 'Let's all get inside.'

Faber fixed drinks, pulled all the curtains and switched on a heater, rubbing his hands together. 'Not long till I have to get wood for the log burner.' Sandrine and Derek clutched their mugs of tea; Bu had refused Faber's second offer of a drink; Faber settled down on the couch with a coffee. Little informal rituals, she thought, as they all checked each other out, making careful character or mood assessments. At last the way was cleared for business.

'Thanks for doing this, Faber,' she said.

He looked at her expectantly over his cup.

She turned to Derek, hoping for some help. He was

impassive, his big gardener's hands around the mug chapped, dry and marked with nicks and soil.

'Like I said, all we really need is somewhere for Bu to stay while we gather our thoughts tonight and decide on a plan,' she said. 'I'd use my place but given my flatmates...'

Faber shook his head, waved her on. She set her mug down on a table that was piled with fine arts books and design magazines. Faber was the marketing manager for a dealer gallery in town.

'It would also be good,' she said, 'if I could do some work here — phone calls, emails and so on. I think I can do a bit to defuse things, if I could just have some time.' She checked her watch. 'I can do something tonight, but I'll need to catch some people when they're at work. If it's all right, I think I'll stay here for the night too, and carry on in the morning.' She studied Faber's face. 'Is that too much of an imposition?'

His eyes were lit with excitement. She knew the same kind of charge: it was the thrill of being in on the latest development, in the know. Affection for him rushed through her. 'Not at all,' he said, grinning. 'I'll make up the bed in the spare room. And someone can sleep on the fold-out couch.'

Derek set his empty mug down. 'I'll be getting back to The Gables,' he said. 'I'll do a bit of a food shop on the way back so we're prepared for the farmhouse. Happy to run you back to The Gables at any stage if you need to collect your car though, love,' he said to Sandrine. She looked up quickly at the endearment. Maia wouldn't have approved. 'And I'll give you my mobile number.'

He frowned slightly after they'd exchanged contacts. 'You told Keith Peterson you'd keep in touch. When are you going to talk to him again?'

She glanced uncomfortably at Bu. 'Perhaps if Bu wants to . . .?'

Bu gave her another of his hazy, just-surfacing-from-somewhere looks. She felt the silence unfurl. Slowly, he spoke. 'Dr Peterson helps eh-sick people. I am not eh-sick.'

The fall of his accent underlined the mystery of his origins and his condition. The relief Sandrine had felt at Faber's support sank under a heavy weight. But Faber shrugged his shoulders at her, eyes still playful with curiosity. It made her pull herself up. Problem-solving. That's what they were here for. Time to get on with it.

❈ ❈ ❈

AFTER DEREK LEFT, FABER said he'd start preparing a meal while Sandrine set to work. When Bu was offered the spare room he nodded, but chose for now to stay out in the shared living space, gazing at the pictures, the small bronze castings and ceramic sculptures. Eventually he found a brainteaser in a rimu tray and began trying to fit the jumbled pieces back in order. Sandrine would have said he showed grim absorption, only every now and then she realised he was listening as she left a message on someone's voice mail, or talked under her breath while typing in emails on Faber's laptop.

When Faber brought out some focaccia and large bowls of pasta with pesto, olives and sun-dried tomatoes, Sandrine stretched for the ceiling, then swung her arms down again. 'Feels like I've put in another eight hours on top of a normal working day,' she said. She rubbed at the tightness at the back of her neck. 'This looks great, Faber, thanks. You're a life saver.'

As they pulled up chairs, Bu sniffing with cautious interest at the food, Faber opened a bottle of wine. He then gestured to ask Bu if he would like some, all just done with posture and head movements, yet each action excessively polite, as if Bu's presence had made Faber at once hypersensitive to etiquette and yet unsure of what exactly it could be in this situation. He poured two more glasses, then quietly put the bottle aside.

'So. Do you really think all this will work?' he asked, nodding at the laptop.

Sandrine sighed. 'Yes. I'm pretty sure that most people in the trade will have been sceptical, anyway.' She carefully avoided Bu's stare. 'And they won't want to go hunting a story that could either turn into a wild goose chase, or completely show them up, either as suckers, or as . . . arseholes.'

'Would most of your colleagues really care about that, though?'

'*Faber*,' she said, hearing just the tone her mother used on her father. 'We're talking the serious media, here. We're not talking tabloid hacks, paparazzi. Okay?'

'Yeah, well. Heaven help us if *they* get hold of it, right?'

The prospect was too irritating for her to tolerate even discussing it. Sandrine frowned. 'Let's just enjoy dinner.'

They both looked sideways, curious to see how Bu managed with a fork and spaghetti. Perfectly well, was the answer.

'So, Bu,' said Faber jovially, 'whereabouts do you come from?'

Sandrine sat with her fork suspended mid-air. Bu nodded to say that he'd heard the question, as he finished neatly sucking up the last strands of his pasta. He cleared his throat with a grumble that reminded her of an old, dreaming dog.

'Nepal,' he said. 'I was born in Nepal.'

Sandrine tried to catch Faber's eye, so she could frown — *Stop. Don't encourage him.*

'Really? Oh wow. I've been to Nepal. I went trekking there with some friends. It's an amazing place.'

Bu raised his great head, eyes warm with wonder. 'I d-hon't remember it. I left when I was too eh-small. I d-hon't remember Nepal, or my parents.'

Sandrine stared at him. 'But your parents died in the fire, here,' she said quietly. 'In New Zealand. South Westland.'

His chin fell to his chest, as if she had accused him of something. He nodded. 'My people-parents. The ones who raised me.'

Faber's jaunty posture and open smile said he wanted the story, but she felt a cold unrolling of dread for how far Bu would travel into his own delusion.

PART TWO
Hide

Bu's Mother, Lillian

LILLIAN'S MOST VIVID MEMORIES of the early weeks back in her native home with the little child had no 'best bits'. Not a one. The first outing in town with the infant was the toughest. She and her husband, Andy, had both worked hard to steel themselves for comments, for disturbed questions:

'Oh, what's wrong with the baby?'

'You poor wretches. Is there anything you can do about it?'

'Do you know what caused it?'

They worked out how they would answer: 'There's nothing at all seriously wrong with him, really. It's cosmetic. He's healthy and growing and that's all we could want. We don't need to do anything, not unless he wants, when he's older. No cause. No reason. No blame. It's just one of those things.'

She told her husband she could handle their pity. From pity might come compassion, and that was surely why Bu had been sent to them, the lesson he was to teach. It seemed the least of the problems she could bear, though she knew it would be hard at first. She even told Andy they should brace themselves for the flatness, the tears in private, when they would be able to drop their guise of coping admirably.

Telling yourself you can cope is one thing, reality another. She expected prurient interest to fade, but it didn't.

She was braced for scorn the minute she left the house. She knew she was meant to bear it, that every word, every look, was a little poison dart released to teach her humility. After months of it, she just wished that God would let her rest. Wondered why she had to encounter unkindness every day, every time she and the child went out together. Wasn't the child himself enough of a punishment? No. That was the wrong word. Such slips were why she had to suffer again. Bu was a blessing, a gift.

But there was no relief. You'd think people in a small town would grow used to you and your ways, your foibles, even if you started out as a newcomer. She'd thought the casual generosity so many strangers had shown each time she was pregnant, before each loss, would expand easily into sympathy, or even into a curiosity that could lead to a better appreciation of what she and Andy were going through. But people didn't seem to be able to help it. Even those who'd seen the child before.

Lillian tried to keep him covered with muslins and hats but he was an energetic little thing, feet kicking and hands dancing on the air, always squirming out of the layers with which she'd try to conceal his shame. And then he was a freak exhibit, a one-child sideshow. Cafés fell silent, pedestrians slowed down, heads turned, eyes followed him as smiles faded. Children dared each other to swing their orbits closer and closer to the baby's stroller, or his place kicking on the picnic rug, before they ran away squealing, thrilled by the terror of it: a play terror, because the *Ape Baby! Kiddy Kong!* was so small.

Initially, the Plunket nurse and the GP assured Lillian and Andy that excessive hair at birth was actually a known phenomenon: although usually it disappeared around six weeks.

'You know, I read about it just the other day. Elizabeth *Taylor* was born with six inches of dark hair coating her entire body!' said the nurse, cradling the baby before she weighed him for his three-month check. (That was the age Lillian and Andy guessed he was and the nurse didn't dispute it.) 'And didn't she turn into a beauty?'

As time drew on, though, both the doctor and the nurse wanted to run any number of tests, monitor Bu's development — the skull measurements were *unusual* — take photos and X-rays, send the family away to a clinic in the city, seek specialist advice.

But Lillian used her nursing background to deflect them. It was harder for them to argue with someone who knew how to use their own language, of course, but she also said she knew, she just *knew*, that as far as the *little soul inside* went, he was fine. Any mother could tell, from the way her baby met her eyes and held them, the inquisitive, attentive, even knowing sparkle. Mentally, intellectually, he was absolutely fine. And if there were other issues — health problems — that came with the damaged genes the doctor kept talking about, well, they could consult with a specialist then. '*If* we need to,' she said, keeping Bu's brief past to herself. 'Not now. There's enough for us to deal with.'

Her husband was inclined to agree. Actually, as Lillian knew, he was too stunned to have an independent opinion. He was in a kind of drawn-out state of paternal post-natal shock. She had been through so many difficult labours. Last time he had been convinced that he was going to lose her as well, not to mention the child he had begun to believe they could never keep. This little blighted miracle, Bu, had chanced into their lives after ten years of wanting a child.

'He's feeding well, he's soiling properly, he's sleeping like an angel. Why should we fill him full of pinholes from needles and prick tests? I've seen enough of that in my day, most of it pointless. He's got enough to go through in his life, already.' And she caressed his silken fur, from the bridge of his nose, back up to the top of his sloping scalp.

When the babe was about a year old, Lillian and Andy decided to buy some land on the south-west coast. Andy had spoken of it many times before. He loved the purity and ruggedness of the place, admired all the stories he'd heard of the people there and their resolute independence. Until now, Lillian had resisted, saying only, 'Maybe one day. Maybe.' Yet twelve months after their return home — following their two years working for the Christian mission overseas — she was the one who pushed the idea. Maybe she was weak, but she wanted desperately to be out of town, somewhere remote, away from the prying eyes, the catcalls and sniggers, the people who hurried their own children past, trying to conceal their rudeness with faux-kind reprimands: 'Don't stare. It's bad manners.'

Andy said surely she must have expected as much, with a child so marked.

'But we believed he would help to teach God's love for all things,' Lillian replied.

Andy paused in his task of ordering tools in the shed. Lillian stood in the doorway, with Bu in a sling on her back, a basket of wet nappies on her hip.

'Well, we might be the only pupils,' Andy said, grimly.

Lillian felt the weight of the child bearing down on the small bones in her back. 'So we'll move?'

His hands returned to his tools, but pointedly she waited. She knew she had such lessons to learn herself. She had been so innocent, yet so arrogant at the same time. Not taking God in. Thinking she had, but then He had to teach her. As if even her soul had a 'skite': like the fancy foyer of a colonial villa, all for show, with its architraves and twirls, and she'd allowed God in only that far. All the dank, cramped rooms of failure and weakness were hidden away behind it. But He knew they were there.

'I think, now, it's what's best for Bu,' she said.

Andy kept his head bowed to his tools, but he nodded.

※ ※ ※

BU WAS BOTH PUNISHMENT and reward, she came to see. He was a sign of how far she had erred, but a covenant, too: a promise that He would bring her His love, if only she would open her heart wide enough. She had seen how she had failed the other children. God blessed her for this recognition, but lest she stray again, He sent her one of His own, a child touched by His hand — a constant reminder.

Prideful, that's what she had been, thinking it would all be so easy, thinking no harm could come to her or her children, as if being a nurse was some sort of protection. Disease and mind sickness happened to other people, 'Not on *our* street,' as her own mother had often said. 'Not to those who pray, and keep God in their hearts.'

When Lillian's first baby came — a boy, badly jaundiced

and underweight — so did guilt. It sat with her like a sour matron, tatting in the corner of her mind, always watching and measuring her. *You're not good enough. You don't love that child the way you should.*

But she thought she'd wanted a baby. Too much, perhaps: her heart too tied to earthly things. For when her first child was born, a strange grief came on her, and she felt God withdraw. The child's cries dragged at her like a frightening riptide that she only wanted to struggle against, pull away from. At nights when the little boy woke she didn't want to get up to feed him. Sometimes Andy had to bring the child to her, put him to her breast while she lay there, trying to wish it all away. During the day, when the baby slept, she feared the sound of his surfacing cries. One day, she even said aloud, 'Please, please, don't wake again.'

The child drank misery from Lillian's milk. He died before he was three months old. The doctors said cot death, but Lillian knew it was her fault. She hadn't loved her son with a natural mother's love.

She felt so ashamed that when Andy said they should try for another baby she just let him have his way. There were two miscarriages after that, then a full-term labour where she lost too much blood, and the baby soon after. She deserved it all, she knew that, but it was so hard.

She wanted Andy to be happy again, to look at her the way he once did, as if she could do no wrong. Sometimes it was even hard to believe that God was love, and not judgement and anger.

But perhaps that is how He works, she thought. He teaches you the true sweetness of hope, by placing it against loss and doubt.

For when she and Andy were both in a state of terrible questioning, there came a chance encounter with Isaac Roberts, who led them to the mission that took them to Nepal. His church there needed builders, teachers, doctors, nurses. As a primary school teacher and woodturner, Andy could assist in many ways. With his skills, and Lillian's nursing background, Isaac said, 'This is no chance encounter. God's sovereign work is to place persons together, to complete His plan.' Isaac's acceptance that their losses were part of the Lord's great scheme was such a comfort. So simple, yet it lifted a leaden care from them both. After meeting him, both Lillian and Andy sensed the call. Helping others, Andy said, in such a beautiful place and with such warm people, would be just the right distraction from their troubles.

There were times when Lillian wondered if even that was sinful. Was finding solace in this way profiting from other people's pain? Really, she asked too many questions, in all aspects of life. She was made of doubt, a difficult lamb for anyone to shepherd. And so He found new and marvellous ways to instruct her. He brought to her a Prodigy.

In Nepal, somehow she and Andy had both believed that the child was an answer to their prayers. *An* answer, not *the* answer. Yet it hadn't seemed such a terrible cross to bear, when the child came to them deep in the midst of others' deprivation and travails. Lillian and Andy both accompanied the roving surgeries that the mission took from one remote location to another. The doctors were badly needed, to name and mend all kinds of ailments, from appendicitis to goitre to the disfigurement of severely cleft palates, and worse: people with their bodies and faces all jumbled, as if when He made them, He had been blindfolded and spun on the spot. Some of the children made you weep as soon as you looked at them. But, oddly, Lillian had never felt that way about Bu. When he came, love leapt from her like a live current. She wondered, later, if that was part of her curse, too — God's sly enchantment.

But the real leaching away of her trust in God didn't start till they had been back in their own country for many months. Distrust of her fellows came first. She sometimes wondered why she and Andy had moved away from Nepal, left the ordinary people she had met there who were at once more fatalistic, and more tolerant; more used to overcoming — or even just living with — afflictions. Perhaps she and Andy had made their decision too quickly. They had leapt at the mission's offer of help to pull strings with the right people, get the little one put on Lillian's passport. Perhaps they should have spent more time thinking it all through.

In the small New Zealand town they chose at first, people left messages for them on their lawn, their trees, in their letterbox. They left cat's faeces on the mail; once a dog bowl and bone on the doorstep, with a note that said *For the mongrel*; toilet paper strung from the trees — a harmless, kids' practical joke, Andy said, but to Lillian the strands looked sinister, like bandages trailing from some massive wound. So they agreed to seek out some land and after they made the purchase, they spent less and less time together in town. There were still days she travelled in to do errands, but often beforehand she'd stand in the middle of the room, paralysed with indecision, thinking about all the things people might say about Bu. Andy got used to her changing her mind at the last minute, giving him a list of things she needed, then saying, 'You go on without me. I'll be all right till next time.'

At first he tried to persuade and cajole her. Then one day she said, 'When Bu can talk properly, and show how clever he is, then it will be easier.'

Andy stood watching her as he slowly snapped the domes closed on his waterproof coat. His hands fell to his sides. She held his gaze. 'All right,' he'd said quietly, and let her keep Bu home too.

They lived on the land in a tent at first. They felled wood where it grew, used horses to ferry in heavy items like solar panels, parts for their small hydro system, a bath tub and sink, through the bush, sometimes taking days to transport things from the rutted dirt road, where they left the ute concealed in scrub and trees. It was well over a year before they could finally stand back and say the rudiments of a three-bedroom house and workshop were done. Andy was to work from home, making furniture to sell. Lillian was to grow herbs, to supply health food shops. They had built a chicken coop, already had the two horses, slowly acquired a nanny goat, a cow and two piglets. Together Lillian and Andy would teach Bu until they felt he was ready to enter the world on his own.

That spring, Lillian was standing in a patch of sunshine, after hanging out the washing, scrutinising the weatherboards still left to paint on this side of the house, but feeling something in her settle at last: the beginnings of the old sense of safety she'd had before she was chosen to be Bu's earthly guardian. *We'll be all right. We'll pull through now.*

Through what? Squinting against the sunshine, she

scanned the trees, the vegetable garden, heard Andy chipping and scraping away in his workshop.

Bu came toddling precariously round the corner, pulling a Buzzy Bee in one hand, dragging a bucket in the other.

Through Bu's life, the internal voice answered.

His life. She sat down heavily on the upturned washing basket, forehead propped on her hand. She felt despair tower over and dwarf her, reduce her to a granule of dirt. Could God even see her there?

Bu spied her, then came puddling over. 'Eh-sad Mummy,' he said, his own little fur-face tragically rumpled, as he held out a flowering weed for her.

'Excuse me?' a male voice said.

Lillian reacted as if to a ghost. She grabbed Bu to her, shielded him with her body. She didn't speak, just stared at the three men who stood there with guns, packs and a panting, but obedient, black Labrador.

'Sorry, we didn't mean to frighten you. We've just lost our bearings. We've been out pig hunting and Tommo here threw our map in the river.'

'I didn't bloody *throw* it, Dad, it was an accident.' The one called Tommo looked angry, hot-headed. She saw now that there was one man with two tall teenage sons. They had the air of three people who had been carrying a fight around with them for days.

'Do you folks have a decent map of this area? We want to head back to the track, and —'

'Andy!' Lillian's cry brought her husband from his workshop. The sight of the visitors pulled him up short.

Once Andy was there, Lillian kept her eyes on the men. 'There are no tracks close by here.' Her voice thinned with fear.

Andy blinked at her tone, slowly began to unroll his shirt sleeves. 'Sorry, friend. My wife means this is private land.'

The black Lab whined and panted. Lillian's lips and fingertips went cold. She remembered the 'gifts' left for the baby boy, back in the town they had abandoned. 'I don't like dogs on our property. I don't like them.'

The father looked awkward, and although the Lab was still perfectly compliant, he put one hand through its collar. 'Sorry, we didn't know. Have you got stock round here?'

'Some,' said Andy.

'She's a good bitch, is Tessie,' said one of the teenage boys. 'She'd never hurt a fly.'

The silence was icy, and under it Lillian thought, *Then why do you take her hunting?*

Andy stepped forward, apology and dismissal both in his shrug. 'If you go back and follow the river south-west, you'll come to a fork. There's a makeshift sort of footbridge over one side. Cross it and follow that part of the river down. You'll hit a track eventually.'

Throughout this scene, Bu had been shielded by his mother's body. Now that his father spoke more politely to the men, he slipped out from behind her legs.

The dog's body narrowed into a lean, dark arrow. At the back of her throat, she hummed, then whined. 'Quiet, Tessie,' said the man. The dog growled, begging to be let nearer.

'Please get the dog away,' Lillian said, trying to sound smooth as metal.

'She's just curious. She wants to play.' The man and his sons were embarrassed, baffled, curious themselves, staring without meaning to, perhaps, or because they thought it would hide their astonishment, if they didn't flinch, didn't quickly look away.

'What's this?' one of the teenage boys asked. 'What's this, hey Tessie? You found a little buddy?'

The dog caught some kind of intoxication from the boy's voice, and from Bu's sudden spurt of curiosity. Bu, his mouth full of flower, stem, a tiny dry stick, and trailing a dark drool line of dirt that matted his chin fur, started to totter over towards the dog, saying carefully, *d-hoorgie, d-hoorgie*, trying to get the word right, voice crammed with the marvel of recognising a real dog, one that wasn't just in a storybook.

'No, Bu. Come here,' Lillian said.

Andy stopped her from snatching up the child, barring her across the waist with an arm as he stepped forward. 'He's all right, Lillian. The dog's well trained.'

Bu reached out to touch the dog's fur with his bare palms. He squealed with delight at the sensation. Tessie's bark broke, high-pitched with agitation, and she began to bound around.

Lillian saw the bared teeth, saw Bu knocked over by the dog's energetic jumping, saw Bu's enjoyment turn to fear. She'd already felt it along her spine, the moment she'd seen the dog look at Bu. Knew something in it would turn and make it go for the child. The savage, guttural growls, the sight of it biting, sent her mad. She swooped at the teenage boy who had chucked his pack and gun aside to try to drag off the dog.

Lillian felt the supernatural surge she'd read about: mothers who lift Jeeps off their babies, wrench fallen logs off their children, run back into buildings that spill with fire. As if the boy and the dog were a single body, she hauled them in one movement off her son. She tore the gun from the teenager's pack and *crack, crack*, twice, shot the dog through the ribs.

She was sweating, shaking, felt herself expanding, her head inflating, her skin burning as she grew and grew. She knew she gave off heat, a pulsing, scarlet light; the bush surrounding them began to step back from their circle, taking all its song, its clicks, whirrs and rustles with it, muffled in silence, as if in appalled witness. She knew she could do worse. She felt the bones in her skull throbbing while her mind filled and filled with it. She thrust the gun from her as if now it seared her fingers. 'Go,' she said. 'Please. Just go.'

She watched them turn heel. Andy's face was white and sorrowful, white as the strange light that flittered at the side of her vision, as if an angel's wing quickly brushed in and out of view. For Lillian, that sight was the last time she felt sure of God's presence. She hadn't known what she was truly capable of until she heard the sound of the gun. She was not a good woman. God had sent her a final test and she had sinned. She felt the warmth of Him leak away, and if He wasn't there, guiding her, how thin was the crust over chaos? Where did one foot go, and then the next? How could Lillian ever know how to carry on?

The Lost Hunters

THEY TOLD, ALL RIGHT. At first, when they were found by a search party, they were disoriented, dehydrated, the two boys suffering from hypothermia, the father on the verge of it himself. He was too concerned about his sons to talk initially, but after twenty-four hours, his version came out, in private.

He and the boys both told his wife what had happened to their dog. Then the sons told their best mates. The wife told some in her circle, but the man never directly told any friends of his own, nor anyone at his work, nor the authorities. He couldn't get it to come out right, sounding like the truth, the kind the police would swallow. And he still didn't know exactly where it had happened. On the South Westland trip from Christchurch, their wanderings had become so convoluted, followed by the deprivations of near-exposure, that he became less and less sure of the exact location of the block of land.

Still, a rumour swelled from that day, in the townships dotting the edge of the sweeping south-west coast. There was something wrong, something that lived out there, in the bush. Some said just a woman and her unfortunate child. Some said demonic. Some said sick. Whatever the woman really was — witch, head-case — she had a deformed son. A hairy throwback, a kind of pygmy monkey-man: made you feel pretty spooked just to look at it. So the father must be a weirdo too. Subhuman, they were. Insane. They'd shot the pet dog of some poor guys who wound up lost and stumbled on to their property.

When the guys saw the mongrel-kid, saw it fed dirt and weed, they tried to stay calm, but their dog had gone for it. Smelt some sort of danger. Bad spirit coming from it, maybe. The hunter smelt it too, he told his wife. The smell of evil, he called it, and him a banker in his workaday life: sensible, and not a bit religious, not till after he was rescued, anyway. It was years ago now, far more than a decade. And the folk round there still sometimes said mongrel-boy, or wild-man. Sometimes maero. They all said, don't go into the bush past Rory McMaster's without a map, a gun, and a mate. Give the mate a gun, too. You'd be mad to go on your own.

❉ ❉ ❉

SOON BU'S HOME WAS like a castle from myth, surrounded by a tangle of bush that might have grown while the people in the distant towns and villages, who could have explored it, fell under a spell of fear for a forgotten number of years.

Bu's Father, Andy

HE KNEW HIS WIFE wasn't well, of course he did. But he didn't stop loving her, did he? He tried to do something to help. He asked her if she would like to visit a minister, but she announced that she had come to see faith as private: between her and God. Fair enough, Andy had said. The voice of her faith had always been louder than his, but now, he thought, perhaps she was just coming round more to his own, quieter way of expressing it.

Besides, part of him guessed her problem might not be a matter for a minister anyway. Maybe it was like the doctors talked about after she lost her other babies, hormones, something chemical out of order. So he found books from the library in the nearest township. He visited a doctor there too, and asked what it meant when someone had slowly grown so afraid of other people that they faltered altogether, lost themselves.

'It's not fear of big spaces,' Andy said. 'It's not agoraphobia.'

'Agoraphobia's not fear of open spaces as such, either,' said the doctor, an older man with a white-sprinkled red beard and close-cropped ginger-white hair. 'It can be a dread of the bustle, the activity, of normal, daily social discourse.' He plucked a drug manual off his shelves and began shuffling through the thin pages. 'There *are* ways of managing the disorder. Counselling, gradual exposure, assessing the patient for medication . . .'

Andy continued to act as if he was listening. He nodded, said yes in the right places and accepted the leaflets he was given. It was just that following the doctor's advice would mean actually getting Lillian to walk to the ute — at least an hour's tramp from the house — and then convincing her to make the long trip to town.

Andy could see it clearly: an impossible chain of obstacles. He didn't believe that the good, clean-scrubbed, Lancashire-accented GP had ever really encountered the paralysing anxiety that Lillian experienced. It had made Andy fear for his own sanity when she began to shake, stare, cling to the ute's door handle or a lamppost, the one time he'd tried to convince her it was okay to take a bundled-up, disguised Bu to town. It was as if she were fighting against a tempest, struggling to stay upright, to even breathe, while the planet whirled around her.

Andy climbed back into his ute, which was stocked up with town supplies, after this regular monthly trip away from Lillian and Bu. He never left without worrying about his small family, whether they were really doing the right thing by their wrong-born son, and yet he also soaked luxuriously in the time alone. It was a chance to see what the outside world still looked like so he wouldn't be too out of touch when Lillian finally came right.

Because she'd have to come right. There was no way they could carry on like this forever. So he continued, indulging her he supposed it was, in a kind of *folie à deux*. The phrase sprang to mind from his mother's kitchen talk about the mutual madness in bizarre love affairs. It made him think of the old *Folies Bergère* posters in the tearooms his mum had run in Greymouth for a while. Only there were no smiling, high-kicking chorus girls here. It was just him and Lillian: clumsy, slow, clinging together, looking sadly over each other's shoulders, waiting for the music to change.

Bu's Mother, Lillian

BU WAS NOT QUITE five. He stroked his mother's arm. His palm shifted to his own arm. Watching his hand carefully, he asked, 'Mummy, why d-ho I have eh-so much hair, when you are bare?'

Here it is. This is where it starts. We've been lucky he's waited till now. 'You were just born that way.'

'But why was I?'

She felt his stare on her skin as if it were a metal seal pressed against molten wax. She had to look away. 'It's just the way you are. When you were tiny as a bug,' she pinched her fingers together to show him, 'you got a message telling your skin to grow lots and lots of hair.'

'Who was the message from? Was it a message from a bad witch?'

'There are no bad witches.'

She saw Bu's quizzical, rumpled face, and tried to push her own struggle away, speaking more firmly. 'It was a message . . . well, from God first, then from the cells that made you. It was a message from yourself.' She wished she knew more, she wished there were answers. 'That's just the way you are. Everyone is designed to look different, Bu. All God's creatures. You know how a bird has a beak, or Daddy has ears that poke out a bit?' She pushed her own ears out from the side of her head so they protruded like wing mirrors. 'Or how I have this bent finger?' She showed her crooked pinky: its top joint made the tip appear to be pointing inwards. 'We all have things that make us what — who we are. Maybe you can think of it like a name. Our bodies wear their own names on them, so that we won't get confused about who's who, or what's what. Does that make sense?'

Bu's mouth drooped. 'But will it change?'

'Change?'

'Will I look like you one d-hay, when I am grown?'

'No. No, darling, you won't. But that doesn't matter to us. Because it makes you Bu.'

'But I d-hon't want it to. I d-hon't want the fur. I want to look like you, and D-haddy.'

'We love you the way you are, Bu. We're so lucky to have you.'

He gazed into her eyes. 'You hab a freckle in your eye.'

'Do I?'

'Yes. D-hoes it hurt?'

'No. I can't feel it.'

He ran his hand over his scalp, his arm. 'I can feel my fur. I can feel that.'

'Yes. I can too.' She smoothed her own scalp.

He pressed his nose against her cheek. 'You are beautiful, Mummy.'

'And you're my handsome Bu. The most handsome little boy in the world to me.'

'You d-hon't know any other boys. Eh-silly.' Matter of fact, getting the world straight.

'Oh, yes I do!' She could hear the strain and knew he could too.

He smiled, gave her a kiss and wandered off to play. She was grateful the painful discussion seemed to be over, for now; thankful for a few moments to pursue her own thoughts, get some things done around the house. Time truly to herself was such a gift, and she loved to use it for gardening, preparing the cooking and medicinal herbs she grew, or for mending, reading — and most of all for music. Listening to music, singing, playing recorder, flute or guitar, humming her own snatches of composition.

She picked up the guitar, toyed with notes for a while, trying to pare the mingled sadness she and Bu had found down to a single tune. Eventually the crick in her neck told her she must have been playing for an hour or more. Blinking and stretching as if she'd been asleep, she scratched down some notes on paper, set the guitar aside, then went through the house calling, 'Bu? Bu, love?' No answer. That was when she knew she had let the silence go on for too long.

She found him in the main bedroom. Shanks and tufts of his fur lay around him in a pale cloud that seemed to shoot gold from one angle of light. Patchy, raw and scraped with razor bites, he looked like a disgruntled, battered tom, still crazed with hate for his enemy. He stared around the room unseeingly, gasping with emotion. There was so much fur scattered everywhere, and so much still to be hacked and chopped, if he was going to finish the job properly.

'Oh no, *Bu*,' she said.

He glared at her now, the black eyes seeming to take her down, down into infinite darkness. 'It will grow back, won't it? Eb-erywhere it will eh-still grow back.'

Nothing she could say would help.

※ ※ ※

THE QUESTIONS RETURNED, of course, again and again. He wouldn't accept her shying away with *Perhaps*

God wanted you this way; perhaps it just happened.

One day he shouted at her. 'No! It d-hidn't just happen. Tell me the truth. There was a reason. There was a *real reason. A real reason.*' He bunted his head into her stomach; clung to her; then fought to get free of her hands. She had to pin his arms to his sides, and only the promise that she would tell him the true story calmed him down.

The tale Lillian told grew over the years. With every telling she wove in small observations, flecks of colour, new strands, as her memory dropped stitches that she had to rescue and redo, and as she discovered finer detail in the act of narration. Sometimes she felt as transported by, as powerless against, her mind's own elaborations as she did when deep in the river of dreams at night. Bu's increasing hunger for more clues meant that sometimes even she was unsure how much she had witnessed, how much she had been told, and how much she had embroidered to satisfy her son.

The tale was of a man who met a woman in a mountain village, high in the Himalayas. She was of the Sherpa people; he was from a country way on the other side of the world, at the bottom. He came from a place that had mountains too, and forests, but it was surrounded by sea, the sea the woman had never seen.

'First, though, you must know about the man,' Lillian always said.

The man had been in the Himalayas for nearly a month, trekking, taking photographs, writing in his journal, hoping, like hundreds of others, that the mountains would somehow answer his questions about his life — as God might, if He took pity on you.

One day, tired after four hours of hiking under a strong sun, he decided to rest at a stand of boulders, using one as a back support. He was more drained than even a long walk should have made him. It was a hollowness that sat with him each day, even after food and water, even after resting. At nights he had been dreaming of trudging on and on, right up into the snowline, and losing himself like a single crystal in a snowfall. He was a young man, and yet his best friend, whom he'd played with since boyhood, had recently died in the country surrounded by sea. So his hollowness was the kind that loss brings. Perhaps he had thought he should get as far away from the sea as possible, and that he could walk off the furious grief, sweat it out like a toxin.

For weeks he'd not been in the frame of mind to talk to anyone beyond the polite *Namaste* or *Namskara* of passing mountain porters, standing aside for the men who carried enormous packloads of Cokes for the tourists, or even massive wooden beams for buildings farther along the trails. He had mirrored the dogged, quiet acceptance of physical discomfort shown by these men, whose backbreaking burdens were steadied with *topi* straps that sat around their foreheads, forcing their faces to bow towards the dirt. Occasionally he had exchanged a little more conversation, when asking for a room at a lodge, or asking for food from families willing to sell meals to the solitary Westerners who straggled past every day. He had avoided other travellers, though. They repelled him, these Europeans: they were too much like an unflattering image of himself.

When he first heard the scuff of feet behind the boulders he'd chosen for his picnic spot, the young man felt a needle of irritation. He wanted to keep following the twists and turns of his own thoughts. He started to gather up his things quickly, tying his food bag, fastening pack clips, and began to head back to the main trail. When he threw a jealous, frustrated glance over his shoulder, he saw that the intruder was an almond-eyed woman, squatting in the easy way people did here, and curled around a baby tied in a sling that she had swung around to her chest. She wore a straight, striped skirt that reached her ankles, and flimsy jandals, but at least, he saw, she had a thick jacket made of felted wool, its coppery toggles like small bells. So often, in his solid hiking boots, and carrying leggings, fleece, gloves, hat and expensive GORE-TEX jacket, he wondered how the locals in fragile shoes and summer fabrics kept warm, or managed the long treks without wrenching ankles, or getting chilblains.

He might have kept walking after mumbling *Namaste, didi*, if he hadn't seen her wipe her eyes with the back of her hand, and the clear marks of tears on her skin. He realised, too, that one side of her face had a slight swelling, and that there was a large bruise on her jawline from a blow that must have damaged the soft skin inside her mouth.

He stopped, took a step towards her, tried to remember some of the phrases he had been practising.

Tapāī sai hunuhuncha?

She looked at him as if he were the village idiot, then turned her face away, shielding the child even more and cupping one hand over her eyes like a visor.

He knew he'd just asked her if she was well but had hoped that, if said with the right tone, the question would convey his concern. He scrabbled around in his pack for his tiny phrase book.

Ke bhayo? What's the matter?

No response. He scanned the empty trail, then looked up at the steep, scree slope a hundred or so paces away. Far down the trail, a flicker of colour near the cliff edge suggested prayer flags on a wooden pole at a bend in the path. There was no other life on the track. She was a long way from the last village he'd passed, and she didn't seem to be carrying anything other than the tiny child, the top of whose thickly fuzz-covered head was just peeping above the material of the sling.

He felt for an energy bar in one of his pockets, and carefully said one of his small cluster of complete sentences: *Tapāī lāi bhok lāgyo*?

Her glance slid over to the shiny wrapper. She had some struggle with herself, but hesitantly covered her eyes again.

He riffled through his phrase book, English words corking his throat, a feeling of urgency building up behind them. Please. *Kripayā*. The book cautioned him that this was 'very formal, usually reserved for writing', but something insisted, pushing up from under his ribs: *try, at least try*.

Kripayā? Ke bhayo?

She dropped her hand in exasperation, and spoke in a hail of words, from which he could barely catch small, sharp blows of sense: *malai dukhi . . . buwā . . . risāunu . . . chaina, chorā, raksi . . .*

Under his breath, he translated for himself: . . . father . . . no? not? . . . son . . . *raksi, raksi*?

She repeated, *raksi lāgyo, raksi lāgyo*, mimed lifting

a bottle to her lips, then grinned like the turning head of a painted dance mask. Her expression dropped suddenly, and with a whispered run of words he couldn't understand, she shielded her eyes again.

He walked around the boulders and came up to her from the opposite side. He ducked his head and knelt so he could see under the shield she'd made for her eyes. He dropped all pretence of knowing Nepali now, and just said, *Isn't there anything I can do to help?*

Tears smudged the dust on her face and, perhaps a little woozy with the midday sun and the thinning altitude, he was frightened by the sadness in her eyes. The pupils reflected huge vistas of mountains and distance. Again, as often on this long trek, he had the sensation that the rest of the world had vanished, and that miles and miles of indifferent majesty, sheer cliffs reaching higher and higher, crags, snow, ice and crevasses, were all that was left of the known earth. Uncomfortable with his frank stare, she tried to turn away, shuffling on her heels in the dirt.

'Will someone be along to meet you soon?' As if she were waiting at a bus stop.

'It seems wrong, you out here all on your own.' He held out the energy bar again, then dug in his pack for trail mix. He gestured with them at her, then at the baby. Despite herself, she laughed, cupping the baby's skull in one thin-boned hand, shaking her head, saying *hoina*, no. She quickly readjusted the sling, and now, from the movement of the baby's head, he knew that it was suckling.

'*Huncha,*' he said. Okay. '*Khājā?*' Snack?

She bowed her head over the baby but he saw her glance sidle over to the packets and he pushed them towards her, along the ground. They sat silently for a while. When he saw a slight tremor in her hand as she tucked a tendril of dark hair back behind an ear it occurred to him, belatedly, that he could be scaring her. *I should go.* He scrambled up to gather his pack, wishing he'd done it more gracefully when she seemed to shrink away. He drew a wide arc with his arm, as if gathering her and the child in.

'If you are afraid to be alone, please, walk with me. I'll help you find a place to stay, if you need one.' Stupid. She would know the lie of the land and its people — her people — far better than he would.

He took a few steps, looked over his shoulder, found he was bowing his head in a way he'd seen an old dog do when accepting biscuits from a stranger: submissive, grateful. *I won't hurt you.* Then he walked away.

After the next bend in the road, when the woman was out of sight, it was all he could do not to sit down again and hold his head in his hands. *I don't understand anything. I'm no good at this, at people. Useless. Useless piece of shit.* Somehow he kept walking, but a few minutes later the sting on his skin reminded him he hadn't topped up on sunscreen. He threw down his pack and searched his pockets for the small tube.

Like a mirage coalescing from bright light, the woman appeared. She stood several paces from him, watching, then not watching. She scooped a handful of something out of a pocket hidden in her clothing, cupped it to her mouth and chewed it, looking out over the scree and rock. When he started walking again, and shot another look over his shoulder, she set out also.

So it went for the rest of the day. When he stopped, she would stop; she never met up with him, yet never let him out of sight. When they reached a lodge, he thought she would either disappear, or talk to the owners. She did neither, but stood closer to him than she had before so that he knew to book space for three. He knew also to be careful: two rooms, he explained to the proprietor.

❄ ❄ ❄

'THIS IS A LONG eh-story,' Bu might say, when he felt the story was as much his as Lillian's.

'Yes,' said Lillian.

'Get to the best bit,' said Bu.

But if there was a long, cold night to fill, with Bu nowhere near sleep, and Lillian wanted to spin the story out, she might answer, 'I like it long. That's how these things happen sometimes. Slowly, so the people can be sure of each other.'

One night, Bu retorted, 'But following the man wasn't eh-slow.'

Lillian laughed. 'All right then, Bu. You tell the rest.'

Bu slipped off his chair, paced back and forth in a small circle, furry brow crumpled in a serious frown. 'Well, the man was bery careful but also that was because he had trouble understanding her. And also she couldn't understand hardly anything he eh-said, because she was Sherpa. She eh-spoke Tibetan as her first language. She only used Nepali when she had to for people like trabellers. But also his accent was eh-so bad. It made her laugh. And eh-sometimes she would laugh even when she d-hidn't want to, and that would make him grumpy eh-so then he wouldn't talk much. But eh-still the woman followed him all the way to where he wanted to go, just up to the eh-snowline, where everyone mainly eh-spoke the Sherpa language. The man didn't know that language. And then they went to her billage because she realised she would have to go back, there was nowhere else for her.'

'Yes, but Bu, can you say *spoke*?'

'Eh-spoke.'

'Try *travellers*.'

'Trabellers.'

'No. Travellers. And say village.'

'*Billage*!' Bu snapped and she sighed; she should have known there was never any remedying it.

'All right. Carry on.'

'But the woman thought if the man was with her, things would turn out all right. And —' Bu painted an arc in the air with both arms: a voilà sign '— they d-hid!'

Lillian smiled. 'Go on.'

'There were other trabellers bisiting, trabellers from the eh-same country as the man. He could talk to them. And the man worked things out for the woman, to help her, because her family d-hidn't want the child. They thought it was — made wrong. And the trabellers he met, they had always wanted a child but couldn't hab one. When they heard of the woman's little baby, they were bery happy. They eh-said God must hab been watching over them, to bring this gift. The mother who the man had found and helped was glad to gib the child a home where it would be lubbed. And eh-so, the trabellers took the boy all the way back to their own country, the one eh-surrounded by eh-sea.'

'And the best bit is?'

'The best bit is the baby was named Phubu for

Thursday, the day he was gibben. But the baby grew up calling himself Bu for short and his new family called him that anyway because that means boy in Tibetan too.'

Lillian nodded.

'But one bit that's not eh-so good is that the Sherpa woman said Bu wasn't eben her own real baby. The woman had found the baby and the baby wasn't like any other baby. But she knew she had to look after it the moment she eh-saw it, and she gabe it the milk she still had from her own boy, who hadn't libbed. She wanted to care for it eben though it wasn't hers, and eben though she knew that her father who was a d-hrunk would be angry, and her husband would want her to leabe the child. He thought it was like an ebil eh-spirit, and should be left out on the hills to d-hie. Or for its own, um, *kind* to find.'

In a tone that told him not to snare himself in the bleaker parts of his tale, Lillian said, 'But there's another best bit too, isn't there, Bu?'

'Yes. Because the Sherpa woman cared for a baby that wasn't hers, and nursed it like her own for d-hays and d-hays, that means she was better than the real mother. Because a *found* baby and a *found* mother d-hoesn't happen bery much. That means it's more eh-special. Because they d-hon't hab to lub each other, but they choose to. And the other best bit is that for this baby there were two found mothers, eh-so that's two times as good.'

'We love you, Bu.'

'Eben though your only boy is an "out-and-out-original".'

'*Because* our boy is an out-and-out-original.'

'And because *two* not real mothers and one not real father have both lubbed me, that makes me okay.'

'More than okay.'

Bu stared into her eyes. He put up a thumb and stroked her smooth cheek.

'There are probably others like me, eh-somewhere, aren't there? And I might find out, one d-hay.'

'We don't know, Bu.'

'There are eh-stories, though, aren't there?'

'Yes, lots of stories.'

'I might be where the eh-stories come from. I might be a whole new person.'

'Bu. You're a special, lovely little soul. One of God's very own. That's the main thing.'

Bu's mouth pouched into a sorry curve. Whenever he pushed on this question, Lillian felt herself clam up. She saw that he knew better than to try now. 'Let's go back to the best bits,' he said.

'All right. You tell them.'

PART THREE
Seek

Bonnie Peterson, Dunedin

'HEY THERE!' BONNIE CALLED from the TV room, as she heard Keith's tread, and his keys jangling onto the kitchen bench.

'Hi,' he answered, smiling from the doorway. He started to loosen his tie, walking over as if to hug her, but then caught sight of Grenfell's report, which she'd been watching. Stopping short, he lunged for the volume remote, striking his shin against the coffee table.

'Whoops. Are you okay?'

'Sshh,' he hissed. 'I know this guy,' he said, by way of apology as he sat down, rubbing his leg.

There was a particular look on Keith's face. 'An institute patient?' Bonnie left her armchair and took a seat next to her husband on the couch, peering more closely at the screen and pulling her crocheted tunic down over her tucked up legs.

He nodded. 'One of mine. He discharged himself, though I knew he wasn't ready.' When Keith spoke suddenly to the TV, she saw how his face had blanched. 'Christ! They're making a monster out of him. This is unbelievable.'

From his tone, she instantly expected his usual reaction: furious pacing, then a sudden declaration that he had to go for a run. It was the pattern he followed when all the hours and effort he had put into helping a patient were lost, because some sick soul was just too damaged to be rescued by the time he got involved. She wasn't prepared for this, though. His feet kept crossing and uncrossing, just like a boy who was trying to hold in some thought, some urgent need. When he put an arm around her shoulders, she thought, *Oh, okay, so he's not taking this one to heart so much*? When he stayed there, face pressed into her neck, she knew she was wrong.

'Keith? Sweetheart?' She tried to pull away, to see his face, but suddenly he was up again, making a call to someone called Sandrine on his cellphone. Edgily, Bonnie got up to fix some decaf, all the time listening out for some sort of explanation. She returned to the couch and pretended to read a magazine.

Pinch-faced, Keith sat down, letting his hands drop between his knees. 'Grenfell's a complete shyster. He's just — *bastard*.'

Bonnie frowned, toying with the lacquered chopstick she had used to hold her hair in a loose bun. 'So where's the patient now, if he's not in care?'

'Long story. Sandrine says they're taking him somewhere the media won't be able to find him, and she's waiting for the storm to die down. He's probably in safe enough hands, as far as it goes . . .'

'Sandrine?'

He sank back deeper into the couch, and she pushed a mug towards him across the coffee table. He took it without acknowledgement, staring out at the sunset-stained sky.

Bonnie couldn't help prodding. 'Can you tell me about it?'

'If he didn't need help before, he will now.'

Her decaf cooled. She felt an old, now uncharacteristic craving for a cigarette: its comforting rituals for nervous hands, its quick chemical transport away from immediate anxieties. She made to stand up, smoothing the tunic down over her black satin trousers. They were new, expensive. Normally Keith would have noticed, and run his own hands appraisingly over the discreet little embroidered Chinese dragons, pleased she still 'took trouble'. But his hand rubbed at his eyes. 'I think what I feel is ashamed,' he said.

Bonnie felt as if she'd tripped. She sat back down and to regain her sense of balance asked, 'Ashamed that he discharged himself? But if it was within his rights, Keith, you can't ...'

'No, it's not that. It's something else.' The look on his face, his painful hesitations, suddenly reminded her of the night when her first husband had confessed to an affair, just two years into their marriage.

'What is it, Keith?' The quick steeliness in her tone made him look up.

'Sorry.' He reached over and cupped her chin, then drew away. 'I mean I wanted to rescue him.'

The misery in his face made her bite back the words: *Well, sweetheart, that's the way it's been with every one of them — what's new?*

'I formed a dozen preconceptions just like this.' He triple-clicked his fingers. 'Everything I told myself I would never do — everything I'm *trained* not to do. From our first meeting, I wanted him to be a certain kind of case. So I could have a chance to live out *ambition*.' He said it with such a rich, Shakespearean self-disgust, that Bonnie felt as if she barely knew him, as if there were secret histories in that serious head of his, things about himself, and his work, that he didn't, or couldn't, speak of.

'A certain kind of case? What do you mean?'

He whistled out tunelessly. 'My Not-Quite Wolf-Boy. A new twist on Kaspar Hauser.'

'Kaspar Hauser?'

He turned his mug to and fro. 'Famous nineteenth-century case. A German boy raised in solitary confinement for years.' He glanced at her and she shook her head; she still didn't know what he meant.

Keith hunkered down, arms crossed on his knees. 'Hauser was found one day staggering around alone in the streets of Nuremberg. He couldn't answer any questions about himself and despite the fact he was adolescent, he only spoke in a peculiar babble. Some versions of his case say all he could say at first was "I want to be a horseman like my father is". Familiar?'

Bonnie felt a strange prickling along her scalp, but shook her head. 'Go on.'

'There's a theory he was of noble descent — in fact, DNA testing done just a couple of years ago on his clothing shows he probably did come from the aristocracy. When he was eventually taught how to talk, he claimed that he'd been kept in a tiny cell, where food and a small amount of water — he was always thirsty — were placed while he slept. Whoever did it always kept themselves hidden.'

Bonnie gave a small noise of dismay.

'Hauser was murdered years after his discovery, lured away by someone promising to reveal the truth about his birth.'

Keith reached for his mug again, staring into it as if

it might help him to think. 'People now believe that he was probably autistic — and I suppose imprisoned by his family out of ignorance and shame.' He shrugged. 'Or political expediency. Anyway, there are other stories a little like his. Of children raised in severe isolation, or by animals.'

'Feral children.'

'Yes.' He stared out the window, at the darkness filling the gaps between fences and houses like a soft padding. He stood and drew the curtains. 'People used to say feral children were a way around the forbidden experiment.'

'What experiment?'

'Forcing a child into complete seclusion, to test whether it still develops speech, or even the ability to understand language. And to test what else might be seen as specifically human, when all society has been stripped away. It seems insane, impossible, to the modern mind. But people used to think it was a way to discover the difference between what's innate and what's taught.'

A picture came to Bonnie of a child in a dim room, a crack of light showing through a hatch as a large hand passed in a bowl of crusts and milk. Would the clank of the metal lock, the scrape of the bowl along the bare floor, have the giddy sweetness of music, or a grinding sense of bottomless loss and monotony? Would the hand come to mean benevolence to the love-starved child, or cold indifference? Abruptly Bonnie pulled herself back from seeing any more. Horror had come too close.

Keith sat down again. 'A huge amount has been learned since Hauser, of course, about language development, social adjustment, mental deficiency, various disorders, but part of me . . .' He exhaled, gave a sour laugh. 'I've had some ludicrous idea of equity. You know, if I could help *this* young man, then I could somehow spirit away something of the human evil, the depravity and misery, left by those other terrible cases.'

Keith levered himself up and went to the sideboard, where he started to fix them both whiskies in thin blue tumblers.

'When Bu came to us, he exhibited high anxiety, refused to talk.' Keith waved a hand. 'Given his social awkwardness, and his striking appearance, I thought . . .'

Bonnie fiddled again with the chopstick in her hair, then stopped, irritated at her own inability just to 'sit with things', as her yoga teacher always urged.

'I was hugely disappointed when I wasn't the one to help him speak.' Keith gave her a look that seemed not disappointed, but ashamed, and he said, as if in self-mocking italics, '"A semi-feral, terribly damaged adolescent, healed through contemporary psychiatric practice and medication." Huh.' He took a sip of Talisker, let it rest in his mouth for a while, then swallowed. 'He could have been such a gift. So many publishing possibilities. But eventually it became obvious he wasn't going to be my very own Wolf-Boy, a prize find.'

Bonnie thought back over the past few weeks: Keith's intense preoccupation; the occasional day when he even left for work without saying goodbye, or came home without seeking her out in her study, where she did teaching prep. Although he often went through phases like this, she chastised herself for not realising that a particular case was at stake. It seemed like a lack of love on her part.

'But I still thought there might be an important case

history there. And I believed I was making genuine headway with him when there seemed to be some response to drug therapy. I decided it was significant.'

He handed Bonnie her glass and took a large swallow from his own.

'What a bloody idiot.'

Bonnie blinked. Keith was a *healer*. He was a *good* man. 'But that's your vocation. That's what you do, it's how — it's how you *help* people.'

He gave her a hard stare. 'But what's the difference, really? Between me and that jerk on TV? If I really strip away all the fancy wrapping, I'm as big a crock as Grenfell.'

'Keith, it's not the same. Offering someone medical treatment . . . that's completely different from going on national TV and calling him a *yeti*.'

Yeti.

The very word broke up the intense mood. Keith gave a short, appalled laugh. Bonnie looked up at him, sharing his disbelief.

'A yeti,' Keith repeated, shaking his head. 'You know, I've dealt with more than one Jesus. I've looked after people who believe they've been abducted by aliens. Oh, and one woman who was convinced that her five-volume autobiography — never actually written, as far as I could make out — was going to be made into a film by Martin Scorsese and Peter Jackson. But Bu would be my first yeti.'

'You don't think *he* believes he's a yeti, though, do you?'

Keith frowned. 'Well. That's what he told Sandrine.'

'What's her connection to him again?'

'She's just a reporter who's taken a personal interest in him. She passed on a little of what he told her before he left hospital: that his parents died recently, in a bush fire, on the south-west coast. We guessed that post-traumatic shock, as much as anything, had kept him mute. We went through all that in his pre-discharge interviews. I wanted him to carry on having consultations with me once he left the ward. Now Sandrine tells me that he and his family were living in almost complete isolation, for years — for his entire life.'

Bonnie set her whisky glass down firmly on the table. She shouldn't have accepted it: its slow heat was scrambling her thoughts. 'So he is like a wolf-boy, in a way?'

'Not technically. He's been decently fed and kept warm, he's been educated, given literacy. He's been loved. He's a gentle giant, if anything. An innocent.'

'But he's clearly troubled. If he believes what he says.'

Keith sighed. 'If he does believe it, and it's not some story he was spinning for Sandrine.'

'Is that likely? For someone as vulnerable as you say he was, to use his appearance as a kind of — what, confidence or sympathy trick, would be —'

'No.' He paused for a moment, considering. 'I would have thought that if he's an ordinary man with an extreme disfigurement, he's more likely to feel so alien, so terrified, suddenly arriving out of isolation, that exploiting his appearance that way would be impossible.'

'*If* he is an ordinary man?'

Keith hesitated again. 'He could still be very unwell. It might be a rare case of clinical zooanthropy.'

'Zoo —?'

'Like lycanthropy, although that's when someone has the delusion that they've turned into a wolf. Zooanthropy's when someone believes they've turned into any other sort of animal. The yeti story could be a measure of his disordered thoughts.'

'But not a lie?'

'No.'

They sat in silence for a while, thinking.

A short bulletin advertising the late news came on the muted TV. Bonnie watched as quick summaries of the main headlines were run through on screen. Then footage of Keith's former patient came up: he shambled, startled, grimaced, then turned to hurry away. Bonnie moved forward in her seat.

'Unless —?'

'Hmmm?' Keith was staring too.

Bonnie took a long look at her husband, then said, 'What if it's the truth?'

Keith snorted lightly. 'Right.' He sucked grimly at his back teeth. 'And now he's got this *circus* to deal with.'

The eerie uncertainty that Bonnie felt when watching Bu on screen was only partially quelled by Keith's dismissive tone. She switched off the TV. 'Well, he might need your help even more, now. Have you any idea where that woman — Sandrine — is taking him?'

'No. But she said she'd stay in contact.' He began to joggle one foot impatiently, then stood. 'Maybe I should release some sort of statement to the media. As the last person to deal with him professionally.'

Bonnie had scooped up mugs and glasses, and was on her way to the kitchen. She stopped at the living room door. 'Saying what?'

'Saying bloody well leave him alone.'

Arlo Nathan, Dunedin

ARLO NATHAN AND TERI CROCKER sat down to their falafel burgers and spirulina drinks at the Food Revolution Organic Café. Arlo had paid for both meals: he was hoping to persuade Teri (a) into bed and (b) to help him with a film studies essay he had to write in the next two weeks. He'd taken a paper in film genres because he thought he'd mainly be watching heaps of cool old movies, then was totally bummed to discover there was still all the same theory shit of English lit papers. Stuff about the Resurgence of the Suppressed Other, the Abject (he'd worked out that was something to do with why he hated the crinkled skin on warm milk, or hair in the bath's plug hole), the Paeleocentric Autocracy, as Teri liked to call it. Phallocentric, he'd corrected, and she gave him an odd, broken little smile.

Teri was smart, underneath her fun-girl act. She seemed to get all that stuff a lot more easily than he did, so he figured chatting her up would be two birds with one stone. Or one bird, one stoner . . . whatever.

He was trying to work out how to ask exactly what was going on with her and the dufus she'd been hanging around with at the last few gigs and parties he'd seen her at. Some wannabe rock star wearing gigantic, women's-style sunglasses, skin-tight black jeans and orange hoodie, with his hair in a black-dyed, gelled up Tintin tuft. He was doing honours in politics at uni. He really was in a band, apparently. (*So?*)

Teri was chattering about a current events item she'd

seen the night before. Arlo's flat didn't have a TV. Someone had set it alight at a Castle Street party. Threw it onto a bonfire of couches, chairs and last year's lecture notes.

'My flatmates — the guys doing zoology — they just think it's a total scam. Some wind-up from Jake Grenfell, or I don't know, some revenge thing in a secret salary war he's having with the TV station.' She sucked prettily at her straw. 'What do you think?'

'Sorry, what's this?' He wasn't going to tell her there was no TV in his flat. She'd already winced when he said it was an all-male household and they were having a competition to see who caved in first over some strange, misshapen glob stuck to — or growing from — the kitchen wall. Who'd be first to clean it up?

'It was in the paper today, too. And on Radio One.'

He looked out the café window, at the pedestrian traffic. Mums with strollers; guys in suits; groups of students; two hairdresser types, one guy, one girl, curving and arching hands at each other in some kind of private dance.

'I guess I've just been really busy. Kind of stressing about uni, you know?'

She shook her head, lightly. 'Yeah, uni is so *assessive*. I didn't plan on watching any TV last night, but the guys called me in when the yeti item came on.'

He perked up. 'Yeti item?' His essay was already bringing in all three *King Kong* movies. Maybe he could put in some up-to-the-minute-reference to this, too.

'It was on *Witness Stand*. Jake Grenfell showed footage of what he reckons is a southern sasquatch. Apparently there's a Māori legend of a wild man called the maero. Some people think this is proof that the legend is based on a real species. They had these anthropologists and primatologists talking about it, and one American guy — a yeti expert — by satellite link. We looked up more about the whole myth on the net. The guys — Zane and Drew — they were so *into* it.'

She was looking a little too rose-and-twinkle. Could either Zane or Drew also be the rock star jerk? Don't tell him they were sharing a flat already.

'It's just amazing how many cultures have this kind of story, don't you think? But Zane was saying it can't be true. Not in New Zealand. Have you met Zane? He's our new flatmate. Really nice guy. American, from Iowa. One of those *annoying* people, though, who's good at arts and sciences.' She said *annoying* in a kind of admiring way. 'He's doing an MSc in zoology, but he's also a fantastic actor. Did you see the capping show last year?'

Arlo hated him already. 'Is he in a band too?'

'No?'

Oh. So, Mr Pseudo-Rock was someone else altogether. There was twice the competition then. 'What does he mean, it couldn't happen in New Zealand? *The Lord of the Rings* happened in New Zealand. Kind of.'

She tucked in her chin, giving him a sceptical look. 'Well, there are no native land mammals, are there?'

'That we know of.'

She pursed her lips, fussed with her paper serviette. 'What do you mean?'

'Well, how do we *know* there are no native land mammals?'

She stared at him, dumbfounded for a moment. 'Science tells us.'

'What, and we listen?'

'Yes! I mean, scientists know from the living species,

but also the fossil evidence. And you know, from early settler accounts . . . ummm, oral history, written down conversations with Māori at first contact . . .' She looked over her shoulder a little self-consciously, as if to check that there was nobody her answer would disgrace her in front of. No history or anthropology lecturers, no spunky graduate students . . .

'But some of those conversations must have given them the story about the maero, right? So how do they sort out what, say, Māori *science* from Māori *myth*?'

She was cutting up her food into smaller and smaller pieces, frowning. 'The fossil record, Arlo.'

'Yeah, but there are gaps in the fossil record.'

She rolled her eyes. 'There aren't any gaps big enough to fit a *yeti*.'

'How do you know? What about the new find in Indonesia — those small people they've nicknamed hobbits? I read about it in *National Geographic* at the doctor. First of all they thought the bones were a child's, remember? Then they realised there was a whole little race that had lived there thousands of years ago. An entire species of human they knew nothing about till recently.'

She chewed, her frown deepening, then took another sip of her drink. Then with a eureka straightening of her posture, she pointed one finger at the ceiling, took a sudden dive for her satchel and came up with a fat, red-bannered book. '*The Oxford History of New Zealand*. I've got this for an essay I'm doing on the nineteen-thirties depression.' She began skimming through it, muttering half under her breath: '*The first human arrivals were Polynesian . . . archaeological evidence . . . Lapita pottery . . .*' She raised her voice, forcefully and conclusively.

'Everywhere they found an abundance of wildlife — sea mammals and birds, particularly large flightless birds, previously undisturbed by mammalian predators.' She sat back and grinned at him. 'There. You just wouldn't have all those flightless birds if there were land mammals. And look here,' she turned the book around so he could read the type, running her finger along the lines a few pages on. 'All this stuff about the Palliser Bay settlement. The graves, the rubbish dumps, the material for tools . . .'

He stared obligingly but blankly at where she pointed.

'Don't you get it? We leave behind all these traces, even when we die. I mean, in Indonesia, where they found the little people, there would have already been other hominid fossils. If there were maero, yeti, sasquatch, whatever you want to call them here, there would be other big bones. Cultural artefacts. Evidence that there were primates or bipeds here before the Polynesians.' She looked flush with argument. 'Zane says . . .'

Screw Zane.

'Yeah, but what about all the untouched native bush? What about all those mountain regions no one's ever set foot on? Have you ever flown over the Southern Alps? They're *frickin'* huge, man, you just don't get anything like that in the North Island.' (Teri was from Auckland: he felt he needed to remind her of her place.) 'Isn't it kind of arrogant for us to assume we know about all the world's creatures, when there are places we haven't even been?' He jounced in his seat. 'Maybe the yeti is cleverer than we are. Maybe it's kept away from us, till now.'

Teri flipped a few pages in her book, skim-reading again. 'Breeding all that time? Over three thousand years? That's how long some people think there's evidence of

Polynesian contact here. Zane says everyone who's got excited about this is indulging in a little post-millennial fantasy. There would be other traces. Other sightings.'

Arlo slumped back in his chair, speared some burger at arm's length. 'The story's one trace though, isn't it? Oral history. And it sounds like there's one big fat physical piece of evidence right in front of us. Maybe it's time to rewrite the science.'

She stared at him again. 'Oh. Right. Yeah. Like how Barry Brailsford's books on the Waitaha rewrote the entire archaeological history of New Zealand and proved that Celts were here before the Māori. *Peaceful* red-haired Celts, leaving cairns and stone walls.'

'They did?'

She narrowed her eyes. 'Yeah, and they mated with yetis. Deep in the bush. And now that there's global warming, all the Yeti-Celt hybrids are coming out of hiding because their ginger fur makes them too hot.'

'Sarcasm's not a pretty look, Teri.'

She went quiet, eating her falafel, absorbed in the book, trying to find some so-called *irrefutable* fact, he guessed.

A real yeti — that'd have to change some things, wouldn't it? Pretty interesting. Maybe he'd take up an anthropology paper next semester.

Gary Marshall, Wellington

IN WELLINGTON, THE LUNCHTIME crowds rushed along Lambton Quay, on their way to grab sushi and coffee; to transfer funds; get to the dentist on time, the job interview on time, lectures on time; they rushed to sign on, pick up, drop off . . . yet everyone slowed a little, or turned their heads far more than politeness asks, as they passed a small, nuggety man carrying homemade placards.

He wore black-rimmed glasses and a pale green, ill-fitting suit. One placard, made of a large, thick piece of cardboard nailed to an old mop handle, he brandished over his head. He also wore a sandwich board, tied over his shoulders with blue twine. With black paint and a rough brush, he had lettered his warning.

The placard on the handle read:

THE YETI IS A SIGN.

Also on the placard was an odd collage. A feminine, pitying Christ's face, cut from a magazine, was glued in a hovering position next to another picture of a lowland gorilla. A handwritten speech bubble floated from Christ's mouth: REPENT! The collage looked like an art student's joke, but when onlookers scanned down to the sandwich board, they could see it was in earnest:

REPENT OR BE DAMNED.

REPENT!

YETIS ARE DEGENERATION: GOD'S PUNISHMENT FOR HUMAN SIN.

From a small, brown leather satchel, which he wore on

a belt around his hips, the man produced a number of flyers, headed:

GOD HAS MADE A NEW FORM.

In tiny, cramped print, single-spaced and smudged, the body of the text announced:

> The Yeti is the beast from Revelation: heed ye the sign of the Apocalypse! The evil we do in these times of trouble and woe shall be punished. The Yeti is a sign a holy sign beware ye all the sign of the Yeti.
>
> If ye shall not heed the word of our Lord God in the Highest in his BIBLE then He shall cause further degeneration of the species. Yetis shall rule the earth.
>
> If ye drink and gluttonise yourself then God shall make more Yeti.
>
> If ye love thy neighbour wrong then God shall make more Yeti.
>
> If ye shall eat too much protein and experience the sins of lust as fed by too many eggs and cheese then shall God make more Yeti.
>
> If ye wear flagrant and revealing costume that incites men to more lust then God shall make more Yeti.
>
> If ye shall fornicate God shall make more Yeti.
>
> For more teachings, consultations, insights, communication with the world of the spirits and the Lord God Himself as Revealed to Me Gary Marshall please phone 04 455 45454

Gary Marshall called out as he handed flyers to anyone who would take them. 'The Yeti is the savage offspring of our lust and sin! It spells the end, lest ye repent!' He walked over to a teenage couple who had their arms around each other, she shivering in a short skirt and tight T-shirt, he in specially ironed jeans and T-shirt, goofy with his good luck.

'We must tame our lusts!' Marshall said. He frowned as the girl took the leaflet. 'Quell the beast within!'

The boy looked over his shoulder at a group of his mates, who had been trailing around after him with takeaway food and milkshakes, probably in the hope that the girl had friends. He laughed.

'Spot the nutter!'

The other boys joined in but the girl said, 'What *about* that yeti, though? My mum reckons they shouldn't let a monster like that just roam around the country on his own. He could be dangerous.'

Her boyfriend clasped her more tightly. 'Yeah, that thing on telly was like, what, five chimpanzees, don't you reckon? Could rip a man apart.'

'Shit yeah,' said another boy in skate gear. 'Won't catch me going bush till they find that thing.'

He gave an enormous hoick, launching a glob that misfired and landed on the placard-carrying Marshall's shoe.

Marshall's hackles rose. 'Look within! See your sins, cleanse them, rise above your baser self!'

As if it wearied him infinitely, the skater said, 'Go on, y'know y'want it. That's really what all this is about.' He snatched some flyers from Marshall's belt and crumpled them in one hand. 'Having a go at the rest of us, just cause you can't pull.'

A glaze came over Marshall's eyes. Through his teeth he said, 'Sinners!'

Something in the clenched cry made the girl side-step like a bee-stung foal. She pulled on her boyfriend's arm. 'Let's go. I'm sick of this. If he was talking about catching that ape-man I'd listen, but he's got nothing to say. He's weird.'

As if her judgement granted permission, the boys egged each other on and started to pelt Marshall's placard with the remainders of their shakes and burgers, heedless and jubilant as kids with water balloons. But when Marshall snapped, their faces collectively blanked with shock.

Ramming, striking, at full, sudden swing, the self-elected preacher sprang at them as if he could beat them back as easily as midges. The blows from the wooden handle left one boy reeling back, clutching at his eye. Frightened, trembling with disbelief, the girl urged some bystanders who'd intervened, 'Someone call the cops, please.' As two men pinned Marshall against a department store window, she cried out, 'You're the one they should lock up, in the same bloody cell as the yeti. You're *crazy*, mister. Fuckin' crazy.'

Jodie Rata Radcliffe, Auckland

JODIE RATA RADCLIFFE HAD to prepare a debate speech for her year thirteen English class. She could choose one of two topics. Either 'Global peace: the timeless anachronism' or 'The news helps to create the nation; it is not the nation that creates the news'. She'd started out on the first topic, but found herself doodling a whole page of spiders on a piece of scrap paper next to the computer.

Some nights, seventeen just felt too old to be doing this sort of assignment; at other times she felt completely daunted by her academic work and wondered how she'd ever get along at university in just under a year. She checked her watch, sighed, then told herself to knuckle down.

Finally, around eight, she decided if she was going to make any headway, she'd have to choose the other topic after all. The nation and the news. Hokay. She started browsing the TV website to see what she'd missed out on tonight.

'Huh. The yeti story's here too,' she said to herself: a couple of nights ago she'd seen it on *Witness Stand*. Knocking at her teeth gently with the knuckles of one hand, she followed the transcript of the item, then listened to the 'backgrounder' as they called it: a word her mum, a speech and drama tutor, would call a tone deaf neologism.

Even though there hadn't been a sighting of the rumoured southern sasquatch for a couple of days now, the news said that there had been 'unrest' in Wellington over the first sighting: a man had been taken in by police after mounting some sort of protest that had gone wrong, and been charged with assault.

Jodie chewed her lip. 'How can you have a protest about a yeti? Down with yeti, they're taking our jobs?' She scrolled down to see that hunters in the north were organising a search. Legend had it that the maero had once lived in the alpine bush in the South Island, the Whanganui forests and in the Coromandel. A group of mates who lived in various parts of the North Island, and who often got together for tramps and hunts, had decided to form a search party. Calling themselves the Sons of Tukoio, after the man of myth who fought Mohoao the hairy wild man and survived, they were asking people to sponsor their search, and raise funds towards building an outdoors education centre for urban kids. They had named their quest the Great Mohoao Hunt.

'So do you think the maero stories are based on a real ancestor, or is it a fairy tale?' asked the young Pākehā woman journalist, on the fragmented image that kept coming and going on Jodie's home PC.

'Aww, not too sure about that, actually. No, but really, it's all just meant to be a bit of fun,' the leader said. 'This is about fun, isn't it, boys?'

'But what will you do if you find the legendary creature?'

The men laughed.

'Shoot the hairy fairy.'

'Cook 'im.'

'Eat 'im.'

'Nah. Donate his body to science.'

'Run the hell away,' said another, and the men laughed all the harder.

The item troubled Jodie, even though the hunters

weren't taking themselves seriously. She bashed out a few points on the keyboard, ideas for how to link this news to the debate topic, then started searching the web for information about maero and yeti, wondering what had happened before, when people claimed to have seen them. A children's book version of the maero came up, showing a skinny man with tangled dreadlocks, green skin, red eyes: nothing like the abominable snowman from the northern hemisphere. It didn't match what she'd imagined of the maero, either, from the stories her grandmother, Kuia Donna, had told her before she died, about patupaiarehe, fairy folk, the wild man all covered in hair. Kuia Donna had loved to spin the old tales, though said she didn't believe in them the way she believed that the moon was in the sky, and that rain was wet. Jodie felt a sudden pang of missing her. Her dad, Kuia Donna's son, was an immunologist and he said superstitions like that had no place in the modern world. There would be no joy in asking him about them.

Instead she had to click away at her mouse. First of all she stumbled on a website that promised to detect whether there were yetis in your backyard if you plugged in your home camera footage to the website's software. She chuckled, wishing her brother still lived at home so she could show him. Then she found sites that had something to do with bikes, snowgear, outdoors equipment of all kinds, really; people whose usernames and blogs had tags like Messy Yeti, MiketheGentleYeti, Betty the Yeti.

There were loads of sites about conspiracy theories, world mythology, zoology, cryptozoology: sites where people recorded years of their own private research.

Finally she came across a short, mesmerising clip of something they called the Patterson-Gimlin footage, from 1967.

A link to YouTube took her to a thread that ran several versions — not just the original black and white, but also some that were colour enhanced so you could see the autumnal North American leaves in the woods.

Her big-hipped cat swayed in and rubbed against her ankles. 'Wanna see an ape-man?' she asked, plonking the animal on her lap. 'Look. What do you think of that?' The cat presented its bum to the screen and butted her chin with its head. She carried on reading. 'It's like some kind of religion,' she murmured in the cat's swivelling ear, as she went through postings that argued the sasquatch was female. On one link she listened to a radio interview with Jane Goodall, the chimp expert, which was played over the top of the footage. Goodall described herself as a romantic, said she believed that the Big Foot phenomenon was real — because she wanted it to be.

'Jane *Goodall*?' said Jodie. She'd heard about her, in biology. Jodie clicked back onto the undoctored film clip of the Big Foot and watched it again.

She hugged the cat closer to her, pressing its outrageous feather boa of a tail against her throat for warmth. There was something haunting about the film. What was it? Maybe just the effect of black and white footage. The odd yearning feeling it gave her was similar to the mood that all old photographs set off: the melancholy recognition of how inaccessible and mysterious the past was.

She tried to halt the clip and zoom in on the image but everything blurred and fragmented even more.

Did the haunted feeling grow from uncertainty, from not

knowing exactly what she was watching, either because of how fleeting the action was, or because the creature in the image had no clear name? Or was it a kind of basic animal reaction to the physical outline of something that could be a predator? Maybe it was instinct that gave her this spooked sensation, this anticipation mixed with wonder and fear.

She replayed the clip yet again, peering closely at the screen. But the Big Foot did nothing threatening. It was caught walking through the forest, looked over its shoulder — yep, there was a brief glimpse of breasts (and how, Jodie wondered, would you make convincing, pelt-covered, swinging breasts?) but then it — she — kept walking. Faster, if anything. Purposeful, giant strides. Not frightened: she hadn't panicked when she'd noticed the men filming but remained focused. Wanting to get away.

The cat, sated with comfort now, leapt to the floor. Jodie sat back, an uncomfortable sensation in her chest. The Big Foot wanted to keep going, to leave. The way it looked at the camera — as if it knew all about men already, knew all about hunters, humans, their tools and weapons, their mess and disorder, and wanted nothing to do with any of it. No curiosity, no wonderment. Its — her — walk seemed so self-contained, so . . . Jodie chewed her lip again. Aristocratic. Yet at the same time it was as if she were completely refusing such human terms.

Jodie thought back to the night she'd seen the recent *Witness Stand* item picked up on the late news. *Just like the maero*. To check her hunch, she quickly found the news site again.

She clicked on the link and the clip replayed. Her skin tingled with little dots of cold. When seen, the maero-sasquatch startled, grimaced, then turned and lumbered away, as determined as its 1960s cousin. Jodie felt strange, brimming tears of protest. *He doesn't want us. Watchers, voyeurs (like me), TV crews, trappers . . .*

It seemed to her that the creature was turning its back on everything else the website had covered over the past couple of days. Bombings, murder, rape, missing children, assaults, embezzlement, even the photo of a British artist sitting with his chin resting on one of his works: a platinum model of a skull, embedded with diamonds.

Something led her to the memory of watching chimps in a zoo enclosure: chimps fed on cabbage, carrots and bananas from old, blue, plastic Tip Top ice-cream containers; chimps swinging on frayed yellow ropes; balancing on perches, slamming themselves at the walls; clambering up to the perches again, then two of them at once turning their backs on Jodie and her family, and crapping, pissing, volumes of it, so much that it cascaded down the glass viewing wall, outside which the human crowd stood, affronted.

'What a statement,' Jodie's brother had said.

'Poor bastards,' her dad agreed.

One of the chimps sat alone in a corner, shoulders hunched up, hand over its face, rocking. Jodie didn't want to see any of the other animals after that. The chimp's despair sat in her own stomach like a hard lump.

Please don't let any hunters down south have the same idea as those other dorks.

Stirred up, unable to concentrate, she couldn't see how to connect all this to her set topic. She checked her cellphone. Nothing. She checked for emails. One message: something sent out by her friend Ellen giving new contact details to everyone in her address book.

Brainwave. She'd start an email petition, calling for people to rally against the pursuit of the maero. She'd take it to . . . to . . . some government guy. The one in charge of the environment. She'd even ask her brother to help her set up a website so that people could donate funds to protect the poor thing. Maybe she could phone someone at the Department of Conservation and ask them for help. She'd call that animal rights group — the one that had freed all the battery hens somewhere in Southland last month. That had been a big news story, though her dad said that was just because it was a quiet week. What were they called? The Aotearoa Animal something or other . . . she quickly typed in the phrase on Google. Yes, Aotearoa Animal Activists: Southern Peace Militia. They'd probably have a mailing list and advice on how to get information out there.

She'd somehow work out her debate speech so that the website petition was announced as its climax. She could even take a collection bucket to class. She doodled acronyms on scrap paper and quickly hit on what she'd call her group. SHY: Stop Hunting Yeti. Bloody brilliant.

Scribbling madly for her rough draft, she started arguing for the negative team in her speech: if the nation is just a collection of individuals, then one by one, the way the people of the nation react to the news can change the news. She sucked her pen for a while, staring again at a still image of the southern sasquatch on her PC screen. *I wonder where he is, right now? I hope we never know.*

PART FOUR
Hide

Bu

People are mindlessly cruel, his parent-folk always said. *It comes from fear, from ignorance.*

I've seen people marvel over how human the monkeys are at the zoo, his mother-woman told him one day, when as an eleven-year-old he raged and cried at her, demanding to know why he wasn't allowed to travel into the nearest town. He wanted to go with his father-man when he went to buy food supplies and sell the wooden furniture he built. Why was he always kept at home, as invisible as a cricket in the rainy hectares of trees, bush and soil?

You stay here for your own good, she said.

'Such beautiful creatures,' people say about the animals they see in their cages. 'They look so wise.' But I've seen the same people recoil from a boy in a wheelchair with a deformed back and misshapen mouth, or a woman with Down Syndrome crying over an ice-cream she'd dropped. The people looking at them: their faces — so brutal.

Here, you're safe, Bu. You're with people who know and love you. It's a love as strong as you would find anywhere else. The suffering out there — it will teach you nothing of value. All it will do is make you an expert in shame, in hurt. Here, you can be real. Not some monster in a mask.

And how he had cried again, great, angry racking sobs, as he slammed a thick wooden stake through her garden and greenhouse, her flowers and seedlings, and trampled her strawberries, because she had as good as told him he was ugly, a horror, even to her. His father-man had to fight to get the stake from him, pinned his arms behind his back, told him there was no bloody chance he could go into town with him now, if he was going to behave like a hoodlum.

They'd lock you up the minute they saw you, you little vandal. That's food for all of us you've destroyed. Get inside before you make me beat you the way you deserve. I don't want to see you until I get back. And when I do get back from town, this place had better be cleaned up.

But he had never beaten him. The mere threat of it that day had frightened Bu, filled him with a misery so painful it felt like grieving for a father who had gone away for good.

Was it a sound-picture his mind had made up, the first memory of his mother-woman's voice? He swore he could hear her still, whispering sour-sweet endearments to him when he was just a tiny thing. *My funny little fright. My ugly cub. Wee genius beastie.* And his father-man's voice, *Don't say those things to him, Lillian, please. Even if he can't understand, I can.*

Yet what had Sandrine said to him, at the hospital? 'But you're smart, aren't you?'

He wanted to tell her that she was the reason he was here, right here. She and her kind. He'd seen other women in his life, yes, of course he had: on the three or four occasions his father-man had smuggled him into town without his mother-woman knowing he was to go.

He had watched all people with a mixture of fear and longing: old ones with their heavy-sad cheeks, or their skin thatched with lines; babies, children, girls, boys, men or women. As he'd grown older, he'd taken more notice of the pictures of women in books, and in movies his father-man brought home for them to watch on a TV set they could use only for videos.

He had touched himself many times, thinking of the women he had seen in these films, fretted over his desire when he woke from dreams that made him moan with hunger and wonder at the strange worlds where sometimes the women shape-changed, even sprouted long silken beards, which made him cry with recognition, fear, and loss. He would be unable to look at himself in the mirror or meet his parent-folks' eyes until he had groomed, gone to chop wood for the stove and had a first hot mug of tea, feeling as if the dream must cling to him like a meaty smell. He had seen his reflection after one of those dreams once, and was afraid it might be the face of a crazed animal that didn't know it was mad, for his face looked just the same, though there was such a confusion inside him.

You hab to let me leabe, he'd said to his parent-folk on one of the last days he saw them. *I hab to go into the world for myself. I need to find people ob my own.*

From the way sorrow slowed his mother-woman, he knew he had already won. *Why the hurry?*

I'be waited all my life, Bu answered.

We need to talk about this properly, his father-man said, leaning his arms on the table he and Bu had made together. *If you really think the time has come, we can consider it together. Moving as a family. Find the right place. Help you settle in gradually. One step at a time, Bu.*

But there were months of waiting. It was the idea of moving as a family, he decided, that made them delay. *We'll harvest the garden first*, they said. *Lay up the preserves.* Then it was, *We can't sell this place in winter. We need to show it at its best.*

But even at the start of spring: *Your father's got a big order to work on before he goes to town next. He'll speak to an estate agent then.* Bu suspected it was just another excuse. He lost patience. He began to make his own plans.

I'm like a prisoner, he said one night.

His mother-woman slapped down a cloth, snatched up a mixing bowl, clashing it with metal beater and spoon. *You don't know how free you are. Why can't you trust us? It's because we care about you that we want you to wait.*

But the hunger for a companion had grown with him all his days. When he was small it was for another child to play with, to share secrets and games. His parent-folk tried to be decent, to always speak the truth as they saw it, and to satisfy his longing for other playmates by playing with him like children themselves, feeding his imagination with books, songs and even films on an old school projector when he was very young.

Stories are the only reliable friends, his mother-woman once said. *They will never betray you.*

When he asked why he and his parent-folk couldn't live where other people were, why nobody visited — no friends, no family, no deliveries — their answers always slid sideways, tried to slip through cracks, disappear under doors.

He had a strange, bothering memory of men on the land, once, many years ago — men appearing like shapes in a dream ... then came some sharp noise, clamour, and they vanished.

When he was seven, he decided his parents can't have seen the men and that they didn't know why they were stuck in the bush so alone. He would be helping them all if he went away to find out.

One afternoon that year, when the adults were too busy, and a bit short with him, he happily took his chance. Copying what he knew from a picture-book about a man called Dick Whittington, he pared the bark from a thin, fallen branch, laid out an old scarf, and in the middle placed a pocket knife, a compass (which he didn't really know how to use but he thought he would work it out), a raincoat, jersey, a hat and gloves for overnight when even Bu could be cold. He added some bread and cheese, and a book for when it got boring.

While his father-man planed and sandpapered in his workshop, and his mother-woman worked with her back to him in the vegetable garden, he set off with his bundle through the trees, wearing only a kaftan shirt and the loose, patchwork trousers in Indian cottons sewn especially for him — cooler fabrics than his parent-folk usually needed.

After half an hour of walking, it was time for the cheese and bread. When that was all gone, he walked some more, drank from a tiny trickle of waterfall, then sat down in the sun to read his book. The sun made his head too heavy to carry, so he lay down to sleep it light again. When he woke, he was hungry all through. He decided, 'I'll find the world another day and I'll take dinner with me too.'

When he managed to stumble his way home — spying smoke from the chimney — he saw that his mother-woman had been crying. His father-man, sweaty and dusty, and as white as if he'd swung an axe into his shin, was just back from hunting for him for an hour, and was filling up a pack so he could set out again.

Bu felt so terrible that he couldn't tell the truth.

'I was looking for a bear,' he said.

He couldn't let them know he had wanted to find other people, people who really knew about the world. Maybe even his own kind, or those who knew of them.

At nineteen he knew how cruel it would be to leave in total secrecy. Although he readied himself quietly over a number of days as the thin end of summer dwindled into autumn, he had always planned to tell them. Yes, he would steal away with his pack and head torch on a dry, clear night with a full moon, but he would also leave a note, promising to return.

He left about one in the morning, when he knew his parent-folk would be at their hardest to rouse. It was sore leaving: he even risked chinking their door open, and looking at their sleeping forms as tenderly as if they were his own babies. He went back to the note he had left, and by candlelight underlined some of the words, and scrawled again at the bottom: *This is my word. I will come back*. Then he slipped away like his parent-folks' answers through the gaps in the world.

The night he left, he knew he should conserve his energy, but his body sang with freedom, so at first he walked quickly, breaking into a run when he was confident the way was clear of tree roots and half-buried rock.

Bu knew now how to work out the quickest route to the road, but for fear of being too easily found by his father-man, he was making his own dog-leg way through the bush, aiming to spend a night in a disused hut. He planned to start the main walk out the following day. This one night alone was a private ceremony as much as anything: a way of taking his leave of the trees, the birdlife, the bush music that had been his main boyhood companions.

The pack on his back made him sweat and pant hard, even in the dark, as he slowly mounted a rise and came up clear of the trees. He decided to stop briefly, shed the top layer of clothes, slake his thirst and then try to keep moving till dawn. Only of course he looked back, and down, to see if he could judge the distance he had already travelled.

In his stomach came a sickening lurch, as when a tree being culled splits too soon, and falls the wrong way.

Fire glared ragged down in the dip, in the direction of his home. A red devil's eye in the dim, night-clad valley.

He knew straight away: candles, left burning on the wooden shelves in his room. He'd used them to save power and because their soft light wouldn't wake his parent-folk. After he had moved from room to room, gathering, watching, closing up, in his excitement, with the scent of adventure in the night air, he hadn't gone back to blow them out. Guilt swirled in his gut.

Gasping for breath already, he ran back the way he had come, pulling the pack straps on, tying the jersey around his waist as he went, his mind zeroed in on the dreadful target, heart bursting with pain. He slid and stumbled several times; thought of dropping the pack and coming to find it later, but couldn't clear his mind enough of fear to trust that he would remember where he'd left it. The surrounding bush spun, a jagged wheel, as he blundered his way down, wildly snapping twigs, smashing ferns with his boots.

When he finally reached the horrid eye, the thundering air around it drowned out his parent-folks' names. He had to turn his face away from the streaming heat. *What had he done, what had he done?* The fire pushed and pushed him back with angry hands. *Go!* In a futile effort he tried to train the garden hose, fed by their rainwater tanks, onto the flames, but he knew it was madness, and cried out as he smelt the stink of his own fur starting to singe when he moved too close.

Soon there was nothing left of the main house. Everything was twisted and charred beyond recognition. It wasn't until the flames crawled over to his father-man's timber store that Bu finally knew that he was going to have to flee before he could wait for the graves to cool, before he could safely go in to search the ruins.

For the third time that night, Bu ran.

❉ ❉ ❉

AT THE HOUSE OF Sandrine's friend, Bu wondered whether he would always have to run from hideaway to hideaway. The little flames of panic he had felt at the hospital stirred, tried to snatch and engulf him once more, but he breathed in deeply, as he had been taught. He glanced over at Sandrine, and she smiled, deep into his eyes.

Sandrine

'ARE YOU SURE YOU wouldn't like a wine?' asked Faber, after Bu had said he remembered nothing of Nepal or of his birth parents, apart from stories told to him. Bu hesitated long enough for Faber to pour him a finger's width of pinot noir. He sniffed at it, but his lips drew back, baring his teeth, and he shook his head in displeasure.

'So where were you raised by your adoptive parents?' asked Faber.

'You might eh-say Eh-south Westland.'

'Oh yeah? Whereabouts?'

'It has no name. Not exactly. It was bery . . . isolated. My parent-folk, they . . . hmmm. D-hidn't much like to be in towns.'

Sandrine had barely touched her food. 'Faber, maybe Bu doesn't want to talk about all this.'

'Sure. Sorry.'

'It is all right,' said Bu. 'If he is going to help, then he must know eh-some things.'

She and Faber exchanged a look.

Bu smoothed his silken beard with one hand, as if trying to think his way along the lines of a complicated map. 'My parent-folk wanted to keep me from harm. They eh-say, they *eh-said*, in a busy town or eh-city our life would hab been too d-hifficult. They tried, when I was a baby, but they eh-said people were cruel. My mother-woman — could not —' he struggled with the next word — 'abide it.' It sounded to Sandrine as if this were a quotation: the mother's voice embedded in his.

He told them about the bowl and the bone on the doorstep.

Although it had started to rain outside — drops scuttling on the corrugated iron roof like birds' feet — neither Sandrine nor Faber remarked on the change in weather. Bu, so quiet usually, so surrounded in a sadness that gave his great frame an unlikely fragility, now held the floor.

'There was more like that. Bad things. They are what made my mother-woman decide that we would leabe the towns and eh-cities. Try to surbibe on the land.'

He nodded to himself, crouched down a little over his plate and sampled some more of his food.

As if it had only just occurred to him, he raised his head a little and added, 'I hardly eber eh-saw another person when I was growing up. My parents were my teachers. But my father-man trabelled to eh-sell the furniture he made, and he brought back books, records, films. So I knew a little about . . . your world.' He faltered. 'But my mother-woman d-hidn't want me to leabe our land. I think, because she couldn't.'

He watched each of them in turn, lingeringly. Sandrine felt an odd shift: a recognition that he looked at her as if she was beautiful. It seemed he was reminding himself of the dazzlement of being in the presence of other people at all. It brought a sharp reminder of the early way his gaze had made her feel cradled, accepted. Again, some inner dissatisfaction seemed to fall still in his presence. Feeling her cheeks flush, she dropped her stare.

Faber's face was blunt with disapproval, disbelief. 'And you were stranded like that in the back-blocks for how long?'

'A few times I went into towns with my father-man. It was when I was older, and when he could be sure that my mother-woman was busy, in the garden, or asleep — on the times we left. She was bery eh-sad, bery affrighted, afterwards.' He sighed. 'So you eh-see, I d-hid know a bit of people, from behind my mask.'

'Mask?'

'We trabelled in bery early winter, if the roads were open. My father-man felt that it would be best if I were cubbered. In eh-snow gear, I looked like anyone else.'

Sandrine felt the urge to laugh, and was ashamed: it was the laugh of any dumb, genetically blessed kid at the schoolyard scapegoat. The laugh she'd heard at her own expense often enough. She pictured an awkward teenage boy, hanging behind his father in a grocery store, clad from head to toe in balaclava, goggles, snowsuit, gloves, the sweat from the shop's heating system gathering in his palms till the gloves were clammy, his breath short with discomfort. She pictured, too, the checkout girls' nervous sidelong glances at him, their efforts to see more than their own reflections in the lenses of the goggles. She wondered whether Bu and his father had gone to the same town for each visit, and whether anyone recognised him: the bundled-up boy who said nothing, who loomed behind his dad like a mummified shadow.

Faber was squirming in his seat, restless with something he wanted to say. Sandrine tilted her glass to and fro, watching the wine slip up and down, deliberately ignoring him, in the hope that Bu would speak first.

'That's bloody awful.' Faber leaned back in his chair. 'Granted your parents must've had their reasons. But it seems so extreme. I mean, surely there were things they could have done — steps they could have taken —'

'Faber.' She warned him off.

He apologised a little. 'Well, I mean, I don't want this to come out the wrong way . . .' He turned back to Bu. 'But if they were so concerned about the way you'd be treated, couldn't they have seen a doctor?'

'Faber, really, no . . .'

'Seriously. There are some incredible things doctors can do now. Full-on metal braces inserted into the skull and the jaw . . .'

'*Fa*ber! It's such a sensitive subject.' Unexpectedly Sandrine wanted to protect Faber as much as she did Bu: as if she wanted him to present well in front of this quiet, mystifying figure.

Bu stared at the melting lip of wax edging the tall, white candle on the table. 'I think I understand,' he said slowly. He looked down at the backs of his hands, the digits splayed, turned them over to the fleshy palms, and over again, to the pelt. 'A disguise. Of eh-skin and bone.'

Faber pulled in his chin. 'A disguise?'

'A human costume.' Bu tilted his head. 'But the d-hoctors could not hab made me human.'

Sandrine felt it again: the awful threat of embarrassment from unintended laughter. The silence seemed to ripple out as Faber waited patiently for an explanation.

She flicked her thumb and index finger against each other nervously. 'Bu's mother told him stories about Nepal, and he — well, he thinks he's a yeti.'

Faber sat back in his chair. 'But that just . . .' He trailed off at the sight of her expression.

'He believes it.' She saw a mingled fear and something close to reverence expand over Faber's face. He stared at Bu for an uncomfortably long time.

'*Wow*,' he whispered. '*Wow*.'

Bu lowered his head, like a Buddhist monk acknowledging an offering, then carried on with his meal: placid, content.

Sandrine realised her right foot was pressing hard into the floor as if she were a front-seat passenger trying to control the speed of an erratic driver. But Faber sank into a cautious silence, eating steadily and slipping Bu increasingly wary looks.

When they had finished the meal Sandrine and Faber took the empty plates into the kitchen. Faber bailed her up at the sink, hissing under his breath, 'What in Christ's name do you think you're doing? He's unbalanced, Sandy. You shouldn't be managing this on your own. You need a shrink. I mean *he* needs a shrink.'

She darted a nervous glance at the doorway. 'Well, like I said, he was in a psych ward for a while, but he doesn't think he's ill.' She started running some water to cover the sound of their voices. 'And if he's not dangerous — I mean, to himself or anyone else — I mean, if he's functioning perfectly well, apart from the fact . . .'

'Apart from the fact he thinks he's a bloody fairytale creature.'

'Well, yeah. But you know, Faber, his heart really is in the right place, and if he's not doing any harm, nobody can force him to . . .'

'How can you *say* that? Are you out of your own mind? How is the poor beggar going to live a life if he walks around telling people he's a flippin' *yeti*? Who will talk to him, sell him food, employ him? What's he going to put on his job applications? How's he . . . how's he . . . I don't know, going to fill out the bloody ethnicity section when he registers to vote? How's . . .'

Perversely, she felt the corners of her mouth twitch. 'He'll choose "other" and he'll write "yeti".'

'Sandrine. You've been wandering around with some poor, deluded guy, thinking you're helping to save the world or something, I don't know, when all you're probably doing is making things way worse for him.'

'But I *am* helping him, Faber. I'm going to try to call off the press. When I do that, he'll have privacy to sort himself out.'

'He can't *do* that on his own. He's delusional.'

They stared at each other, and Sandrine ran a hand over her eyes. 'Okay. This has all just been — I got swept up in the moment, with the mob outside his place. There's something so defenceless about him, something compelling, I don't know, despite . . .'

Faber gripped the back of his neck with one hand, and she could see he was about to explode. 'Okay, okay,' she said hastily. She checked her watch. 'I'll make another call to the doctor who was treating him. He knows Derek and I have been sheltering Bu since the news broke. I'll call him first thing in the morning. It's too late now.'

Faber had begun noisily rinsing dishes. 'Are you sure we're safe with him overnight?'

'Perfectly safe,' said Sandrine. 'I think.'

'Right,' said Faber, face reddening. 'He sleeps in the spare room. It has an external lock. You sleep in my room, and put a chair under the door handle. I sleep out here on the couch, next to the axe.'

Sandrine rolled her eyes.

'What? You're still treating this as a joke?'

'No, no, I'm not. But he's hardly the Incredible Hulk, is he?'

Faber clenched his jaw at her. 'He's bloody well bigger.'

'Okay!' She flung up her hands. 'We'll do what you say.'

Knowing she was barricaded in for the night, Sandrine slept fitfully. She kept wondering what they'd do if Bu woke and had to go to the bathroom, or did turn psychotic and start to jimmy the bolt they'd secured once he was asleep. She imagined him trying to batter down her bedroom door, and exact some kind of revenge, his ragged shadow looming on the wall . . . When she woke the next day, late for her, it was to relief that nothing had happened overnight, and to a sheepish concession that she had been caught up in Faber's overreaction.

Although it was after nine, she was the first up, clothes creased, head foggy as she padded over to Bu's door to slide the bolt quietly, so he'd be left unaware that he'd been a temporary prisoner. She stumbled over Faber's shoes in the living room and saw that he was still asleep on the couch. She slung on an old denim jacket she found on a coat hook near the front door and stepped out into the daylight, to collect the morning paper.

Several of the people gathered in front of the house were familiar. *How the bloody . . .*

'Sandrine Moreau!'

'Sandrine, your flatmates had a hunch we might find you here. Nice girls. Tell me, how was your night with the Beast of Dunedin?'

Bloody Chelsea and Eileen . . .

'Ms Moreau, are you all right? Is the beast dangerous? Are you sure you don't want him taken in?'

A short, blonde woman, whose Botox and collagen made her appear startled and petulant at the same time, muscled her way to the front. 'I'm a features writer at *Style*.'

'Of *what*?'

'*Style*. The fashion magazine.'

'What the *hell*?' Sandrine turned away in disbelief, snatched the paper out of Faber's letterbox.

'It's a fascinating case, Sandrine.' A balding man pushed closer to the gate. 'As you can see, it's created quite a stir. National Radio has just finished an interview with some research scientists who'd like to meet with your acquaintance. Apparently he was discharged from hospital before they could get permission forms signed to run a number of tests on him.'

'Tests?'

Journalists were angling their mikes or scribbling furiously; one woman urged a photographer to get closer to the balding man.

'This is a complete invasion of privacy. You're . . .'

The *Style* woman spoke again. 'If you change your mind, my contact details are on the card.' Her blue eyes shone with a doll's hard, plastic stare.

'I have nothing to say to any of you, and neither does Bu.' Sandrine felt her voice rise.

A man laughed. 'Boo? His name's Boo?'

She marched inside, slammed and bolted the door.

Faber lifted himself up groggily and untwisted his T-shirt. 'What's happening?'

Sandrine unfolded the morning paper. On the front page the smaller item running like a banner at the bottom wore the headline 'Yeti Hoax: Psychiatrist Condemns *Witness Stand*'. There was an artist's impression of Bu — it looked like a criminal Wookie — and a photo of Dr Keith Peterson. Sandrine groaned, dropping herself down on the couch. Faber leaned across and read over her shoulder.

A psychiatrist who treated a man who fits the description of the so-called 'Southern Sasquatch' has attacked current events show *Witness Stand* for misinforming the public. While Dr Keith Peterson refused to give any further information on the patient's name or case details, he said that the recent news item on *Witness Stand* was 'blatantly exploitative of a highly vulnerable young man'. Peterson said he would be investigating official avenues of complaint.

Dr Peterson specialises in the treatment of anxiety and personality disorders and depressive illness. When asked if the man in question had himself suffered from any of these conditions, Peterson would not elaborate. He said 'the kind of public scrutiny and pressure that *Witness Stand* has placed this man under is highly morally questionable. Should the individual in the recent TV footage go on to suffer from psychological distress caused by this inappropriate attention, I will do my best to make the network liable for the costs of his health care.' When asked why he had come to the media himself, Dr Peterson said, 'To insist that he be left alone.'

Faber whistled out through his teeth. 'Maybe you should call Peterson again.'

'To let him know his statement hasn't done any good?'

She put the paper aside. 'Poor Bu.'

Faber watched her for a moment, then reached out as if to touch her hair, but pulled back. 'He's lucky to have you looking out for him, Sandrine.'

She brushed a feather that had escaped from the down sleeping bag off his chest.

'Not that lucky,' she said. 'This is all well out of control. There's a fresh mob outside the door.'

Holding the sleeping bag up under his armpits, Faber shuffled to the window and peered out through the gap in the curtains. 'Holy shit. How the hell did they work out ...?'

'My flatmates.'

'Shouldn't you know half these people? Can't you call them off?'

'What a mess.' She covered her face briefly with her hands. 'I'm sorry, Faber. I'm the one who's got us all in to this. Poor bloody Bu.'

'Look, that crowd's not your fault.' He pulled the curtains together. 'Let's just call Dr Peterson. Get him to take over again.' He shuffled closer. 'It's okay, Sandrine.' He put an arm around her and she felt her pulse quicken. 'Why don't we sit down for a sec.'

They sat, and when he didn't give up his embrace, she finally lowered a last defence, wondering fleetingly if the quietening of self-criticism she had felt last night under Bu's gaze had led her here, after what seemed like years of self-restraint and withholding. Her head rested on Faber's shoulder. *Am I really risking this? He's meant to be a friend* ... Yet some stronger impulse in her was sliding, letting go ...

Faber's mouth was speaking into hers, gently. 'I really missed you.'

She felt made of warm, dry sand: the old Sandrine slumping, sighing into herself. Of course, of *course*. So many people had guessed about Faber before she had: so what, you're really *just friends*? She found herself answering him, 'Do you know how long you were away? Ten days, seven hours and twenty-five minutes.'

'I've missed you for longer than that. Every time I've seen you. Even when you drove me to the airport before the trip, I was thinking, if Sandrine said *don't go*, I'd have stayed.'

She laughed, then saw his doubt as he wondered if he'd misinterpreted the last few moments. Fingering the pocket on his T-shirt, she said, 'Our timing isn't great, is it? In the middle of this farce.' Yet she shook her head, astounded: the blond hair at Faber's freckled wrists, the solid feel of his hip against hers, the warm skin of his neck...

'Now is good,' he grinned. Their kiss seemed to shift and translate all the years they'd known each other: every glance, every conversation, funnelled towards this.

Eventually they had to pull apart. 'I better make that call,' Sandrine said reluctantly.

'Yep. I'll grab a shower then make us some breakfast.'

She frowned. 'Is Bu moving around yet? If he is, it might be better if I phone from the bedroom.'

'Not sure.'

They passed down the corridor together. Bu's door was open, and the slept-in bed was empty. He was gone.

Bu

WHEN HE SAW THEM on the couch, it was like when he'd watched some of the movies his father-man had brought home — where the kisses made him feel swollen with waiting, ugly and happy-sad all at once; where he was glad there was a kiss, but he wished it was him, and knew it couldn't be, perhaps not ever.

Only now it was worse. He wanted to run out of the house like the child he had been when he'd smashed plants in his mother-woman's garden.

He had dreamt for so long of the *rest of the world*, of finding someone who would cradle his jaw in her hand the way Sandrine cradled Faber's, just as if she knew all the movies, too, and had practised to get them perfectly under her skin.

He wished he could storm down the street and splinter all the windows, crack them so the glass wore tears like shattered cobwebs.

Bu had let himself be carried here, drawn by some light gleaming only in his own mind. Sandrine filled his eyes, even beat in his head, when he lay down and waited for sleep. When she was in the room, turning his gaze from her took a huge effort. It was as if there were a live current in her, drawing his eyes back and back. When he watched her, he forgot the heavy bones of his face, his huge mitts and feet, his muzzle. Yet now they seemed to return, at twice their original size and awkwardness.

Throwing on a lightweight balaclava, sunglasses and thin, black silk gloves to conceal as much of himself as he could — and with all his other worldly goods in the pack he'd brought from home — Bu clambered stiffly from the bedroom window at the side of the house. He turned away from the crush of people, straddled the neighbour's low fence, eased himself slowly down — still not sure how strong his ankle was — and began his solo walk.

Nobody seemed to notice him go. He was listening for his name, half wanting Sandrine — or anyone — to run after him, and say, *Don't leave* . . .

He shuffled his way from street to street till he found a bus stop. He knew how to catch a bus, though he was surprised to find it really did work. The driver let him on, asked no questions, although his eyes sometimes found Bu in the rear-view mirror.

When the bus dropped him in the middle of the city, Bu slowly made his way, partly by chance, partly by smell, sense of light and air, to some public gardens. Like old friends, the trees, shrubs and flowers released him from the need to be brave. He curled up underneath a giant trunk and its swaying green light. With his head on his pack, he cradled the hurt in his stomach, waiting for it to pass as if it were just a bodily illness; waiting for some sort of plan to make its way through the ache.

The Crowd

'D'YOU THINK THAT GUY'S all right?'
  'Just napping, probably.'

'Look at him.'
  'Wow. He's *huge*. Is he for real?'
  'It's probably some sort of costume. Did you see those students on Great King Street today? There were about forty of them — Batmen and Supermen and Shreks and someone on stilts — all heading off to the Cook for happy hour.'
  'Huh. He's probably sleeping off the party.'

'Check out the freak.'
  'What do you think's wrong with him?'
  'Everything, I'd say. Watch he doesn't bite you. Could be catching.'
  'Very funny.'

'Hey, that guy's still there.'
  'Sun's going down.'
  'Oh well. It's not as if he's hurting anyone.'
  'True.'

Bu

PART OF HIM WOULD have liked to have lain there forever, put roots down into the soil, let all his thoughts and dreams untangle and stretch out, tender as bud-skin. Then his past could peel away, merge with the ground and he could change from the shape of a beast to the shape of a tree, never mourning for any loss.

But eventually he felt the cold. He moved only because his body made him; it dragged his mind back along the streets, the thick, black cuts they made through the occasional swatches of green, past the thin, scraggly trees poked into the pavements here and there. He worked his way to a main road. Bristling with trepidation, limbs taut with readiness to dart away, he approached a man, asking if he knew the way to a *motel*. He said the word carefully, precisely: it was one of the many he had read and heard but till now had never used.

The man had a goatee beard, sunken cheeks and forearms covered in blue swirls and words. Head back, chin up, eyes drilling, he kept his distance, but Bu could still smell his breath, sour as an old dishcloth. The man turned on the spot, looking north and south. 'Uh, go straight along this street, then hang a right at the set of stone steps going up the hill. There's a backpackers' there.'

Hang a right? 'You mean go right?'

'That's what I said.'

Bu thanked him and moved off. The man still stood there now, watching. Bu caught the odour of a thin hostility seep into the air and with quick instinct, knew to feign calm. He kept walking, slowing his step a fraction beneath his normal pace, to conceal the rising panic he felt.

Without his parent-folk, without nurses, doctors, Derek, Sandrine, *Sandrine*, what would he do? How would he manage the city, this life?

Bu trudged through the compact city centre, his head down, trying to ignore the people who stopped and stared, looked over their shoulders, or glanced at him, then hurried past as quickly as they could. Where did they all learn so much distrust, these ones who had surely never been as alone as Bu? What had taught them to be so affrighted? Shouldn't they feel safe, tucked in tight to their skins?

At the top of the stone steps he'd been directed to, and along the rise, Bu found a blocky-looking wooden building, painted white: The Done Inn. A hand-printed sign on cardboard in the window said *B&B and long-term lets*. Bu went in through a door with another sign saying *Office*, then through a curtain made of strings of a dry, hollow reed, where he found the reception desk empty. There was the sound of a TV coming from another room. He tapped the bell, then waited, noticing all the paintings of albatrosses, royal spoonbills, seagulls, penguins, on the blue walls. The birds appeared misshapen, overfed. Bu found he didn't really like to look at them for long, as if they were real, might feel his stare.

Someone came in slowly from the TV room. The man — another who had blue patterns on his arms — had thick, glossy black hair that sat on his head like a fat, contented mallard nestled into itself for a sleep. He wore a gold link bracelet and tartan slippers. His skin was very brown, and his shirt, which was loose and big on him, had a picture of a car shooting flames. Somehow these things — and the bad paintings — made Bu feel that the man might have had hard times. Or maybe it was the way he didn't meet Bu's eyes, didn't ask any needless questions. He didn't recoil — and so Bu felt his dread grow smaller.

'Room? For the night? Or you want to take lodgings?'

Bu saw that the motel owner wanted to be left to himself, and was unlikely to trouble him for anything more than the cost of the room, so he arranged to stay indefinitely. He could leave any time, as long as he gave two weeks' notice. The man, leading him outside then round the back of the building, shot information over his shoulder.

'You have to share a bathroom, kitchen and living room with rooms seventeen and eighteen. All the rooms have their own TV. Too much aggro over channels otherwise. There's nobody in those rooms at the moment. Hasn't been for a month or more. These are my long term places. Mostly I get backpackers. Germans, Aussies and Brits.' Every sentence sounded as if the man wanted to put an end to any further conversation yet quickly another fact demanded that he bark it out. 'You do your own laundry. Cook your own food. Supply your own bog roll. Supermarkets aren't far from here. New World or Countdown. Cumberland Street. Paper delivery in the morning. Once I've read it, I drop it in the communal living room here. For free. That's about it.'

He opened the door for Bu, went in ahead of him, put milk in the fridge, threw open two windows. 'Needs airing,' he said, tossed the key on the coffee table and left.

Bu liked him.

When he had gone, Bu took off his extra layers and sat

with his head in his hands. But thinking soon made him so weary again, that after drinking the full carton of milk as his evening meal, he slept.

His dreams were confused and jarring. He woke several times in the night with a sore neck, his body twisted at the angles nightmares grew from. When he finally slipped back into an even sleep, his dreams invented Sandrine's body: the body he had never seen, but here it was, near to him, smooth, pale, tender as something for which he had no language. She was over him, around him, let him be over her, staring down into her eyes, the sweetness in him reaching and reaching for the sweetness in her.

When she touched him, it was like the old story: Bu felt altered, his fur and brow diminishing. Although for some reason he couldn't look down at himself, through the strange telescope of dreams he knew that he was handsome, his own skin bare and lucent as the inside of a sea shell. Her hands had changed him from beast to man. Yet suddenly her eyes grew scared, shuttered. '*Who are you?*'

When he woke, he knew from the sun through the curtains that it must be late, and his stomach growled with hunger. He pulled on his disguise, and mind raw with night images, stumbled out of the lodgings to find food.

The dream was still too real for him: he walked through its haze rather than through the city streets. Yet he found it protected him, in a way, from the odd looks. Perhaps people recognised the dull pang in him, now: there were no questions, not even any taunts, just the checkout girl with her inky blue hair tied up like a feathery fountain and funny colours painted on her (orange mouth, lavender eyelids) dishing him change as fast as she could. He used the small store of money he had withdrawn from a bank in a wall using his secret number, all the while scared someone would say he wasn't allowed, and what did he think he was doing? When he had taken his change, the girl turned her back on him for the next customer, her shoulders hunched.

He lugged the food home, began to set himself up in the small kitchen. When he took his breakfast to the dining table, he saw that true to his word, the proprietor had left the newspaper there on the table. Only it was yesterday's: and there was a photo of Dr Keith Peterson, and an 'artist's impression' of someone who looked a little like Bu himself.

Another one? his heart asked with a leap. Then he read the words, and although he felt his old, resigned, distanced fondness for the troubled doctor, he realised with a slump that the drawing was meant to be him.

All through breakfast he thought about his hospital days, and how Sandrine's presence had started to turn away the grief for his parent-folk, and the wringing misery of guilt over the candles, the fire. 'It was an accident,' Sandrine had told him on one of her visits. 'I understand how you feel, but accidents aren't about blame. They're about bad luck. Not bad deeds.' He had let the look in her eyes begin to free him. Yet the sadness tugged at him again now that he was truly on his own.

Back in his room his fingers closed around the pocket knife and the alarm clock in the inner pocket of his backpack, pulled them out. He remembered the mornings when he had opened these gifts from his father-man: the clock in particular. They had little need for alarm clocks — they rose with the birds, went to bed with the sun —

though his father-man owned a wristwatch for the times he went to town. When Bu received the clock, he felt it was a sign: perhaps an acknowledgement that one day, he too would be living by city rhythms.

Sometimes his father-man had spoken of how Bu was equipped to learn almost any trade: he'd not only taught him woodturning, but also how to fix up the wiring in simple circuits, the basic principles of plumbing and construction. He told Bu that he was a damn sight cleverer than he and Lillian put together, that he would, one day, 'get by' in the world.

Now Bu caressed the clock's ordinary black plastic edges, wondering how much longer his father-man would have delayed his departure from their land. Automatically, he reached for the photo of his parent-folk, as if he might be able to read in his father-man's expression, from all those years ago, what he really intended for him. He dug his hand into the pocket for the cool wood of the small case that held his mother-woman's locket. Nothing. He dug again. He peered in, shook the pack upside down, searched all the other compartments. He groped through all his pockets, flung clothes up off the floor, shook them too. Still nothing.

He sat down on the bed, mind racing. When was the last time he'd seen it? The Gables? He closed his eyes, racked his memory. The Gables, his room there . . . he hadn't taken it out of his bag. Then his stomach sank. The ward with Dr Peterson. That was the last time he was sure he'd seen it. Somehow the box must have slipped from his pack. He had to have it back. The locket was the only thing of his mother's he owned.

He fetched the newspaper, looked at Peterson's photo

again to confirm to himself that he meant no harm. Rummaging once more through his clothes and pack, he found the little piece of printed cardboard the doctor had given him, fingered it thoughtfully, turning it over and over.

He would phone him.

Keith Peterson

CLICKING HIS TONGUE IN irritation — it was the third interruption to his research time in half an hour — Keith snatched up the phone. 'Yes?'

At Bu's hesitant, low-crouching voice, 'Hello? D-hoctor? It is Bu eh-speaking,' Keith instantly felt lightly, cheerfully shaken, as if a dozen rudely strewn parts of him had fallen back in place. An unease he'd sat with for days began to clear.

'Hel-*lo*, Bu! How good to hear from you!' He realised he was standing up, as if expecting him to say, like a young son, *Can you come and get me*? *I'm scared*. 'You're safe and well?'

'Yes. I am. But . . .'

When Bu explained what he had lost, and wondered whether the doctor could hunt it down for him, Peterson was only slightly diverted from his fresh happiness and the expectation that Bu would ask to see him again for treatment. *He's talking fluently. Maybe more open to contact . . .* 'Just one moment, Bu. Wait while I speak to the institute's lost and found.'

He willed the switchboard to hurry, thinking Bu might grow confused, and hang up. He paced back and forth, then as soon as the woman answering started her spiel, he leapt in with, 'Yes, hello, Dr Peterson here, I'm looking for something mislaid by a patient of mine. Is there a slim, oblong wooden box with a necklace in it anywhere in your collection?'

'One moment.'

Keith waited.

'Yes, are you there, sir? We do have something like that here.'

'Marvellous! I'll come and get it.' He hit the hold switch off again. 'Bu, are you still there?'

'I am.'

'It's your lucky day. We have the box.' Peterson clutched the phone tightly. 'I'd be more than happy to collect it for you and return it.'

He waited for Bu to release some clues of his whereabouts and state of mind. Sandrine Moreau had phoned him as soon as she'd discovered that the unfortunate fellow had absconded, though that was too strong a word. Bu hadn't committed any crime, hadn't harmed anyone, wasn't in anyone's custody. Peterson had informed the police that Bu had disappeared, and the officer he had spoken to had thanked him and said, 'We'll make a note of it', at which Peterson had felt despondent. He imagined a yellow Post-it note stuck to a desk lamp, gathering dust, then finally thrown out when the officer came to do an end-of-year purge.

Bu gave a rumbling sound that somehow made Peterson's defences weaken. 'Please,' he said. 'I would very much like to see you.' He pinched at his temples. 'I still think it's important, for your own good.'

The rumble lightened into a kind of hum. 'I will come tomorrow, perhaps. If it is not too eh-sunny.'

'I beg your pardon?'

There was a pause. 'It is easier for me to cubber myself in the d-hay if the weather is cold.'

Another pause as Peterson registered what he meant. 'Ah. Of course.'

Both men hung up, and Peterson, open-mouthed, looked out at the clouds brought in by a freezing sou'wester. 'He could be the only warm man in Dunedin,' he said aloud, then bit his lip in happy self-mortification.

He sat down at his computer screen and pulled up the email from Professor Caroline Braze, a geneticist at Wellington Public Hospital.

He knew Caroline from med school — had been sorely disappointed when she fell for an actor working on a touring production and followed him up to the capital. She reminded him of a piece of Clarice Cliff from his great-aunt's china cabinet. Her skin was creamy and clear; her clothes were cut at eccentric angles and she wore chunky beads and bracelets in a bright jumble of parrot colours. You knew she was walking towards you in a crowd before you had quite seen her face.

He had left her message marked unread, liking the way the bold type spotlit her name.

From>>	To>>	Subject	Size	Received
Caroline Braze	Keith Peterson	Consultation	4 k	10../../0

Dear Keith

I recently heard through Afshana Ali from Dunedin Public orthopaedics that you've had dealings with a patient I'd be very interested in assessing. I understand the patient (NH # 5779) is male, exhibits hypertrichosis, pronounced cranial abnormalities and suspected gigantism. (Of course I've also been made further aware of the man's condition through the recent unfortunate media speculation.)

I'm going to be down in Dunedin for three days next

month for a mobile clinic, and wondered if you would
be so good as to provide a referral for this man. I have
a two-day paediatrics clinic from the 14th to the 15th,
but have booked in an extra day to enable me to see
a couple of older patients too. I've managed to secure
a consulting/research room in the endocrinology
department at Dunedin Public, and will be there from 9
to 3 on the 16th. I have a one-hour slot free at 1 p.m. If
your patient could agree to see me then, that would be
ideal. As you'll no doubt understand, an investigation into
this man's case could greatly extend our knowledge in a
number of areas. Of course I'll send you a formal letter
after any assessment he agrees to undergo.

It would also be great to catch up with you in person,
if we can arrange it.

Trusting that you and Bonnie are both well
Caroline

Peterson typed his reply.

Dear Caroline
Very good to hear from you. I'm more than happy to
discuss my patient (Bu Finlayson) with you. First of all,
I should let you know that Bu discharged himself from
hospital, and my consultations with him ceased, as he felt
that he had made a successful recovery. However, I've
just recently had renewed contact with him, and I'm very
keen for regular meetings with him to recommence.

My angle on this case is that the man is delusional.
Although I have by no means been able to consult with
or analyse him as extensively as I'd like, my preliminary
thoughts are that he probably exhibits a form of clinical

zooanthropy. I suspect he suffers from some kind of endocrinological disorder, and that the isolation of his upbringing, and distorted beliefs formed under unusual parental influence, have led him to enter a psychotic state where he believes he has certain mythical animal characteristics.

Given the obviously abnormal physical features he presents with, I'm tempted to resort to a kind of clinical metaphor, and say it's as if he exhibits an inverse version of body dysmorphobia: in that he's translated a definite disfigurement into a fantasy identity. (Should you wish to know more about the normal course of either clinical zooanthropy or body dysmorphobia, I'd be happy to elaborate in a more formal sense, as you say, at a later date.) I'll certainly recommend to him that he consult with you, and I'm more than happy to help set up an appointment for him. My view is that it may well help him on the road to full psychological health if he meets with you and learns more about the parameters and prognosis of his physical condition.

Please do call me when you're in town. It'd be great to catch up.

Best as ever —
Keith

Done, he said to himself as he pressed send, although even putting Bu's situation into this casual version of patient notes left him perplexed, chasing all the proliferate questions, and all the more aware that the case was nowhere near resolution.

❉ ❉ ❉

DESPITE THE FACT THAT he was expecting Bu, Peterson couldn't help but start at the sight of him. His height and breadth made the furniture seem flimsy. He seemed like a gigantic cat burglar, or maybe some sort of eco-warrior vigilante, the pack and outdoor gear giving him a look that was at once rebellious and fugitive.

Once inside the consulting room, Bu slipped off his balaclava and gloves and unbuttoned his raincoat. He asked for a window to be opened and gulped down the offered water as if stifled.

'Have you been well?' Peterson asked.

Bu narrowed his eyes: the expression, Peterson thought, was contented, sphinx-like. He took it to mean yes.

'I've heard from Sandrine Moreau,' Peterson said, leaning against the side of his desk, arms crossed. 'She says you just vanished from her friend's house.' He took in the way Bu's gaze switched from Peterson to the small oval side table with its tissues, the glass paperweight containing bright twists of molten colour, the artwork on the walls — a pale man curled around a woman curled around a child — and finally to the window, where the sky seemed to flutter like flags between the scudding clouds.

'Both of us want to help in any way we can. If you have any more calls from people wanting interviews, just direct them to one of us. We'll deal with them.' He softened his voice. 'If you let us handle this professionally, we can protect you, and I'm convinced this ridiculous fuss will die down.' He went to sit in the squat leather armchair next to Bu's. 'What's most important at this stage, of course, is how you feel about what's happened.' A silence pooled between them. 'As I mentioned on the phone, I also think it would be a very good idea if I continued to see you, so that we can discuss the loss of your parents, and your — your sense of *yourself*.'

'I would like to hab the necklace case I came for. Please.'

Waiting a couple of beats, Peterson concealed his disappointment. 'Yes. Yes, of course. It's just here.' He reached over from the chair and opened a desk drawer. He passed the box to Bu, who caught at it with those somehow heart-wrenchingly bare palms, hungry for the metal of the locket inside. He fingered the necklace as if its shape could be sealed into his touch in a kind of memory tattoo, then prised open the locket.

Peterson craned over slightly. 'The photo — is it of your parents?'

'Yes.'

'May I see?'

Bu hesitated, but then he passed it to him.

'Bu —' Peterson gazed at the image, then passed it back. He tried to say the next words gently. 'They're not like you, are they?' He rested his fingertips briefly on his shaven cheeks. 'They're like me.'

Bu looked from him to the fading Polaroid of his parents, then up again.

Peterson leaned forward a little, resting his arms on his knees. 'I think we need to talk about your family. It's very important for your health that we do so, Bu. The anxiety, the depression . . . these may well be acute reactions to the crisis of the fire. But I strongly suspect you won't be entirely free of them unless you confront some other . . . facts. Your emotions may well have been there as a kind of general dysphoria — mood imbalance — for much longer, as part of another underlying condition.'

Had he said too much, too quickly? Bu gave a small

involuntary moan. Hearing that isolated half-cry, and despite knowing its probable psychiatric provenance, Peterson felt the need for some sort of distraction or protection. His fingers pianoed on his knees, searching for the comfort of papers, books, pen, keyboard. But he pushed on. The painful encounter with facts was necessary, like birth pangs. If he was to achieve anything like a full self-knowledge, Bu had to bear down on the past and the delusions he had built on it for his short-term, but unwittingly self-sabotaging, salvation.

'There's another thing, which I'd like to mention as soon as possible.' Peterson heard the flatness of falsehood in his own voice. It might be too soon to raise the point, but a swift dose of reality might have a curative effect and Caroline Braze's roving clinic was only two weeks away.

He handed over an envelope that contained a blue appointment card he had filled out by hand. 'A colleague of mine has heard about you. She would be very interested in having a consultation with you.'

Bu opened the envelope, looked at the card. 'A clinical geneti-eh-cist,' he read aloud. His eyes — big, liquid, black — glinted, and Peterson had an irrational intuition that Bu was poised on the threshold of some momentous change. What would this huge, looming man-boy, who believed himself to be some kind of beast walking out of the oral legends of prehistoric time, be like if he were pushed too far, enraged? Now Peterson felt the thrill of a lead. He wanted to write down *anger, or the mask of anger* in his notes, but suppressed his eagerness and nodded at the card. 'Yes, she's a geneticist,' he said. 'Do you know the term?'

Bu turned the card over, as if he might find the definition

printed on the back. He cocked his head to one side: Peterson imagined that if he had upright ears, they would be rotating this way, that way, an early detection system for catching any surprises hidden behind the words. He felt a little ashamed of his own animal metaphor, yet it was not impossible that the impression of feline alertness and agility, even in the man's massive bulk, was something Bu had cultivated, consciously or otherwise.

'A clinical geneticist looks at various aspects of growth and development — how they might be affected by chromosomal abnormalities. They study our physical make-up. Caroline Braze has a particular interest in disorders or syndromes which . . .' again he felt the mental effort of trying to find the most delicate way of phrasing things '. . . which might mean she would be of help to you.'

'Chromosomal? Eh-syndromes? What d-ho you mean?'

A question snagged at the edge of Keith's concentration. Did the accent grow exaggerated when he was confused, annoyed? He'd spoken so little, overall, that Keith had been unable to think through all the implications of his halting pronunciation. He quickly scrawled a note — *speech impediment*? — then tapped the pencil end on end as he answered. 'Well, to work out what the condition of your health is, she would want to take a blood sample, some measurements — say of your height, the size of your skull, the nature of your hair and skin, and so on — and she'd compare these to other information she has on people who . . . are similar to you. She might then be able to offer some sort of prognosis and support.'

'Prognosis, eh-syndromes — these are eh-strange words.' Bu seemed to mean not unfamiliar, but uneasy, untoward. The way the lightly coiled locks on his forehead lifted with the cast of his eyebrows; the widened eyes; the clenching and unclenching of his hands on the armrests: he was frightened.

Peterson, unsure now whether Bu had said *strange* or *strong*, spoke carefully. 'I should explain. There's no need to see her until you're ready. The chief reason for agreeing would be to establish your medical profile so that we — she — could ascertain whether there might be any future health issues for you.' He took a deep breath. 'Bu — I gather, from the things Sandrine says you confided in her, that you would have rarely, if ever, seen a doctor while you were growing up?'

Bu shook his head. 'My mother-woman was a nurse. When I was eh-sick she cared for me.'

Peterson frowned, letting this piece of information slot into what else he had heard about Bu's past. 'Did she ever suggest to you that, given some of the signs you show —' Peterson again quickly gestured with his hand, touching his chin, cheek, the backs of his hands '— there could be health concerns for you? In the sense that often a cluster of features *such* as these can have other associated problems. We don't know this in your case, of course, because you seem fit and healthy. But there are various syndromes where more serious internal complications arise.'

'What d-ho you mean, eh-serious?'

'If we take, say, acromegaly or gigantism — conditions where there is abnormal growth of the features or the limbs — untreated, they can lead to diabetes, heart failure, muscular problems and so on.'

He gave Bu a moment to absorb all this. He seemed to be mouthing over some of the words to himself, eyes roaming the room like someone trying to think their way through a foreign language. When he dropped his gaze, it was steady, but his hands still gripped the arms of his seat, like someone in a plane bracing themselves through turbulence.

'This d-hoctor, she has met others like me?'

Peterson took time choosing his words.

'She will have seen people with attributes such as yours, yes. But they would have had them with varying degrees.'

Bu's large lower jaw jutted out, an exaggerated picture of adolescent sulk. 'But she d-hoesn't know another of my kind.'

Peterson made a steeple of his index fingers, resting them against his mouth.

'You know, Sandrine also passed on something of the story about your birth parents. And I should make it clear, she only told me out of real concern for you.'

Bu seemed impassive.

'She said that you believe you were fostered by human parents. That you believe you are — something other than human.' Peterson leaned forward slightly. 'Do you feel safer, that way? Is it, perhaps, better than being a man?'

Bu's eyes glittered.

'I am not bery much like a man.'

The hardness of his tone drove Peterson to make a calculated feint. He nodded. 'Perhaps Professor Braze's tests will show something unexpected. Perhaps they'll prove you're right. But seeing her is, of course, your decision.'

Bu's fingers alternately plucked and smoothed at the arms of his chair as he stared out the large window onto the beautifully kept grounds and a perfectly framed view of a tall blue gum. Peterson himself found the tree soothing as he walked through the grounds every morning and evening. In spring there were magnolias, rhododendrons, azaleas, daffodils. He wondered, now, as he watched Bu search the view, whether he found any comfort in it — this man who spent his childhood surrounded by native bush — or whether the setting seemed artificial, alien.

Bu seemed to draw himself back into the room. 'All right. I will eh-see her.'

Peterson nodded animatedly. 'I think that's an excellent decision, Bu. And I hope that you'll also agree to meet with me again?' He felt the return of that hot dart of energy he always experienced at the start of new research, and a quiet kind of vindication. The shame he'd told Bonnie about vanished now that Bu *wanted* help — perhaps vanished the moment Bu made his phone call.

Bu straightened. 'Perhaps,' he said. 'If I feel . . .'

Their separate silences met and merged.

Peterson wrote out another appointment card, giving the same day and time for the following week, and handed it to Bu, feeling as unsure as a boy handing flowers to a girl he's barely met. 'If you're able to attend I'll ensure I keep this time free for you, every week. I'll be here.'

Bu took the card, slipping it into the envelope with the one for Caroline's clinic.

With the combination of care and matter-of-factness that a mountaineer shows preparing for a climb, Bu kitted himself up again. Standing at the window, Peterson saw Bu's languid, heavy gait take him across the grounds, across the drive, through the gates and out. Watching him leave was painful. He feared for him out in the streets, in the world.

Bu

'DARE YOU TO SPEAK to him.'
 'You.'
 'No way.'

'Mum, what's wrong with that man's face? Is he really a lion?'
 'Be quiet, Ben. Stop staring.'

'Oi! Man-panzee! What lab did you escape from?'
 'Check out the beardie-weirdie.'

Bu tried to imagine drawing quiet into his ears the way eyelids could draw darkness into his head. Concentrating on not hearing the comments, the laughter, he walked past a building with a large, red W on the side: Westpac. A bank. The family bank where Bu had an account now, too, though it only held the benefit payments Sandrine and Derek had helped to organise. His father-man had been careful to explain to him about banks, lawyers, the government, church, police, schools — all the machinery of the great, ostensibly faraway world from which Bu had felt himself banned like an ogre under a hex.

When he was about seventeen, Andy, his father-man, had begun to drill him on some of these facts — fiercely at times. It began after Andy had experienced a dizzy spell, had felt one side of his face and body go numb, and for several days afterwards found it difficult to pick up anything with his left hand. Some weeks later, when the sensation in his arm was returning, he and Bu were in his workshop together. With Lillian far off, pruning the fruit trees she had cultivated beyond the potager's perimeter, Andy tested Bu again and again. How to find his way to the main road in an emergency; the name of the family lawyer; the town his practice was in; the street address. 'This is the man who has our wills: mine and your mother's. He has copies of all our other papers, too. The land title, our marriage certificate, and so on. If anything happens to us, you contact this man.'

It wasn't a conversation to have in front of Lillian. Bu knew there were reasons his father-man kept certain secrets; reasons for him to talk in low tones even when she was barely within hollering distance; reasons that the only times Bu had been allowed to leave the land were when Andy had virtually smuggled him out. Each time they came back, Lillian was so eerily erased by fear, that after the last foray Bu had said to his father that they oughtn't to try it again without her.

Bu stayed halted by the bank's sign. It set off some near-chime in his memory. *Westlake*. The lawyer. Martin Westlake. He hadn't even realised he'd been waiting for the name to re-emerge.

It was time to write to him about his parent-folks' papers and to find out if he knew — as his father seemed to think he would — what Bu should do, once part of the old enchantment was irreparably, miserably lifted.

Bu made his slow, preoccupied way back to his lodgings. He would have to explain about the fire, and his time in hospital. If he were to be believed, he would probably need to give the lawyer Dr Peterson's name, and maybe even Sandrine's. Maybe.

He reached a sloping patch of grass made colourful with pansies, marigolds and other plants he couldn't name, all set out in the shape of two church bells. Another strange city-dream of plants — a small grave of flowers to mark the original green the buildings and footpath must have buried. As the sight made him pause, there was the sudden, ear-splitting shriek of a car braking, then a muffled thud. He jolted around, and saw a crumpled bicycle and basket in the street, books and papers strewn in the gutter, and a young Chinese woman lying flung to the side, half on the road, half on the footpath. She was draped awkwardly over the kerb, limp as the scarecrow he and his parent-folk had made for their potager. The car's driver still sat in the vehicle, grey-faced and immobilised with shock. A cluster of pedestrians hung back uncertainly, although a van driver who had climbed out of his vehicle stood near the woman and started to redirect traffic as he spoke into his cellphone.

Bu didn't think: he was floating above himself, seeing at once the frail, discarded woman, and his own form prostrate in the bush, with a woman kneeling next to him, saying, under her breath, *Oh, my God*. A physical memory of touch seemed to brush along his wrist and across his temples. Then came the recollection of voices: like lights that were strung along the darkness he'd slipped into, guiding him back to himself for a moment. More buried memory came to him: first the sounds of the couple's urgent conversation, and then the man continuing to talk to him as he lay there, slipping in and out of consciousness. The voice had given him the strength to hold on, as if it were drawing him from beneath a crushing weight of water, before pain wiped him blank again.

Although a voice in the present gasped, 'Don't touch her! You mustn't move her!' Bu found himself kneeling down and gently adjusting the woman's body so that she wasn't lying over the concrete ridge. Her eyelids fluttered and then she looked directly at Bu. In a moment her gaze darted from side to side, as if she were watching the world from a fast-travelling vehicle; then her eyes rolled and closed again and her body began to shudder.

Bu heard the van driver call out to the general crowd, 'Has anyone got a blanket or a jacket?' When nobody volunteered he strode back round to look in his van. 'Shit. Nothing in there. Anyone spare a *jersey*, a *sweater*?' He turned on the spot, agitated. 'She needs to be kept warm.' There was a stir and at last a young woman ran off towards a first cluster of shops and cafés, saying she'd find something. The onlookers saw her duck into a corner food shop, then come out again and duck into a knick-knack store. As if the sight of her empty-handed sent him a command, Bu again lowered his enormous form, then lay down and gingerly stretched himself the length of the unconscious woman's side. He narrated his movements to her as he cupped her head in one arm, and held his balaclavaed cheek near hers. Willing the heat of his pelt to travel through the fabric, he tried, too, to will himself invisible, closing his eyes as if to block out the low electricity of disbelief he could hear spitting through the crowd.

'What's going on?'
'What's he doing?'
'Maybe he knows her.'

Yet in that moment he wasn't afraid of them: all that mattered was the broken form of the woman. Until the ambulance arrived he talked to her, tried to guess her name, told her who he imagined must be waiting for her, said over and over again that she would be all right.

When the siren shrilled along the street, and the paramedics hunched down next to them both, taking over in their quick, efficient way, Bu clambered up from the footpath. His scalp tightened as he scanned the disbelieving faces of the gathered crowd.

An ambulance officer had been listening to the van driver's version of events. He turned on his heels where he squatted and asked Bu, 'Did you see what happened? Was she definitely hit by a car?' His tone said that Bu's very presence was suspect. The facts the van driver had given him were cast in shadow by the monstrousness of Bu: his size, his face changed the story.

What had he done wrong? His heartbeat sputtered like a bulb about to blow out. *Out*, his mind said. *Out*. He turned around and around, frantic.

'Hey!' demanded the paramedic, wanting his answer.

Bu, mouth dry, tried to remember which direction the B&B was in. He heard a sound come from the woman and her eyes opened. Everyone's attention swung from the agitated figure of Bu.

'Did she say something?' asked the second ambulance officer.

'Sweetheart, can you speak to us?'

'Chen Mei-li,' she said. 'Mei-li, my given name. Can you tell him?'

'She's conscious.' The news rippled up and down the crowd, which parted as police arrived.

Bu felt a man in a peaked cap and with gold-edged teeth staring at him. 'What a frickin' weirdo,' the man said, slyly, as if he were promising Bu something, something he didn't want. But now that there was a gap in the crowd, Bu took the chance to flee. Grasping at half-recognised landmarks, he strode up the road, had to turn around, found the right steps, took the hill to The Done Inn, ignoring the twinge in his ankle, driven by a powerful instinct to take cover. All he wanted was the sweet protection of walls and door.

He would not go out into the daylight again.

❊ ❊ ❊

OVER THE WEEKS OF waiting for a reply from Martin Westlake, he tried to manage on the benefit. In order to afford his room, and to keep out of sight, Bu started to forage for food after sunset. He fed off discarded meals he found in rubbish tins or, most often, off supplies he'd filched from supermarket loading bays: a burst carton of cereal; squashed, leaking juice containers. He began to sleep when he could during the day, leaving his room only at night when hunger — or the strange energy still seeded by the thought of Sandrine — forced him.

After almost a fortnight of this, he was feeling light-headed, drifty from poor diet and lack of sleep. He was often restless and wakeful even after returning from his night-time foraging, and would nap fitfully, well into the afternoon. The city still excited and confused him, in equal measure, and he went out in it with his senses as vigilant as a wolf's to any movement, odour: ready always to merge back into the shadows. Sometimes what he'd seen in the dark-time carnival as he stood alone at an empty corner, crouched behind skips or perched on fire escapes, was what kept him tossing and turning back in his rented room.

He had seen fireworks that shattered and peeled the night like thunder and lightning; an old blind man sitting on a stool, playing guitar, a cap full of coins at his feet — the man himself unafraid of Bu, though his dog growled and made Bu quickly move on; a street-fight; a very thin, bent woman with white hair and pink-rimmed eyes jeered at by three men; tiny insects made of red stones and silver in a jeweller's window; a very tired, small boy walking holding his parents' hands and swung up on *one-two-three* between them; the city's own lights like a night garden, its gleaming flowers repeated in the harbour. Bu decided a city was heaven and hell in one place: no sky or time divided them.

One morning a knock on his door roused him from the ends of a ragged, turning dream full of mocking mouths and thin lights lying on the water like long, golden foxgloves. A sou'westerly flung rain and hail at the windows, rattling the room as if desperate to get inside and shelter from itself. He padded to the door to reassure himself that it was just the wind and stood there, dazed, an unintentional mirror of the two police officers. Was he to be punished?

'Bu . . . er . . . Finlayson?' one asked.

He hadn't heard anyone speak his father-man's surname for so long. 'Yes,' he said, as if they had brought him some news, some deeper recognition.

The officers introduced themselves — Bradley and Hall — and explained that they wanted to ask him a few questions. There was a stiff, cautious formality to everything they said. The lawyers had received his letter notifying them of the deaths of his parents. In the way of these things, certain procedures had to be followed.

It had been far from easy to track down his family's property, but fire safety officers had already concluded that the blaze was not suspicious. The police understood from the lawyer's contact with them and a Dr Keith Peterson that Bu hadn't reported the deaths for some time because there were ... err ... until recently, serious health complications. It took Bu a moment to realise the police weren't there to take him away.

The woman officer, Constable Bradley, made an aside: 'In fact, sir, I think I recognise you from an incident outside the public hospital. You were in a wheelchair.'

Constable Hall gave her a look that Bu knew meant 'How can you *think* you recognise him?'

Nevertheless, Hall added, there were some questions they had to ask.

The officers were mild, probing gently but insistently over certain puzzles regarding Bu's departure and the time lag since the deaths.

He hardly realised what he'd said when it was all over, but his answers must have held true, for the police said there was no further need to trouble him.

When they left, Bu felt an unlikely coolness eddy around him. He wrapped a blanket over his shoulders and crept into a chair. He had the desolate feeling of an ending that had come without notice, without ceremony. *Accident*, they had said: they understood. Just an accident. He sat there for minutes on end, thinking *But who can I tell?* His fingers went to the top of his head. A patch there grew with a slight kink to it: it was wiry, a little darker than the rest. He traced his fingers along each crooked fibre, got to the base, then gave a sharp pull. Each sting and tug was good pain, as if he were digging out an imperfection, clearing away some troublesome, persistent, inner doubt.

Constable Fliss Bradley

FLISS BRADLEY SAT WITH her hand on the police car's ignition key for several seconds before she could start up the engine again.

'Problem?' Hall asked.

'He's not guilty now,' she said.

Hall glanced at her profile, then stared back at the B&B's front entrance. 'But?'

'But a guy like that, how's he going to keep out of trouble?'

'How old would you say he was? Twenty?' He fastened his seatbelt. 'Doesn't matter, I guess. He seemed untouched, to me, either way. Kind of naïve.'

'Or corruptible,' corrected Bradley. 'That kind of innocence, in that kind of face . . .' She shrugged, then started up the car. 'We'll be seeing him again.'

Hall sank back in his seat. 'On TV, maybe.' When that got no reaction, he rolled his head on the headrest so he could gauge Bradley's expression. 'You could tell he's the sasquatch guy, right? That whole thing was a set-up.'

'No bull,' said Bradley, more interested in the turning traffic.

'Yeah. My girlfriend's a friend of one of the flatmates of the journalist who . . .'

'Now *that* doesn't sound like an urban myth.'

'Seriously, I've met her. And *she* says the guy thinks he's a yeti, but he's probably just got some genetic thing. I reckon it could probably be treated with some nip and tuck, a shave and maybe some hormone tablets. As it were.'

'You going to tell that to all the other yeti?'

'Eh?'

Fliss Bradley shook her head. 'Nothing. Just a joke.' But as they wound up the street and she saw the bulky outline of Mount Cargill lift in the distance, she thought of the mountains she'd climbed: peaks in the Southern Alps, the Himalayas, the Canadian Rockies. In her mind's eye she watched, as if from the window of a plane, as a tiny mannikin worked his way over the great white flanks of the mountains. He was lithe, fleet, his mind clear of all the petty ugliness and the outright, twisted violence she'd seen over her fifteen years as a cop. His thoughts were filled with sky, stone, the arc and swoop of a bird's flight, grass fluttering its seedheads like prayer flags over harsh rock. He walked on as if there would never be any need to stop.

'What's up, Brads?' Hall pushed at his unnecessary sunglasses so they sat atop his head.

She sighed. 'Nothing. I just hope that you're right about him, and I'm not. Hope we don't see him again.'

Hall barked a short laugh. 'He sure was no oil painting.'

She shook her head, tiring of him, as usual, before their shift was even halfway finished, and took the car through a right turn, off the hill and down towards the busy student quarter, its streets glittering with broken glass, its stained couches spilling stuffing on wooden verandas, its population of sulky jaywalkers in tight jeans. She could do without the way Hall leered at the young girls, but today it felt like the lesser of two irritations. And if he was distracted, she might be able to summons that image of the Himalayas again, drink from its cold, clarifying silence.

Bu

IT WAS HARD FOR BU not to feel some link between the officers' visit and the sickness that struck him late that night. It was some gut bug, probably picked up from food he'd fished out of a bin at dusk in the Woodhaugh Gardens, when the ducks were tucked into their feather beds and the sparse light on the paddling pool made it black and gelid. The gripe felt like a punishment: his body telling him it had been wrong not to notify the police sooner, wrong to keep the secret he hadn't even wanted to own.

He was ill for nearly six days, retching himself dry, sleeping for hours, occasionally waking up only to wonder whether he should feel grateful that he was in no need of food, or worried about how he could go on like this, what the next foraged meal would do to him, how he'd manage till the money came through: the government benefit seemed to run out all the time.

In his semi-feverish state, the arguments went round and round in his head like trapped mosquitoes. By the end of the six days, the high, whining drill of anxiety had just one question left. *How to live? How to live?*

As he surfaced a little, and managed to keep down some of the milk that Desmond, the B&B owner, kept bringing to the communal kitchen, Bu grew more mentally weary at the thought of having to go back to his night-time scavenging. He told himself he should be brave, go out among ordinary folk again, explore all the wonders he had dreamed of as a child: concerts, markets, circuses, shops, fairs, schools, theatres, playgrounds . . . Yet his heart felt scoured out at the thought of the gaping stares he would attract, the ring of empty space that would form around him, as if his face gave out some poisonous vapour that drove life back.

In the end, it was the hard fact of hunger that made the decision for him, dragging him out, weak under a fat moon. His senses were dulled: he couldn't pick up all the minor changes in the air around him, so a cat startled him by running across his path well before he noticed its scent. He felt he might faint before he found the skip full of old bread behind a bakery. As he climbed out of the massive bin, a car of young guys hooted and yelled at him — maybe half in fright at his balaclava- and glove-clad bulk — so he began a clumsy, depleted jog, telling himself he'd eat as soon as he was safely in his room again.

Gasping with the effort of the run, and with twinges biting at his ankle, he stumbled over the stoop of The Done Inn, still clutching his bread. It was the wrong entrance, he knew, but the last few paces to his own door could have been kilometres, impossible.

Desmond eased his way through the reed curtains, to see who had arrived so late.

'Mate,' he said, over half-rim spectacles that somehow didn't seem to fit with his tattoos, Harley Davidson T-shirt, weathered face, slick dark hair swept back from a widow's peak. 'You look like you took the name of this place literal.'

Then he moved back a small step. 'You all right? Hey, let me give you a hand.' In the stark light of the reception area, Bu could see mould showing through the clear plastic bags of the bread. With a frenzied, involuntary 'No!' he clutched the packets to him, trying to lurch away, but the world skidded. Darkness rushed into his head.

❊ ❊ ❊

WHEN BU CAME TO AGAIN, he was on the floor, but in a new room, with Desmond smoking and reading a paperback book with a cover that matched his T-shirt — another motorbike. His manner barely changed when he saw that Bu was awake. He drew another puff, put out the cigarette, marked his place in his book with a folded sheet of cigarette paper, took a long pull at a mug of tea. 'Morning, mate,' he said, finally. 'You've slept the sleep of the innocent, eh? Right through.'

Bu levered himself up awkwardly on his elbows, pain beating on one side of his head. 'What happened?' he peered at something shining in the corner. Gradually the cube of orange and red assembled into a window, curtains, sunlight burning through.

Desmond scrutinised him. 'You've let yourself get dead beat.' He stood up from his chair in one simple movement that showed how much muscle and power were compacted into his small frame. Bu sensed that he was being deliberately reminded, *I am not afraid*.

After watching him for a moment, the man left the room, saying, 'You'd best get some food down you.'

Soon there were the sounds and achingly good smells of cooking. Bu had to shut his eyes again to stop himself being overwhelmed: together the hot butter scent and the sun were too much. Desmond came in with a small plate of scrambled eggs and a mug that steamed with peppermint and honey. He helped Bu up to a small table.

'Easy, easy,' he warned, quickly handing Bu a fork. 'Slow down, mate.' Bu dropped his head, embarrassed, then he found a smile stealing up as the food in his belly sent out its tendrils of warmth.

When he sopped up the last of the butter and eggs on his plate with a piece of wholemeal toast, he nodded to Desmond. 'Thank you.'

They sat in expectant silence. Bu knew the questions would come; Desmond, probably, knew that the answers wouldn't be easily given. Bu looked around the room: at the posters and framed photos of motorbikes, a calendar with a picture of a man inside the gigantic curled hand of a wave; a glass cabinet filled with odd bits and pieces.

They both spoke at once.

'How d-hid I get here?'

'I call that my museum.'

An abrupt pause, then, 'I dragged you by the shoulders.'

'They are eh-special, those things?'

'You're a heavy bastard. Even when you don't eat.'

Bu looked at the floor.

'What's this all about, eh mate? I hear you come and go. Or I see the lights go on and off. *And* I got a sixth sense about who's in and who's not after umpteen years of running this place. You're never out for long, are you? And only at night.'

Des swung up from his seat, went to the kitchen and came back with six loaves of bread, which were now completely covered in a rash of mould. The memory of his dread that they might be taken from him came back to Bu with raw humiliation.

'Why you acting like a thief, hey? Sneaking about at night.

And getting yourself in a bad way. You'll turn yourself not right in the head if you carry on like a hairy vampire.' There wasn't a flicker of regret from Des at the words. 'Come on mate, out with it. What mess are you in? Nothing could surprise me. I've had all sorts through here. Trannies, priests, cops, prostitutes. Even one of them bloody animal imitators.'

'Animal — what?'

'Imitators. You know. That lot who get operations so they look like cats or lizards or whatever the hell else they fancy. Thought you were one of them, first, didn't I? Thought there might be a bloody convention on.'

Bu put a hand to the side of his skull, his earlier headache ghosting there again.

'We get plenty of convention types here, too, y'see. For university gigs. Some of them seem a bit put out when they realise I'm not going to wipe their arses for them. I say, "Excuse me, but going by the name, this ain't the bloody Ritz. And it seems to me you *know* where your own arse is, seeing as how you're up it already."'

Desmond rolled himself another cigarette, using tobacco from a packet in his trouser pocket. He tapped it on the table.

'A letter came for you this morning,' he said. 'Big fat one. Return address sounds like a lawyer's.' He eyed Bu. 'You in trouble with the courts?'

'Courts . . . no. No trouble. May I eh-see it?'

Desmond quirked up his mouth, shrugged. 'Course. It's yours, innit.' He left the room, brought back the envelope and watched unabashedly while Bu read the contents.

Bu's hands shook a little as he smoothed out the pages. He raised his eyes to Desmond's. 'Family papers, and a letter. About money,' he said quietly, then tucked everything away again.

Yet Des must have caught sight of the cheque. He winked. 'That's your way out of here, eh?'

Bu stared. Realisation opened in him like bubbles rising in water. 'Yes. Of course. You are right.' He clutched the letter tightly to him, leaned across the table. 'How d-ho I . . .?'

Desmond lit the cigarette. 'If you want help, you tell me what you're running from.' He drew smoke into his lungs, blew out. 'Then maybe, I help. For a price.'

Bu watched him. 'How much?'

'Negotiable. But you spill the beans. I like to know what I'm getting myself into.'

Bu's hands dabbed at the knees of his trousers. He tried to find the few-enough words that Des might have patience for. 'I'm running from . . . the people who want photos. The news people.'

Desmond didn't lose a beat. 'Thought so. You saw the papers I've been leaving you? Thought you might need to know what was up with all that.' He sat back in his seat. 'I recognised you in them, didn't I?' He waited, as if expecting congratulations. 'Just thought someone'd got the wrong end of the stick about you, that's all. Like I say, I've had one of them animal imitators in here — well, two really — they was a couple, but he looked more of a dog than her.' He grinned, showing a jumble of bad, yellow teeth. 'I figured you'd want to be left alone. Thing is, in my business, in a city this small, if y'can't keep quiet about who's staying here for the odd, you know, this an' that, you ain't going far. Customers'll dry up quick. So I like to pride myself on my *discretion*.' He savoured the word.

'Mind you, the pictures in the newspaper — they look nothing like you, to be honest. Those artist's impressions, they look more like — well, thugs, really. Boneheads.'

He sat back in his chair to take the full measure of Bu, then sucked at his teeth. 'You've done a good job, mate. Lying low, I mean. In a place like this. Must be the bush knowledge, eh? Nah, only kidding. The papers and all are saying you were a beat-up. Well, not you, but the yeti.'

Bu's eyes sheered away from his.

'Actually, they're not saying much any more. The story's sort of gone off the boil over the past week or so. As they do, when the next film star ODs or drink-drives.' He rubbed at an itch on his nose. 'Yeah, last Saturday, maybe, was the last time I heard anything. It was all over the news then, mate. All sorts about you. There was a group of boffins — zoologists and what-not — on the telly arguing about whether the yeti could still be around. Some reckoned the stories about yeti might originally have come from some man-ape or ape-man — they don't even know which way round it goes — but that's all died out now. Would've been some sort of anthra-logical cousin of ours. But for there to be a yeti here — well, one of them said, short of you being smuggled in by someone, like they say about the puma or whatever it is in Canterbury — sorry, mate, but impossible. Unless you're — I mean it's — a throwback. Like that Turkish family where every one of the kids walks on all fours. Heard of them?'

Desmond grinned again, as if Bu would see the fun of it all — the great, fascinating joke. 'Like I say, there was all sorts going on about you. Some young girl up in Auckland's got a website raising money to protect you. Should give her our address, eh? She's hooked up with that group, whatch-a-ma-call-them, the Aotearoa Animal Activists.' Desmond gave a jungle yell, beating his chest, then grinned again. 'They say they want to liberate you. Don't ask me what they mean by that. It's not like you're some battery chook they can set free into a nice backyard, now, is it?'

Bu fingered the rough patch of hair on his scalp, gave a swift tug.

Des frowned at him. 'Doesn't that hurt?'

Bu shook his head.

Desmond sat quietly for a while. 'There was more, too, mate. Apparently there's been some unexplained stock deaths round Southland way. Sheep and cattle savaged. Most people reckon it's a pair of stray dogs but a couple of fruit-loops on talkback were saying police should investigate links to sightings of the southern sasquatch.' Desmond picked a fleck of tobacco from his tongue. 'Not exactly pretty out there for someone like you to go wandering around, eh?'

He stared at Bu with gritted teeth, as if he'd already bitten down on some unchangeable decision. 'But you can't carry on like some kind of bloody zombie of the night. What is it you want help with?'

It was all Bu could do not to bolt right then. He just wanted to leave and start again, where none of the cameras and questions would follow him; where nobody would want him to change, until he had found out for himself what his mother-woman's stories meant. He wanted to go into the mountains of the north, the great spaces on the other side of the world. He wanted to walk there, clamber over the rock, taste the dust, read the marks of wolf, marmot, yak, listen to the wind, climb higher into the wild realm of snow and ice. He wanted to know the place, that edge of the world where Lillian's stories had grown. There might be Nepali people who would know him, be unafraid and welcome him in. Lead him to others, like himself: a tribe of Bu, of yeti.

'I need help to leabe the country.'

Desmond stubbed out his cigarette, squinting at Bu in a way that made him think he was going to turn him down.

'Too easy,' he said. 'It's fate that you and me met. Traveller's cheques, plane ticket. I can sort the lot.' He frowned at the ashtray, as if some complication had come to mind even so. 'You got a passport?'

Bu's heart faltered. 'No. But I trabelled on my mother-woman's, when I was eh-small.'

'That in the papers from the lawyers?'

'Err . . . yes.'

'Got a birth certificate?'

'No.'

Desmond nodded. 'Thought as much. Folks in a fix never do. Never mind. I've got a mate up north. Works in immigration. I'll have a word. Give us y'mother's passport, and we'd better get you a fresh photo downtown. Should be able to sort something out. This mate owes me, and I know he's got a few string-pulls owed him.' He let a grin flit up again. 'It'll cost you, of course. Meantime, if there's things you need, and you don't want to go out on your own during the day, just ask. I'll buy in food and so on, if you like. We'll sort the money as we go.'

Bu nodded. 'Thank you,' he mumbled.

'No problem.' Desmond leaned over, gripping him on the upper arm. 'You keep it together. I been down in the black places, too, mate. No need for it. We've all got to help each other out, eh?' He flexed his bicep clownishly, then slapped Bu on the shoulder. 'Right. I got jobs to do. Have to see a man about a right dog's breakfast. Dodgy plumbing in the other block. You leave me a shopping list and I'll get on to those other things.'

❋ ❋ ❋

ALTHOUGH HE HAD DECIDED to leave, Bu still wondered what it would be like to meet Sandrine again, to walk past her in the compact city centre when he was on some errand, as when he went out in daylight to get a passport photo taken. (Des came with him, and though there were no catcalls, no laughter on the streets, the man who took the photo seemed to spend a long time staring through the camera each time before the flash went. When the photos were done, he wouldn't meet Bu's eye, spoke only to Des.) Des had told him Dunedin was a small place, just 100,000 permanent residents, with another 20,000 or so during university terms. He said he was always bumping into people he knew. But to Bu, raised with just two people in his world, the numbers seemed almost too huge to fit in his head. He wondered if Sandrine was trying to trace him. How hard would it be? He knew that if he stayed here, it would because he wished for one particular thing: the impossible. Better to run, better to keep away from the stab of hope. Yet he was unsettled as he waited for the friend Des talked about to 'come up with the goods', and was made more so by the travel books Des bought and borrowed for him, and the pictures of Nepal he showed him on his computer.

'Shall we look up yeti?' Des asked once, a glint in his

eye. But Bu knew now to call his bluff. He must pretend to think he was a man. There would be less curiosity, then; less eagerness to persuade him that his belief — his very *self* — was false, his travels to the origins of his mother-woman's story were just, in one of her phrases, a *pipe dream*. He knew it wasn't a pipe dream. It was the way to truth.

Though Desmond was keeping him supplied with everything he needed, a terrible restlessness stirred in Bu. He still slipped out at night, compulsively walking the streets, clad in his habitual camouflage gear, trying to exhaust himself so that sleep would come more easily, with its relief from his questions about his upcoming departure, and its balm for thinking of Sandrine. Her name kept returning like a whisper deep in his head, heat along his limbs. It filled him randomly, suddenly, with a vigour that made him want to run down the street, mad and racing — away from seeing, in his mind's eye, the curve of her neck, the line of her collarbone, the swell of her breasts.

Over the next fortnight the sun set earlier and earlier so he didn't have to wait so long for the evening's generous disguise. He constantly tried new routes: along the cold valleys; out to the harbour; once staying out so late that he saw the sun come up and hit the glass panes of houses on the far slope, as if an entire hillside had been set on fire: a sight that made him want to turn and run. Other nights he wandered up hills and through the green belt, often leaving the road and weaving his way through the bush, persuading himself that he was back on the southwest coast, trying not to let the occasional sweep of headlights along the edge of the reserve ruin the illusion. A favourite resting place was the Woodhaugh Gardens, down on the flat, fifteen minutes' or so walk from the steep street where The Done Inn perched. Very rarely did anyone pass through here in the dark. Bu liked to sit there, by the children's paddling pool or the pond, and listen to the ducks chuttering and creaking to each other in their sleep. Or he leaned on the low fence to gaze down at the Leith River, feeling strangely calmed as the water fanned and folded the moon's reflection.

On a Sunday night, as a light rain began to mist through the trees, he levered himself up from a bench and made his way back to the B&B. Only one or two people scurried past, hidden by coats and umbrellas themselves, so when his balaclava grew uncomfortably damp, he risked pushing it halfway up his forehead for the rest of the route home, though he kept his hood on.

As he came alongside a Thai restaurant on a street corner, he was aware of a sleek, low-slung, silver car growling slowly past him and heading south, but his attention was quickly taken by a gust of wind. He stopped under the restaurant's awning to zip his coat up higher. He glanced in the window. As if his imagination had polished the idea of Sandrine for so long that finally it conjured her up, he looked straight at the table where she sat alone, reading a menu.

He pressed a gloved hand to the window, then had to clear the condensation of his breath from the glass so he could still see her. His movements caught a waitress's eye. In disbelief she slapped one hand to her mouth and slopped the contents of a water pitcher onto the floor. Sandrine, startled now too, looked over to the window, then stared at him with an unexpected stillness. He pushed his hood right back. He saw — and heard, slightly muffled — the waitress scream, but at last Sandrine slid back her chair and stood up. Faber appeared from the rear of the restaurant, reached her and cupped a hand to her waist questioningly. His easy intimacy dropped a knife clean through Bu's heart. Forgetting to cover his face again, he turned back to the street with an involuntary, guttural yawl. He caught sight of the silver car that had passed him earlier coming back the other way. It pulled up to idle beside the pavement, a cluster of young men's faces under peaked caps and beanies pressing forward at the windows, gawping at him. Trouble prickled between his shoulder blades, stung his eyes. He swung away, wrenching down the balaclava and jerking up his hood.

He heard Sandrine behind him. 'Bu! Wait!'

The sight of her running out into the rain seemed to animate the men in the car. 'Freak-boy!' one of them called. 'Seen you before. Saw you with that Chinese chick the other day. You still chasing skirt? Or you only like them coma-ed?' His friends dutifully laughed.

Some of the words made no sense to Bu, but the menace in them was strong as the taste of blood. He saw Sandrine whip around to the car, body pitched forward, though Faber was trying to remonstrate with her and pull her back. 'Tough guys, aren't you, sitting there and yelling out of windows?' she said. 'Too bloody cowardly to get out though, aren't you?'

'Fiery little thing,' grinned one of them, showing gold-rimmed teeth. Some memory of the man fizzed but didn't quite take. Bu felt that he should say something, something to get them away from Sandrine, but his mind fumbled.

'He could crush you in his fists. You and your weedy sidekicks, but he's *too good* for that, isn't he? He's a better man than you'll ever be. He'd never hurt anyone. He . . .'

'Pussy, pussy, pussy.'

Faber raised his voice. 'Sandrine, just leave it. They're not worth it. Let's just concentrate on Bu.'

Let's just concentrate on Bu. She had to be told. And she was an *us*. He lurched around on his heels.

'Bu! Bu, wait!'

'Boo — boo-hoo!' called another man from the window. 'Don't cry, it's only a talking carpet!'

The car's engine roared and throbbed, and suddenly the car was spinning off, turning around then coming back at Bu over the kerb. He leapt out of its way, as Faber yelled, 'Morons, I've got your plates.'

Bu's stomach wrung with pain. He didn't want to be defended, least of all by Sandrine's lover. He could smell him on her, as if her own scent had switched — and nectar could give out the sourness of onion weed. He swung his head, blind and bull-heavy, and lumbered away, up the hill, hauled himself down a side path and skirted around the back of a house, taking a fox's route up the inner city hillside. Vaulting over fence after fence, he was almost nimble with urgency now, as he wove up Warrender, fled along Queen's Drive, back down several streets and then uphill again. Finally he found himself slumped next to a wheelie bin in an unfamiliar backyard at the end of his own street, lungs searing, ears ringing, but sure, at last, that the silver car couldn't have tracked him.

He had to catch his breath before he could carry on, but even when his chest had stopped heaving, he found himself hunched there still, driving the heel of his hand into his forehead to a rhythmic, '*Eh-stupid cub, you eh-stupid cub.*'

A flood of light from the house's back porch and the scrape of footsteps made him flinch. A thin woman stood there, limp umbrella in one hand, rubbish bag in the other.

'Oh God,' she said to herself, 'I thought it was him.'

Bu started to scramble up, ready to sprint again. He felt a strange, backwards gliding sensation when he realised that the initial look of fright on the woman's face was ebbing away, to be replaced by confusion. He hesitated.

'Eh-some men were after me,' he said. 'I d-hidn't mean . . .'

She dropped the rubbish bag and touched fingertips to the right side of her head. 'He's really gone and done it now.' She kept her fingers pressed delicately to her temples and bent at the knees while apparently trying to keep her head still. 'It's all right,' she counselled herself. Moving carefully, she approached the wheelie bin, lifted the lid and got rid of the rubbish bag.

Deliberately not looking at Bu, body curved defensively, she shuffled back to the porch. When she neared the back step, she turned to look straight at him, where he stood — at his full height now — in the pool of light that spilled from the house.

Yet when the woman spoke, it was in an abstracted way, as if Bu were merely her reflection. 'I've got to get out. Got to.' Her voice made him think of something wooden and worn: a table with years of burns and stains, scribbles and nicks gouged into it. It seemed too old for her. And although her skin had none of Sandrine's sheen and softness, Bu could still marvel at how smooth it was. Even as he noticed this, he was already registering something else.

Now that she stood directly under the porch light and its stuttering halo of moths, he saw the bruising on her collarbone. She tucked her long brown hair behind her ears, still talking to herself, 'Maybe he's right. Maybe I am crazy.' She checked nervously over her shoulder and before her hair fell forward again, Bu glimpsed a long scratch at the side of her neck. She began to weep, but as if she barely noticed.

Impulsively, recklessly, he stepped forward, reached out and lifted her hair again.

The woman's eyes told Bu that she didn't care any more whether he was a figment of her distress, or some unexplained visitation. She looked at him with terrible resignation. The edges of the scratch were seamed with red where infection was spidering along her skin. He had seen something similar on his father-man's arm, after a spike from a thorn: cellulitis, his mother-woman called it, the germs only needing a pinprick entry point.

'Eh-someone must eh-see this. It needs medicine.'

'He'll kill me next time,' she said, from a long way off.

Trying to bring her back again, he cupped her head in one hand. 'Who?'

She closed her eyes and he felt the slightest relaxation of her weight as she leaned a little more into his palm. The seconds swelled.

'Len,' she whispered. 'My husband. I make him angry. He used to be so . . .' Bu felt a rush of anticipation and a honeyed kind of fear tingle in the fork of him. He moved his thumb slowly over her cheek now, wishing her sadness were a coating he could lift off like dust. He traced the planes of her face as if his own actions hypnotised him, and yet how vividly awake he was.

He didn't quite understand why there was the wetness of tears in the woman's eyes as one of her hands stroked his forehead up and over, up and over. She gave a small sound, a hum that drew him closer. With a warm shock he felt his body and hers press against one another. She murmured again, then the back door clicked open and a man stood there, the biggest he'd ever seen, pale eyebrows and dome-like head gleaming in the porch light.

'What the f —'

The woman sprang from Bu, staring at him in mortification, seeing at last that he was real. 'Len,' she said, as the man came towards her. 'Please. Please don't.'

Bu spun around and loped away, into the safety of the shadows. Yet from the street he could still hear the abuse the man flung at his wife. 'You cunt.'

Alice and Rennie, Dunedin

ON A STREET NEAR The Done Inn, in a house adjacent to the roughcast villa with the peeling white paint and the chipped terracotta pots of geraniums, the young neighbours called the police. The couple, postgrad students in a rented dive, had begun to suspect just two weeks after they'd moved in that the man next door hit his wife. There were fights that carried over the fence and into their own rooms: blurred, but unmistakable.

They'd seen the woman just last week, with a bruised face, weeping at the end of the bar in a local pub, while her barmaid friend brought her coffee and a muffin and passed her a sheaf of paper napkins for her tears. The woman made out that she didn't recognise them when they stood shuffling their feet at the counter, shocked into silence by her face. When the barmaid took their orders, Alice asked, stupidly, 'Is she all right?' Then, as if in explanation, 'She's our neighbour.'

The barmaid swiped at some invisible marks on the counter with a cloth. 'Kindest thing you could do right now is give her some privacy.' Her tone said Alice's naïvety was an embarrassment. When Alice slipped over the money for the drinks, she felt as if she was offering payment as an apology. Only then did the barmaid lower her voice, in flat, yet forgiving, complicity. 'Some arseholes, eh?'

Rennie and Alice took their glasses to a tucked away corner, feigning not to notice when the woman left.

The fight that made Rennie and Alice call the police started well after sundown. They were both wide awake after too much black coffee, still trying to get some preparation done for undergrad tutorials they were teaching the next day. After she'd left the coffee pot on an element, Alice had to open windows and the back door to get rid of the smell of burning. Exposing the house to the air was like throwing a volume switch. Rennie immediately came to join her in the back doorway, his arm going around her shoulders protectively.

Before, when the fracas had woken them at night, the darkness had been paralysing, as if what they heard was somehow happening in the underwater realm of dreams. Their hazy, disoriented selves, drenched in sleep, sometimes fogged with wine, might have been inventing, or distorting something harmless.

Yet now the shouts, the sickening thuds and the high, splintering sound of something breaking, filled them both with shame. They'd helped to let this go on, hadn't they? By being too timid, too wet behind the ears, to take a stance and act.

'We have to do something.' Alice started down the steps.

'Alice, no.'

'What?' She whirled angrily on Rennie.

'We can't go over there ourselves. I'll call the police.'

After Rennie put the call through, Alice shrugged on an old jersey to try to stop the chill working deeper under her skin. Rennie kept vigil at their bedroom window, standing where he could see the street and the neighbours' letterbox. When he made quickly for the door once the police arrived, and went out to accompany them to the neighbouring house, Alice felt sick that her lack of faith had pushed him to make his face known to the vicious bully inside.

'Ren,' she called out, to bring him back, but he ignored her.

The police gestured for him to stay away. They could hear it all too. But by the time they got inside, the man had vanished. He must have fled through the back door and out across the tangle of blackberry and wild grasses that grew in the cramped yard, skidding down the huge clay bank, then on to who knows where — to hide out in the green belt, hitch a ride to one of the small coastal settlements outside the town boundaries, maybe hole up in some condemned house in the city's neglected south.

The offender, police called him — not the woman's husband, nor her boyfriend — when they came to question Alice and Rennie the next day.

'She says the attacker was unknown to her,' one of the officers revealed. He was a fit, trim-looking man with a grey, bristling hair cut and a way of writing quick lines and dashes on the air when he spoke.

'Unknown?' Rennie pushed his fringe out of his eyes, looking at Alice as if she might be able to explain.

'Did you see the assailant?' asked the police officer.

'I recognised his voice,' Alice answered, dismissing the misunderstanding. 'The things he called her . . . We've heard them fight before, you see. And we've seen him a couple of times — out in the yard, or just, you know, coming and going.'

'Can you describe him?'

Rennie nodded for Alice to go first.

'He's much taller than Rennie — so over six foot. He's solid — muscly. He shaves his head sometimes. He's pale, has sort of white-blond eyebrows. He'd be in his forties, I'd say.'

Rennie watched the officer write on a pad. 'He's nearly

always in black jeans and a black fleece vest thing over a pale blue shirt — some kind of work outfit, I think. Don't know who he works for, though.'

'Did either of you actually see him on the night of the disturbance?'

Alice waited, hoping Rennie would say he'd caught sight of him through the bedroom window: pacing, pointing at his wife, hurling something. Or that he'd noticed his shape, then yes, definitely his face, as the man made his way to the front of the house, but then turned and ran as soon as he saw Rennie, or the patrol car.

'No.' It was like an admission of failure.

Alice's hand worried at her leather watch strap. 'Neither did I.'

They could both see their usefulness was over, although the officer ran through a few more questions, then thanked them courteously for their time, telling them to contact him if they happened to remember anything else.

❋ ❋ ❋

ALICE COULDN'T LET RENNIE touch her when they went to bed that evening. She kept thinking of the woman, the fact that she'd been interviewed from her bed at public hospital. It was as if the man was outside the house, a thick clump of hate bulked in the dark, squatting under the windowsill, clammy breath sneaking through the gaps in the weatherboards.

Over the next few days he seemed to be between her and Rennie still. Although they stuck to their usual daily rhythms of cooking together, walking to seminars together, taking it as a given that when one was invited somewhere, the other would tag along, their conversation was cool and they had trouble meeting each other's eyes.

Then a description and an accompanying police sketch of the attacker appeared in the paper two or three days after the woman was interviewed.

The report said the assailant was well over six foot, had a heavy, overhanging eyebrow ridge, a large jaw and long, dark-blond hair growing over the entire surface of his face, neck and the backs of his hands.

'What?' Alice cried aloud at the student café table in The Link.

Rennie's head lifted from an academic article he was highlighting; he turned the newspaper so he could read it.

'Shit. Why would she do this?'

Alice rested her elbows on the table, gripped them tightly with both hands, trying to stop the unexpected smarting in her eyes. 'She's protecting that bastard.'

'Yeah, but I mean, why? With such a transparent lie?'

She looked away, unable to answer coherently. She bent closer to the newspaper to examine the description and identikit picture again.

Rennie's arm went around her. 'Insane,' he said.

'No one will believe this.' In her tone was an apology to Rennie, and she let his arm rest where it was. The frost that separated them melted away, yet the relief and warmth could only spread so far.

Overnight, stories of the southern sasquatch had set in and they had a new, punitive tone that made Alice feel a seeping unease. It followed her throughout the next few days, well after the newspaper was folded away, or the radio turned off. She walked her own street now with a strangely haunted feeling, as if the very way the light fell from the sky on those houses, their tiny, grudging courtyards, was untoward.

Bu

PERHAPS BU SHOULD HAVE been set more on edge by the second police visit, even though there was a sense, in their questions, that they were visiting reluctantly — that it was part of a routine they had to follow, despite their own better instincts. When the hostel cleaner, the B&B's security camera footage, and Des all backed up Bu's alibi — that he'd been home about half an hour before the police overheard the disturbance — Constable Fliss Bradley said, 'Sorry to trouble you again, sir. We suspect the woman is disoriented, confused. There are competing descriptions of the assailant. It sometimes happens after these things, sadly.' The two officers exchanged a look and a nod which conveyed there was more that they wouldn't, or couldn't, discuss. They left curtly, off to some other line of inquiry.

When they had gone, Des gave Bu a hard, knowing stare. 'Trouble's got a nose for you. You're best off out of here, eh mate?'

It was true. Their visit made Bu feel his departure for the north was even more necessary and urgent. Yet both the knowledge that he was leaving — and the knowledge of how a woman's body could glide beneath his hands — also gave him a loose kind of confidence. Two days later, when Desmond finally brought Bu his tickets, passport, foreign currency and Travellers Cheques, and took his fee — telling him to make sure he didn't sleep in the next day or he'd miss his flight, reassuring him that he'd drive Bu to the airport — Bu knew he wouldn't be able to sleep at all.

He went over and over the little booklet of his passport, fretting about what the inside of a real plane would be like, how people would stare; he kept checking the airline information, counting the money, reading the fine print on the Travellers Cheques, flicking through his travel guides again, then pacing in a nervous excitement so irrational and distracting that by midnight it had driven him right out of the B&B.

In his routine disguise, he slipped out of his room, following an urge to walk the streets one last time: a quiet yet defiant, celebratory farewell. Nobody would see him in the dark, he told himself; nobody would recognise him through his camouflage gear.

When he turned away down his street, his back to her house, he thought of the sad, porch-light woman, yet only in a hasty, furtive way: as if even the idea of her might bring him more trouble — or send her more grief.

He wanted to go to all the places he had been in this city, record each spot, really see each one: to rehearse his own story for himself, so that one day, he could tell it more clearly. And he wanted to say to each landmark, *See how strong I grow?* He could barely acknowledge to himself that the city, the listener in his mind, was really Sandrine. Even the porch-light woman hadn't filled her absence the way he had expected.

He would be quick. Although there were hours before Desmond would call for him, he knew that the same jumpy excitement that had driven him out into the streets wouldn't let him linger there, either, and before long his thoughts would begin to fidget with worry.

He made his way along the empty streets, then through a thin stretch of remnant native bush that made the green belt. The familiar sound of cracking twigs, and memories of trying to mimic patches of darkness in games of hide and seek with his father-man, gave him a burst of nostalgia and happiness that sped him down the hill.

Under a moon netted with cloud, he passed the bakery where he had stolen bread from the dumpster. He intended to head towards one of the supermarkets from which he had also spirited away spilled food, broken containers. First, though, he would revisit the Woodhaugh Gardens. He wanted to watch the ducks huddled near the pond, grateful for their silent, companionable acceptance of him.

Tonight two ducks slept on the grass near the main barbecue area, perhaps driven away from the pond side by rivals. Bu settled for a bench against the low wall, thinking this was far enough, if he wanted to pace out the full route of his night wanderings before morning.

Almost as soon as he sat, two men in hoods appeared along a path that led through trees from the road to the barbecue area and toilet block. Bu froze. He tried to tell himself to get up and leave right then, but the men seemed oblivious to their surroundings. He would wait it out for a bit: they might turn back. They were arguing, voices slurred and loud. There was the smell of drink, and a trace of something unfamiliar but acrid, reminding him somehow of the cleaning fluid used at the B&B. One man, as big as the one Bu had seen in the porch light the other night, was carrying a piece of wood, a broken fencepost maybe, saying the pills he'd taken hadn't worked. The other was telling him to settle down, did he have no idea what had just happened back there, they'd be lucky if bloody Christie didn't come after them, he was a total psycho, owned firearms, that was what really gave him the shits . . .

'It was just a bit of beer down that chick's front, Jonno. It'll wash out. Stupid dizzy slu—'

'— it was what you were doing with your hand down her dress. Christie's going off his nut. She's his wife. He's going to come after you. And if he doesn't, he'll be grassing on you for that other crap. Tell them he's seen you.' Jonno grabbed his friend by the shirt. 'Not that way, this. He'll guess the other . . .'

The big man grabbed back, angry. 'He won't come after us, y'stupid tosser. And if he does, *I'll* do *him*, won't I?' He brandished the fencepost.

Jonno pulled away, coming out well into the open now. 'Get stuffed. Find some other suck to hide you from the cops. I'm off.'

He stopped in his tracks at the sight of Bu's shape shouldering the dark.

Jonno

'SHITE.' JONNO'S VOICE went thick with a mixture of awe and fear. 'Len! That's it. Look, that's him,' he said. He was thinking, *How would a mutant like that expect to hide in a town this size, even in the dark*, and said again, 'Him!' Len had his back turned; was taking a leak up the side of the public access barbecue. Jonno meant, *It's what they're calling the sasquatch: the one in the papers, the one fingered for the number you did on your woman* . . . He thought the obvious thing would be to run from a bastard that big, but nothing was obvious to Len right then. Jonno could almost see how lights popped on and off in his mate's head, how the night ballooned and warped, the way his hands grew huge to him, throbbing with power.

Len saw the creature. It stared back at him. Then, as if anyone even looking at Len for too long was asking for a fight, he went for it on a berserk, hate-filled high, a Catherine wheel of boots and fencepost, grunting out words with each blow.

In fragmented panic and misunderstanding, Jonno hung back for a split second before he realised how badly Len had lost it. Then at last he hauled on Len's shoulders, yelling. But he was so far gone. The thing he'd attacked shielded its face from the blows, and while Jonno was pulling at Len, it bellowed, and with a horrible, lurching step, turned in a circle as if trying to work out which way to run. Huge, but it didn't know how to fight. It could have dropped its shoulder and bowled Len, bowled both of them, but it just stood there dazed, chest heaving, muzzle stretched in a grimace of disbelief as the rain of blows paused while Jonno lugged Len back. Len easily broke free, and swung at Jonno first, knocking him off his feet so that he could be left alone to finish the job.

Jonno picked himself up and ran at the sound of wood meeting skull. Out on the street corner, under the lights of the Willowbank Dairy, he put a call through to 111 on his cellphone. 'There's been a beating,' he said, but not what instinct told him, that help might come too late.

Bu

BU WISHED THE MOON would warm him, as the sun could. He felt its cool light like a palm over his eyes. He couldn't see it fully: just a broken gleam, as if through gaps between fingers. He wondered briefly where he was, wished he were lying on the patch of grass near the red clover, nasturtiums and evening primrose his mother-woman grew beside her herbs, wished he were watching mountainous clouds in an immense sky that told him how vast the world really was. He strained to hear the cook-pook-cook of the bantams, the music box phrase of bellbirds, the sound of his father-man's tools chipping away at the last minutes between morning and lunchtime.

Although he could not get warm, he found a small bead of clarity deep in his mind. Like a magnifying glass that focused his thoughts into a steady ray, it burnt away the doubt that people's questions had bred in him. He knew now, far down inside himself, what in fact he had always known. He would never be like one of those bare-skins. It was sad, but no matter how much he loved his parent-folk, he was not one of their kind.

The clarity helped him as he strained to catch the warmth that the sun had once stirred in him. He had the sensation of trying to remember a vivid, gliding happiness from a dream, before he was fully awake, even as the tale it told lost definition and colour, bled away into the dirt hard beneath his head.

Too cold, now. Too cold.

Professor Caroline Braze

SOMETIMES THE WHEELS in an institution turn with a beautiful efficiency, if the need is pressing enough. Keith Peterson and Caroline Braze acted quickly to make the right calls, click on the right buttons, fill in the right forms, so that a team of pathologists, geneticists and endocrinologists could examine Bu's massive, damaged body thoroughly. Just forty-eight hours after she had been notified of the death, Professor Braze was on a flight from the capital to Dunedin, to meet with colleagues for their initial briefing.

As she walked into the small meeting room set aside in the endocrinology department, a light sweat made her shirt cling to her back. The unreadable faces and the stillness in the room did nothing to help her relax.

She'd expected this to be a good, lively discussion. She'd worked with some of these people before, and this was a thoroughly unprecedented, internationally significant situation. She glanced from face to face, the eyes cast down in diffidence, or perhaps in the sort of respectful deference she'd expect from students, not from colleagues.

'Caroline, how was your flight?' A lean man with a grey-specked moustache cupped her briefly by the elbow and gestured to a chair. You could always rely on Paul.

'Fine, thank you.' She beamed back at him gratefully, and he brought her a coffee from the automatic dispenser. He seemed to have nominated himself as a kind of host-cum-chairman: he welcomed in another senior pathologist, helped him to a tea, then sat down, pulling up the arms of his navy blue jersey as he said, 'Well, given that Jean Silvio can't make it, that's everyone now. Though, taking latest events into account, I'm afraid absences aren't quite so significant any more.'

A series of glances quickly travelled around the room, as those already in the know tried to work out who else was too.

Caroline pulled the sides of her boxy red jacket a little closer. 'Some obstacle? What's happened?'

'It's difficult to say exactly how, at this stage,' Paul shuffled some papers in front of him, a pinched look on his face, 'but the body of the individual we're all meeting to discuss is — ah — no longer accounted for.'

Silence.

Caroline stared at him. 'Disappeared?'

'I'm afraid so. I —'

'Some administrative balls-up.' Caroline pushed her coffee cup away. 'It'll be something simple. Someone's mixed up the labels in the morgue. Or misread them.' She leaned over and snapped open her briefcase so that she could find her ID card. 'I'll head down there.'

'Caroline, it won't help.' Paul lifted up a close-typed piece of paper from the sheaf he had on the table in front of him. 'This was left taped to the morgue door this morning. It's been printed out from the web.' He passed it to Caroline first, though a few heads craned to read it with her.

<http://Aotearoa.Animal.Activists/news_rescue_maero_liberated_in_death>

Aotearoa Animal Activists have received the following anonymous message:

On the night of Sunday the 4th of May, we of the Southern Peace Militia rescued the mortal remains of our cousin, known to some of us as the maero or sasquatch of the south.

Dunedin and Christchurch comrades received word that the body of this tragic figure was to undergo dissection for medical research purposes.

It is our view that this research was unauthorised as our cousin did not agree to any after-life procedure. The issue here is one of universal individual rights and consent. We all have the right to have our bodies treated with respect, dignity and according to our last will and testaments. Nowhere has there been any mention of what our cousin would have wanted. He died from a brutal beating, abandoned and alone. He did not sign any documents. It was our duty to give him the dignity of a decent committal service.

Thanks to our close informant, after we heard of the intentions for our noble cousin, we swiftly mobilised and gained entry to the morgue, through means we cannot disclose for fear of reprisals. We removed the body. Rest assured we treated our noble cousin in the most respectful way possible in the circumstances. We removed him from the land of his suffering and in a symbolic act of liberation in death we held a dawn burial at sea. On board we had a qualified celebrant who was able to conduct a very powerful and moving ceremony.

We feel that the treatment of our maero/sasquatch cousin highlights the despicable attitude in modern society towards all our fellow creatures. All beings deserve the right to live and die free from the tyranny of our species.

Remember, the only thing in the way of total animal liberty is your fear. Face it, erase it, replace it with salvation! The planet's animals need you today.

Aotearoa Animal Activists — Southern Peace Militia

'Jesus,' said Caroline. She was still staring at the sheet of paper, but her mind had locked on an image of the sea as she had seen it from the plane early that morning. Miles and miles of changeable ocean had stretched beneath her plane, its blue-grey depths almost unimaginable to a timid swimmer.

She bent forward to rest her forehead in her hand, something between delayed vertigo and motion sickness hitting her in this stuffy, inauspicious meeting room. And she knew that if she looked up, she'd only see her own utter disappointment reflected in all the faces around the room.

Sandrine Moreau

SANDRINE HAD A CALL from a work colleague shortly after she'd arrived home at the end of her shift. Her foot was aching, her head throbbing after a bad day, yet the insistence of both paled as she heard what he said. Her hand flew to her chest as if her heart might startle from its roost, and she sat quickly on one of the kitchen chairs to steady herself. The moment she put the phone down, it rang again. This time it was Keith Peterson.

'Do you know how it happened?' Numbness seeped into her hands. 'Yes, yes. Thanks for letting me know. Yes, fine. I'll be fine. And you?' As if she were listening through a thick glass wall, she heard Keith tell her that he felt he was grieving for someone he knew better than he could really claim. That it was as if he'd lost a rare opportunity to understand the splitting and masking caused by trauma.

Sandrine tried to keep up as he confided that Bu had taught him more than he'd realised, and that this whole experience had made him decide to concentrate entirely on adolescent psychiatry. Head still ringing with shock, she found Keith's unexpected warmth and openness hard to take on board. Stupidly, she nodded down the phone, but he didn't seem to notice that she'd gone quiet on the other end.

Eventually Sandrine excused herself, then hung up and sat for several minutes, staring out the window to the harbour. On the water, flocks of shadows raced towards her like live things, as if more than the weather and the light were at work here — as if phalanx after phalanx of souls were skimming over the surface of the visible, to the ineffable, the unknowable.

❄ ❄ ❄

IT MIGHT HAVE BEEN hours later when Faber let himself into her flat.

'Sandrine? Are you okay?' He placed his keys and phone on the bench, then came and rested a hand on her shoulder. 'It's so dark in here.' She turned from where she had been staring at the screensaver on her laptop, after she'd drawn herself away from the harbour view to do some desultory searching online. She pressed her face against his chest, not wanting to admit that the compulsion that had passed between her and Bu might have even been a strange-shaped love. Or compassion. Was there a difference? Perhaps one lined the other, each acting like the soft, white felt inside a leather glove.

Epilogue

Liam Seabrook, London

FOR WEEKS NOW, ONE man in England had been following the New Zealand story about the death of the so-called yeti. Liam Seabrook was alternately curious and detached, guilt-ridden and dismissive of faulty conscience. Memories of an incident just after he'd left New Zealand, twenty years before, gnawed at him, so that after work each night, he found himself hopping off the 73 bus a couple of stops sooner than usual and slipping into The Rose and Crown for a pint that became three, four, sometimes five before he found the blunting effect he wanted. He'd strike up a conversation with anyone, becoming loquacious, intimate about all sorts of fabricated situations: a recent relationship break-up; a bad accident that had lost him his job and family as he recovered from the head injury. All the time he talked, winning sympathy, or secrets in exchange, even a one-night stand that promised to turn into something more if he played it right . . .

He'd only been twenty-one himself back then; it was before he met the Nepali wife he had brought with him over to London. (Things with her hadn't worked out, as it happened. People had said it wouldn't: the two cultures too different. She'd taken the children back to her own country. Liam often thought of following, but his own sense of failure, his fear of what his children would think of him now, kept him back, kept him saying, *Next summer*.)

Twenty-one, and he hadn't known much, was still caught up in the maze of grief for his best mate, hadn't fully considered the consequences for other people at that time. Hadn't thought what it might mean to take a child away from its mother — even a strange troll of a child like the one he had helped to . . . well, pass on to someone. That couple from back home, they almost seemed like some sort of missionaries. Do-gooders, anyway, and they were desperate for kids of their own. She was a nurse, he was a carpenter or builder, maybe; certain facts were vague to him now. There was the Nepali woman from his own, soon-to-be-wife's home village, who had miscarried her own first baby and in the final week of her second pregnancy had gone wandering for several days. She came back no longer pregnant, and with the little monster boy. Wanted to keep it, though her family would have none of it. Some villagers said she'd lost her own child again, had come across the creature abandoned on a hillside to die. Others said no, it was hers, but denied by her husband.

His Nepali was fairly rudimentary — he and his wife would go on to speak only English at home — but he picked up enough to get the atmosphere of fear, some whispered talk of spells, curses. Maybe they were talking about the old myths; maybe they were talking about the way things were now. He couldn't tell. He acted as a go-between for the childless couple and the woman's family. The Nepali people didn't want to harm the creature, but they didn't want it in their village and certainly not in their homes. His compatriots were mad, he thought, fanatical. About all sorts of things. Bits of watered down religion — God is Love and Only Love; raw, organic food; herbal remedies; weird therapies. But mostly love. Yeah, fanatical about how it could heal anything. Nutters, he told himself; but then again he'd really thought he could be doing good by helping them out, giving an unwanted child a home. Healing a loss, not deepening it.

He was never exactly sure who or what the child really was, and neither was his wife. The village woman's? Some other family's illegitimate spawn, cast out to be eaten by rats and eagles, but surviving by chance? He'd pushed away these and other thoughts whenever they came too close.

But then he'd gone on to have his own children. From the very day his son was born, he began to wonder about what he'd done back then, what sort of life the little ape-boy had. Whether the fanatics had found that love really did cure all. He doubted it. Daren't think too hard about what might have come of it, just as he hardly dared tell himself now, that he had once been a father. And would be again if he had the spine.

He'd make peace with his past some day, and when he did, the night terrors of a little, wailing bear cub with blue eyes, or the dreams of the strange, humanoid baby he feared because he knew it might turn to show his own son's face, would stop. Till then, alcohol was an acceptable anaesthetic. And it spoke to him, made promises. It always said, *Plenty of time, Liam. Plenty of time.*

References

Teri Crocker reads a passage to Arlo Nathan from Janet M. Davidson's chapter, 'The Polynesian Foundation', in Geoffrey W. Rice (ed.), *Oxford History of New Zealand*, 2nd edn (Oxford: Oxford University Press, 1992), p. 7. She skim-reads and summarises other information from the same chapter.

Jodie Rata Radcliffe comes across images of *The Maero, the Very Fierce People*, retold by Ron Bacon and illustrated by Manu Smith (Auckland: Waiataura Publishing, 2004) and of *Mohoao, the Fierce Fairy Person*, retold by Ron Bacon, illustrated by Manu Smith (Auckland: Waiatarua Publishing, 2004).

Background Material

Books

Michael Newton, *Savage Girls and Wild Boys: A History of Feral Children* (London: Faber and Faber, 2002)

Russ Rymer, *Genie: A Scientific Tragedy* (London: Penguin, 1994)

Roger Shattuck, *The Forbidden Experiment: The Wild Boy of Aveyron* (New York: Farrar, Straus and Giroux, 1980)

Articles

Rick Blau, 'The Older Child or Teen with Selective Mutism' at <www.selectivemutism.org/resources/library (accessed 2 December 2008)

Ashok Kumar Jainer, Mohammed Quasim and M. David, 'Elective Mutism: A Case Study' in *International Journal of Psychiatry in Clinical Practice*, Vol. 6 No. 1, March 2002. pp. 49–51

Other

Francois Truffaut (director) *The Wild Child* (*L'Enfant Sauvage*) (1970)

Andrew Ward, www.feralchildren.com

Summer Seibert, Tammy Qualls, Viki Johnson, Tara Butterworth, Crystal Glenn and Alexandra Hudson, 'What is Selective Mutism?' <www5.esc13.net/speechlang/docs/meetings_materials/08_09/SLP/Sep08/> (accessed 2 December 2008)

Acknowledgements

THIS MANUSCRIPT WAS WRITTEN WITH the financial and practical assistance of a Creative New Zealand New Work Grant; a Writer's Residency at the Varuna Writers' House in the Blue Mountains, 2006 Sydney Writers' Festival; and the New Zealand Society of Authors/Janet Frame Memorial Award for Literature 2008. I'm very grateful for the generosity of all these funding bodies.

My thanks to Barbara and Chris Else of Total Fiction Services, for their ongoing support and vital critical feedback. Thanks to Barbara Larson and Simon Cunliffe for astute readings of a late draft. Thanks to Lorraine Scott, Dr Michael Newton, Dr Roy Craig and Rob Neale for early discussions about some of the subject matter here, to Harriet Allan for her valuable comments, and to Anna Rogers for her gimlet-eyed editing. Many thanks to Danny Baillie for wide-ranging, patient conversations throughout the novel's development — and for so much more besides.